The fear rose within her. *Dieu*, but she had been a fool to speak! Sir Giles was English and this was England. She had told Sir Giles because she loved him; *oui*, even her life she would give for him. But, *parbleu*, she must make him understand.

Her eyes rose to his in appeal. 'Sir Giles, please do not test my word. Forget what I said. The truth is useless to anyone.' Trembling, she was so close to tears she had to pause to choke them back.

Sir Giles' hand tightened upon hers. 'You can bear anything. I've seen your courage. Come The duc is waiting for us. He will be alone.'

Also by Deborah Chester in Sphere Books:

A LOVE SO WILD
SUMMER'S RAPTURE

Burning Secrets
DEBORAH CHESTER

SPHERE BOOKS LIMITED
London and Sydney

First published in Great Britain by
Sphere Books Ltd 1984
30–32 Gray's Inn Road, London WC1X 8JL
Copyright © 1982 by Deborah Chester
First published in the United States of America by
Dell Publishing Co. Inc., 1982

TRADE
MARK

Printed and bound in Great Britain by
Cox & Wyman Ltd, Reading

This book is affectionately
dedicated to my parents . . .
who made me possible

'Don't you believe in love? This is love,
you know. There are people, men and women,
who love each other against whatever odds,
and who continue to.'
                    – John Dos Passos

PROLOGUE

Terror lay upon the face illumined by the glow of a poorly trimmed taper; the man gulped his wine and caught the dicebox hard against his chest before clenching his teeth and making the cast.

Muret sighed and forced his gaze away from the scene; why should he remain fascinated with a fool who had lost so steadily all these hours and now fell back fainting in the arms of those crowded about the hazard table? A fool and, *sacredieu*, the hole was filled with fools. Muret's thin lips sneered a bit, and he reminded himself to lounge a bit more in his chair, to fondle the stem of his glass just so, as he had once seen a great seigneur do in the old days. It was hard to play the gentleman, not that any of the creatures dicing so lustily in this gloom- and smoke-filled salon took any heed of him in his corner.

The muscles in his neck ached from the strain of holding his head at a supercilious angle, and he writhed in his cravat. *Merde*, but he longed for the comfort of his uniform and braid, with the weight of his weapons upon him! But wait and watch, Monsieur le Colonel had commanded. Muret blinked several times to ease his eyes. Quickly he took a sip of his wine, which was a thin, unsatisfying stuff – rather like the charms of a *grande dame* – and glanced at the comte to make sure he had not slipped out while all eyes were watching the one ruined by dice.

Ah, *bon*, the rogue was still in his place, looking aloof and undistressed by the warmth of the overcrowded chambers. And how did he keep his linen so crisp? Muret

1

tugged a bit at his own cravat, which had gradually transformed itself from a stiff prison into a limp bandage.

Watch the comte, Monsieur le Colonel had said. *Eh bien*, he had watched and watched for close onto five hours now. And to what purpose? Muret shrugged and pushed his glass away, only to gulp as he realised he had naught now to occupy his hand. Frowning, he glared at the glass, not daring to pull it back to him, and in another moment a passing servant scooped it away.

'Muret!'

His name came as a hiss in his ear, startling him, for he had convinced himself he could watch all from this corner. Looking around, he gaped a bit at Céreau, who appeared burly and constricted in his civilian clothes.

'What? Oh, you!' he said stupidly and received Céreau's frown.

'Oaf! Where is he?'

A shaft of eagerness pierced through Muret's daze, and his head came up. 'There has been the order?'

'I have a brace of gendarmes without the door.' Céreau glanced about with a quiver of impatience. '*Mon Dieu!* Let us not be all hours with this. Which is he? And on your life do not point!'

'The man in the coat of saffron,' said Muret with a shrug to hide his pique. Playing spy was not to his taste, he assured himself, although Monsieur le Colonel said he did well at it. No, he much preferred to be in his uniform, snapping, 'Monsieur, consider yourself under arrest!' with a bold hand upon the butt of his pistol.

Céreau snorted. 'The one there at the faro table?'

'Yes.' Wearily Muret stood up, wishing himself at liberty to stretch and grunt. His task was finished; now perhaps he would have a day of leave, and tonight he would find Marie and take her to a café. With measured steps he followed Céreau outside into the gloom of twilight. The blow of cool air was a delight; he gulped in a lungful of it and gusted it out with pleasure. What relief to put his square hands in his pockets at last! 'I smell rain,' he commented

Céreau grunted and paused on the steps to beckon to the two soldiers, who came up smartly. While he murmured their instructions Muret glared at them beneath his brows. Boys, yet to shave – was the Emperor mad to take such green cabbages into his ranks?

Saluting, the pair entered through the portal, and Céreau gave one of his low, mirthless laughs. 'That is done. *En avant*, Muret.' He pressed a coin into Muret's ready palm. 'The colonel's compliments. Take your woman somewhere tonight, eh? *Au revoir.*'

He turned away, but Muret lingered a moment longer on the steps, gazing at the Emperor's bold profile on the coin. His father and brother had died in the Revolution; Muret himself had witnessed the king's head fall – sneezing into the sack, they had called the process. Now he served the Emperor, who arrested seigneurs or common men as he pleased. *Eh bien*, it was well enough.

CHAPTER ONE

Mademoiselle Catherine de Bleu sat in her aunt's narrow drawing room, attempting to alleviate her boredom by sketching a vase. In two hours she was engaged to dine at the Hôtel Monteau, but her heart was not in the occasion. Catherine's hand faltered as rebellion grappled with her sense of obedience. She knew her aunt meant well for her, but, in truth, she found the life of a debutante tedious in the extreme. Etienne du Monteau bored her; if she never saw him and his mother and sister again, it would not matter one jot. Almost she wished to be twelve again and in boy's clothes. Ah, that had been a grand time of life.

Roaming like vagabonds from one European capital to another, often with a paste diamond and a horse as their only wealth, she and Armand playing pranks as madcap brothers, Aunt Eustacie preserving her dignity heaven knew how, and Milord himself devising any number of audacious schemes for their survival. But they were respectable now, living in a respectable quarter of Paris, almost within sight of the Tuileries, and doing well enough on the proceeds from Milord's luck at the faro table. Catherine herself was grown up, her breeches long ago exchanged for muslins, sarsenets, and low bodices. A wicked thought curved her lips, and she thought of Etienne du Monteau. He was just beginning to fancy himself in love with her. What would he say if he knew she had once swaggered, and stolen snuffboxes, and talked bosky gentlemen into betting on the wrong bird at cockfights?

Abruptly she frowned. Let Aunt Eustacie consign her to the evils of spinsterhood; she cared not a sou for her rôle of the *jeune fille*. There was no life to it, no spark of danger to excite her, no promise of anything more than the same old round of demure glances and simpers performed for a surreptitious clasp of a gentleman's nervous hand and the hope of a declaration. A pox on her dreams of belonging somewhere and being settled with a country house and a man to take care of her. If settlement meant Du Monteau, she would far rather end her days as a dirty gypsy.

She tossed down her sketchbook and was about to go and beg off from the evening when her aunt entered the room.

'Catherine.'

Above the sombre hue of her taffeta the Comtesse de Chalier's face was deathly white. She clutched a letter in her hand, and the expression in her dark eyes struck instant alarm in Catherine, who hurried to her.

'Aunt! What is it? News from Vienna? Never say Armand has gotten himself called out over that silly heiress he's dangling after. If he has –'

'*Mon Dieu*, will you cease acting like a spaniel dog in need of discipline?' Milady held out the letter. 'Read this. It came for Armand but minutes ago.'

Catherine paused in the act of unfolding the paper. 'We should not pry.'

'Bah!' Milady gestured. 'It bears the seal of the Emperor. Do you think I dare ignore such a thing?'

'No. No, of course not.' Catherine stared at the missive, resisting the shrinking of her fingers from any contact with the imperial seal. 'Surely he is not arrested –'

'Don't be an idiot. Robert has taught you to exercise your wits to better purpose than this.' Milady's dark eyes pierced through Catherine, yet there stood a misery in their depths that touched Catherine's growing alarm. 'I have

6

glanced at it, but read it to me. I must hear those words aloud before I can believe them.'

Obediently Catherine spread out the page and frowned over the flourished writing. 'Subject to His Majesty the Emperor's disapproval, Monsieur le Comte de Chalier is submitted to arrest and imprisonment. Regarding this matter, one Armand de Chalier shall appear tonight at the Tuileries upon the hour of eleven and a quarter. By the hand of His Majesty's secretary, et cetera.'

Catherine attempted without much success to swallow the dryness in her throat. 'So it has come at last, just when we were growing fat in our security.' Fear stabbed her, then anger blazed over it and sent her across the room to clasp her aunt's shaking hand. 'And we are without that wretched Armand! *Mon Dieu*, of all the times for him to be off on one of his escapades –'

'Silence!' commanded Milady with a sharpness not to be disobeyed, but her hand pressed Catherine's as though to soften the rebuke. 'We must be grateful the fire-eater is out of the way. But do the spies not yet know he has left Paris?' Brushing Catherine aside, she began to walk slowly about the room, her thin, elegant hands clasped before her. 'This letter is a trap to snare him. *Grâce à Dieu*, it has come too late!'

Catherine frowned at her. 'Surely you do not suggest we pack our things and flee without Milord?'

'Do not be a fool!' Milady withered her with a look, then drooped and made a despairing gesture. 'I could never desert Robert. But what are we to do? I feared disaster yesterday when he sent Joseph home to say he would spend the night gaming. And now that dog of a Corsican has guessed at last who he is!'

'No, I think not,' said Catherine. 'The letter is not phrased in that way. Perhaps there is another reason for this move. We must learn what it is.'

7

'Yes, and how?' retorted Milady with raised brows. 'We have no Armand to risk.'

'Perhaps we do not need Armand.' Catherine spoke in a slow voice, trying to marshal her thoughts. She reread the letter and frowned. 'I see little choice but for someone to go tonight in his stead. To stay away is to throw a taunt in their faces.'

'A stupid move,' agreed Milady, becoming thoughtful too. 'At all costs we must not lose Robert by our clumsiness. He is our life.'

A pang wrenched through Catherine, making her glance at her aunt with a rush of compassion. Dear Aunt Eustacie, so fierce and strong-minded, but who gave all her heart and soul to Milord; how she would die inside were he to be lost! Catherine put out her hand, then let it fall before her aunt could notice. Sympathy would be spurned by Milady, who preferred action. With a sigh Catherine turned instead to repairing her own loss of heart. She must employ her wits at this moment of crisis and not fall into any womanish vapours. To do less was to defy her years of tutelage at Milord's hand.

Drawing in a deep breath, she clasped her hands together and made herself speak in the firm, composed manner which had been taught her as one's greatest resource. 'Why should I not go in Armand's place? I can listen as well as he.' Encouraged by her aunt's arrested expression, Catherine permitted a flush of excitement to fan the flames of her imagination. 'Better yet, I can don the clothes Armand left behind and carry one of Milord's pistols, to fool them altogether!'

'*Imbécile.*' Milady gripped the edge of the mantel with whitened fingers. 'To play the masquerade at such a time! This is not a game, miss!'

'Indeed I think I realise that, madame,' retorted Catherine with equal spirit. Intrigue was stirring, setting her old instincts aquiver until she was like a filly being brought up to the starting line. And while a part of her paced in anxiety for Milord – who meant everything to her as well as to them all – the rest of her exulted at this chance to shake off missish airs and the restrictions of *ton* circles. *Mon Dieu*, she thought, a little amazed at this unfettered leaping of her spirit. She should have been a man, for in her heart was a yearning for adventure not at all respectable.

'But I am not suggesting any hey-go-mad escapade,' she went on, striving to banish the closed look from her aunt's countenance. 'Will those dogs speak to a china-doll miss?' One contemptuous hand tossed back her long, guinea-gold ringlets. 'I should not learn half as much in this guise.'

'It is not a guise, Catherine,' began Milady in quelling tones. 'You are a young lady of breeding, of –'

'Forgive me if I dare to set you down,' interrupted Catherine, as one might execute a sword thrust *en prime*, 'but we have no time to waste upon quibbling.'

Dull crimson appeared on her aunt's sharply boned cheeks. Biting her lips, Milady glanced away for a moment. 'I agree,' she spoke at last in a low voice. 'But consider also that your woman's skirts could save you from possible assassination. If there is a trap –'

'I have to take the risk, don't I?' said Catherine just as softly, though her heart shrank within her. 'Grant me the intelligence to know what I am stepping into. We dare do nothing else.'

'It is true.' Milady rubbed the knuckles of one hand, the line deeply between her brows. 'But I still wish to see you remain feminine. We women have advantages when we let our womanhood disguise our ruthlessness.'

Catherine smiled. 'Aunt, you are correct, *sans doute*, but I know I am sometimes more actress than real person. If I go as myself I shall be terrified and at their mercy. If I go as a man, I shall feel the bravado I must exhibit. Let me try.

9

And we must send word to Armand immediately.' Falling into thought, she tapped one slim forefinger against her forceful chin. 'How many days to Vienna if Joseph takes the horse and leaves within the hour?'

'No!' Milady's dark head lifted. 'No, and no! Joseph shall accompany you! I will not permit you to enter that den of danger with no one at your side.'

Catherine shook her head, marveling at how this danger to Milord had clouded her aunt's mind. She started to voice her objection, despite a sudden wish that Joseph could stand at her back wherever she was soon to find herself, but before she could do so, Milady sighed.

'*Eh bien*, you are thinking. I am the *imbécile* tonight.' She passed a hand swiftly across her brow and struggled to smile. 'Once you go to that wicked place, there shall be no escaping if they decide to keep you, and it would not matter how many good Josephs we had.' She paused, regarding Catherine a moment with her sharp, dark gaze that missed so little. 'I will give him his orders and command a light supper for us. Go and begin your preparations, child.' Suddenly her thin lips trembled and she clasped Catherine tightly to her. 'I thank God for your courage.'

By the hour of ten a boyish figure stood before the looking-glass in Catherine's private chamber. For the thousandth time she studied the reflection to assure herself that her mouth was wide and firm enough, that the set of her cravat was suitably arranged, and that the masculine cut of her attire concealed any feminine curves. *Dieu*, but it was startling after these past few years of being a girl to see her limbs so boldly encased in pantaloons and boots. Warmth upon her features betrayed her, and she glanced at the floor in confusion as well as annoyance with her qualms.

Aglaé, Milady's maid and dresser, a woman of ample girth and years, paused in the act of sewing in pads to conceal the disparity in the breadth of Catherine's fine shoulders and the fit of Armand's coat. 'Eh, mademoiselle,' she said in her slow provincial accent. 'Do not fidget so. You will make a good young man. Remember the old days and have courage.'

Catherine turned away from the faded dimity curtains she was fingering and gave the woman a grateful smile. Little good it did to repeat self-commands to be calm. One might as well order a dog on the scent to come to heel, or a purebred hunter to turn from a fence. With a frown she held out one slim hand and exclaimed in frustration to see it tremble. Disconcertment undermined her. Had she lost her knack at the old game? Ah, bah! These past five years had been too easy, and she had paid the price for comfort by growing soft.

Accepting the altered coat, she shrugged it on with a sigh. 'I have the nose of my ancestors, but besides that, Aglaé, shall I fool anyone?'

Aglaé's plump lips stretched in a smile. 'It is a haughty nose. A proud one. And you are *parfaite*. Almost I could chase you from Mademoiselle Catherine's room.' Then she frowned. 'The hair is not yet right. Too long in the back.'

Involuntarily Catherine flung up a hand as though to protect her golden ringlets. The memory of the struggle to grow out boyish-cropped curls at a time when the style for young ladies was not short still lingered too strongly within her. 'But I have pinned most carefully,' she said.

'Bah.' Aglaé snapped her broad fingers. 'The night is stormy. What if you get wet, or must doff your hat?' She held up her scissors and clucked reproachfully when Catherine still could not master the last stirrings of rebellion. 'To be cropped is the fashion now. Very modish. But if you will not, I shall get out a walking dress and you may go as Milady desires.'

'No,' said Catherine as much to herself as to Aglaé. 'No, I

11

mustn't show cowardice now. *Alors,* cut.'

In moments a rather angelic young man emerged, one perhaps too slight and sweet with his long lashes and cherubic cap of curls, but when Catherine altered her expression to a haughty sneer, the sweetness became disturbingly sinister. All regret faded, and Catherine gazed at her reflection with delight.

The cut locks were swept into the grate while Catherine adjusted the angle of her hat to a rakish nicety and swept a few practice bows. 'I must make a pretty leg,' she muttered to herself, irritated by her clumsiness. '*Mon Dieu*, Aglaé, I need practice for this part.'

And when have you ever had the luxury of practice before?' demanded Milady, who entered the room without warning.

Startled, Catherine whirled, but the remark piqued her enough to gruff her natural contralto as she replied with one slim straight brow arrogantly lifted, 'Why, madame, one always may long for luxuries.' She flourished a bow, then faced her aunt with a thin smile and one hand shoved into her pocket.

Milady's dark eyes widened, and Catherine heard her draw in a short breath. 'Ah, but for the colouring it might almost be our Armand again.' It seemed to be as near an expression of approval as she was likely to show. She hesitated, still frowning, then handed forth a pistol. 'I have primed it and . . . oh, Catherine, my child, will you not rethink this plan and go as yourself? I sense a false step somewhere.'

Milady's doubts were in general sound, and this one gripped an icy hand around Catherine's resolve. But the faraway chime of the half-hour prevented any faltering now. She was committed; she dared not step back from what could be a possible chance of obtaining Milord's release. The summons had been sent out by the dog

12

Bonaparte, but perhaps she would have only Chief of Police Savary to face. She hoped so; she could not be sure her wits were sharp enough to deal with the man who had crushed Europe into submission.

Catherine headed for the door with a rapid step. 'There is no time to change our minds now. Wish me well. I hope to be back within the space of two hours.' Then, because it was too dangerous for her own composure, she averted her gaze from her aunt's anxious face and went out, shutting the door swiftly behind her.

She turned her thoughts to what lay ahead, for she dared not dwell upon anything but her rôle as Armand de Chalier. Equally consciously she sought to reaccustom herself to the freedom of her attire by lengthening her steps into strides and whisked herself down the dark servant stairs with only the whisper of her hands brushing the wall to accompany her. How lonely and silent the house was as though it, too, waited with bated breath for the fate of the master.

Shivering again, she drew her borrowed cloak more tightly about her before lifting the latch of the tradesmen's door and slipping out as one more shadow in the raw night. The cold seemed especially bitter, tinged as it was with damp and eerie tendrils of fog curling about occasional lampposts along the deserted street, and it bit at her fingers and nose first. Spring was not coming easily this year. She sneezed and pulled the folds of her cloak even closer, quickening pace until her footsteps rang out in echoes between the dark buildings. This street they lodged upon was a reputable one, but she soon turned off from that and thereafter kept a lookout for lurkers and footpads.

But the rapid pace soon spent her, and she realised it would put her at yet another disadvantage to arrive at the Tuileries disheveled and out of breath. A calm and unruffled demeanor must stand with her, and digging out

13

some of the scanty sous she carried in her pocket, she hailed a hackney at the first opportunity. Ensconced within its interior, which smelled strongly of street mire and onions, she heaved a sigh and sagged against the seat with one hand at her breast to ease her pounding heart. She must not fail Milord, if there was anything in her power to be done. She owed him too much not to keep her courage well stuck. He deserved her utmost.

But what sort of situation was she sticking her nose into? *Peste*, the look of it was grim. Biting her lip, she eased one hand over the cold surface of the pistol butt and tried to seek a measure of comfort from its heavy presence in her pocket. At least she could shoot if matters became sticky, although whether she would be obliged to turn her weapon upon an attacker or herself remained to be seen. She prayed to God the decision would not arise.

The pistol was the first thing the guards took from her, when, after showing her letter, she was conducted through the palace corridors – catching glimpses of salons filled with light and elegantly clothed people – and deposited in a narrow antechamber to kick her heels and sit upon a prodigiously uncomfortable chair with not even a meager fire in the grate to warm her. Relieved of her hat and cloak as well, she fidged in her place for a minute or two, then jumped up to pace along the confines of that dreary chamber, striving as she did so to guess the reason for her summons as well as to school herself yet more perfectly in her part.

It was all very puzzling, this arrest of Milord's. *She must remember to clasp her hands behind her, not before.* There was no reason for such an event unless his true identity had been at long last uncovered, and if this were the case, he would be even now upon his way to the executioner instead of reposing in a prison cell while the government interrogated his family. She frowned, wishing there was a

14

mirror in which to check her cravat, and paused to tap her fingers upon the marble top of a candlestand. *Should she lean against the wall? No, better not.* It did not make ready sense. They had done nothing of late to excite the attention of the authorities.

'Armand Chalier.'

Deep in her thoughts, she was startled by the voice, but just in time managed not to respond. The servant advanced a step into the room and repeated himself more loudly.

The moment was upon her, and her heart bolted. Sheer nervousness seemed about to turn her stomach. Swallowing hard, she put the sneer upon her lips and turned to gaze upon the impatient-faced lackey. 'I beg your pardon,' she drawled. 'Were you addressing me? I am De Chalier.'

The man snorted, his pinched, sallow face growing more impatient. 'I beg the pardon of monsieur,' he said with insolence. A typical court servant, thought Catherine. 'Monsieur de Chalier –'

'I style myself merely as Monsieur le Vicomte,' broke in Catherine, then permitted her sneer to ease into the vestige of a smile. 'But I make allowances. Address me as milord if you like. Do I go through there?' She waved a languid hand at the door left ajar behind the man. 'Ah, *merci.*'

Fighting the urge to take her chance and flee, she strolled past his surly person into a larger, blessedly warmer apartment hung in scarlet and white, with the imperial bee engraved over the mantel. The Emperor sat at a long desk carved from mahogany, reading through a stack of reports and scribbling notes from them. He did not look up at her soft-footed entry, but remained intent upon his work, a stray lock of dark hair loose upon his brow and the hint of a smile playing about his lips. Near him on the wall hung a portrait of the Austrian princess he intended to wed this month.

A somberly garbed man who was adding to the stack of

15

papers at Bonaparte's elbow glanced at Catherine and, with an inaudible murmur, bowed and let himself out, leaving only one other gentleman present, a haughty, dark-visaged man in uniform who Catherine recognized at once as General Dessaix. He sent her a measuring, rather peculiar stare, and she knew a flutter of unease. Something *was* awry; the general's manner betrayed it. But he did not speak. For the first time she wished she had come as a woman. This should have been a matter under Savary's jurisdiction, a man she also knew by sight as a consequence of Milord's rule that no one of his household should walk about ignorant. Instead, she, who had need to remain as a nothing in the momentous affairs of Napoleon Bonaparte, stood here in the Emperor's presence with not an inkling of what was afoot to guide her. Gad, but it was devilish!

'Well!' Abruptly Bonaparte tossed down his pen and studied her with dark eyes that seemed to miss no detail. 'The *petit* Chalier at last, I have no doubt.'

Although most of her life Catherine had regarded Bonaparte with the utmost contempt, she now found it impossible not to be awed. He was a small man, but it was as though she faced a presence greater than life. The very set of those pale Corsican features set her heart thundering. By birth, their positions were worlds apart, and yet she could see at once why he had this effect upon her. It was very simple. He possessed power, and she did not. Too uncertain of her tongue at that moment, she nevertheless managed to collect herself enough to flourish a bow.

'Ah!' said Bonaparte and leaned back in his chair with the tips of his fingers together. His dark eyes gleamed with a light which disturbed Catherine so she was hard put not to betray her discomfiture. It seemed he would draw her into the net of his forceful personality and trap her there as yet another of his puppets. Her chin came up; he would find she was not so easily caught.

'Your Majesty,' broke in Dessaix, abruptly coming

16

forward. His face was out of the shadows now, and Catherine saw it was thunderous. 'This is not Armand de Chalier! He was pointed out to me upon one occasion by Savary and is dark, not fair. I would swear to it.'

Dismayed, Catherine made an involuntary gesture, only to see Dessaix whip out a pistol to train upon her. At once she froze. But in desperation she clung to her sneer and her sangfroid and even managed a cool glance in Bonaparte's direction. '*Non*, of course I am not Armand,' she said, praying her voice would not become shrill. Though she kept her gaze upon Bonaparte's frowning countenance, she was certain Dessaix's finger had tightened upon the trigger. A knot gripped her stomach, cramping it until she all but gasped with the pain. She scarcely dared breathe lest he shoot her. But if she was to be blown to bits in the next instant, she must do so with her wits still about her, or she was no pupil of Milord's. 'I am his cousin,' she forced herself to add, just as coolly as before, though she feared she would soon begin to shake. 'Surely it is known that he is gone from Paris.' And then bravado came to her aid and enabled her to throw a challenging glance at Dessaix. 'Or did Savary and his informants seek not to give you that bit of knowledge?'

'Insolent whelp!' Dessaix's face darkened, but Bonaparte lifted one hand to curb his general.

'Go on, cousin to Armand,' said the Emperor. He seemed almost amused, but she was not deceived. At this moment the danger about her was very great.

She sought quickly for what must be an excellent lie. 'I am Jacques-Pierre de Bleu,' she said, managing to put arrogance into the announcement, and was amazed she had not stammered over such a mouthful. 'I have a sister, who is prostrate over this matter–'

'We know of her,' snapped Dessaix. 'Why have you never appeared before?'

Confound the man! Catherine gave him her coolest

glance and hoped she looked enough like an unruly young braggart to satisfy this uniform of suspicion. 'I am kept as much out of the way as possible,' she said in bitter tones and employed her sneer again, wishing she might shove her hands in her pockets, but certain the move would get her shot. 'In fact, I only arrived in Paris today from my school and find this difficulty thrown at me by a hysterical sister and aunt.' She scowled and sank a petulant tooth into her lower lip. 'What must we do to free the old man?'

She could have stamped her foot in frustration to see Dessaix look still unconvinced. He frowned and glanced at the Emperor. 'I suppose Savary could tell us the truth of that arrival in a day or two, Majesty.'

'No.' Bonaparte gestured with impatience. 'This youth does not concern us. It is the girl. Catherine de Bleu.' He spoke her name as though savoring the taste of a sweetmeat, and Catherine thanked God for her notion of appearing in disguise. Surely there would have been worse disaster had she come as herself.

'Your sister is a comely girl, I'm informed,' continued Bonaparte and raised his brows at Catherine for confirmation.

Peste, was he hoping for a seduction? Catherine burned to have a pistol in her grasp at that moment and was hard put to shrug in an offhand manner. 'Handsome, but not pretty,' she said, scowling. 'Not to my taste, these fair *haridelles*.'

'But she *is* clever and quick-witted,' put in Dessaix, who had lowered his pistol, much to Catherine's relief and restored nerve.

She appeared thoughtful. 'I am more so.'

Bonaparte did not trouble to conceal a smile. 'Well enough, young cock! We have a task for her to perform. If she succeeds, your uncle may have his wrongs against France forgotten and his freedom restored.' Rising to his feet, he swaggered round to the side of the desk and leaned

18

against it with his arms crossed over his chest. 'I have not yet given up my intention to invade England. With King George insane, a great deal turns upon the Prince Regent. Your sister shall play upon his fondness for attractive women, gaining a place in society and in his favor. And when she has done so,' said Bonaparte, his eyes suddenly flashing with command, 'she shall assassinate him.'

The silence stretched out. Speechless, Catherine could at first only stare at him. '*Mon Dieu*,' she whispered at last, clenching her fists. *'Mon Dieu!'*

Bonaparte smiled, slowly, winningly, ruthlessly. 'England will be thrown into confusion, and then I shall strike. My army can subjugate those shopkeepers in two months, perhaps less.' He smiled again, and such was the force of his personality, she almost found herself nodding back. Caution, she warned herself. Any other man she would call mad, but Bonaparte could do what he proposed, if he were given the proper chance. And it appeared she was to be his chance.

'Don't look so stricken, my boy,' the Emperor continued, reading her more easily than she liked. 'Simple plans work best; I have no worry concerning the success of this one. But if you think the fair Catherine is too fainthearted for the task, please remind her of how simple it would be to bring your uncle to trial and execution. Savary is convinced his background is not all it should be.'

But by now she had fully grasped what they were asking of her, and rage slapped away her astonishment. What right did these dogs have to command a child of her house to murder? Pride lifted her chin. No one forced her to do his bidding. 'Gad, messieurs, it's an outrageous act you bid us perform! Send a man to do your evil, not a chit of a girl,' she snapped.

Dessaix stiffened, eager to answer the challenge of her tone. 'Do you refuse, then, whelp?'

A sense of danger reined up hard on her temper, and she

realized she dared not give way to scorn at this point. For Milord's sake, she must not. But the more she considered the extent of her helplessness in this matter, the more it maddened her. Her eyes blazed, her lip curled in a sneer unfeigned, and she vowed she would have shot Dessaix dead in his boots at this moment for daring to thrust her into such a corner. As for this Corsican, who gave himself airs above the rest of mankind . . .

'Milord de Chalier would be crushed to see how hard this choice weighs upon you,' said Bonarparte softly, but with an air of menace in his voice which permitted nothing but capitulation. 'It is not your choice, boy. It is the girl's, and I think she would be willing to do anything to save her beloved uncle, *non*?'

If he had not shown himself so dangerous, Catherine would have sneered at the Emperor as well. Did this tiny peacock think she shrank from killing? Why, Milord was worth a dozen English princes; for his sake she would do anything, just as he had done everything for her. One's honor demanded it as much as one's love. But this Bonaparte needed taking down a peg for his impudence in forcing her to skip her feet to his piping, and, by gad, if she could she'd do it at the first opportunity.

'Very well,' she said with a shrug and began at once to think of contingencies. 'We shall need money. The English season won't come cheap.'

Bonaparte nodded at Dessaix, who unlocked a strongbox on a nearby table and tossed Catherine two laden purses. She caught them deftly and slid them into each pocket without offering the insult of looking to see what coin she was paid in. She knew the chink of a gold louis when she heard it. Confidence quickened within her as though to offset the weight in her pockets. With good French gold they might escape anywhere to live their days in comfort, but only if Armand could rescue Milord. That, however, was a plan

20

for the future. For now, she must be out of this den of danger as soon as possible and away to tell Aunt Eustacie of this. It would take time to infiltrate society circles in England, time enough for Armand to free Milord. And if he succeeded, then they could leave the Regent of England in good health and be on their way.

'Remember, my boy, your uncle won't escape us, for all his cleverness,' said Bonaparte. 'And we shall be able to keep watch on you in England. Do not try any false dealings. That is all.' Covering a yawn, he turned away to pick up another report, and Catherine took a hasty leave of the palace, pausing only to recover her cloak, hat, and pistol, which she gripped all the way home out of fear that some chance footpad would choose her conveyance to rob, and there would go her gold pieces.

Breathing hard, as though spent from a long, hard race, she leaned back against the squabs and sighed, brushing the cold perspiration from her brow. She was trembling all over, but at least she had survived.

Assassination... again she knew a spurt of rage. How dare this Corsican nobody, this son of an Italian innkeeper, seek to hold a trump card over her head? Emperor he might be, but he still thought in the manner of scurrilous *banditti*. It was below her pride to think of weaseling her way into a fat prince's graces, of presenting herself for a bussing like any common tavern wench simply for the chance to drill a pistol ball through his royal heart. She gripped her weapon so hard she all but shot it. *Bon Dieu,* she had never been so galled! Bonaparte would pay for the insult. On her honor she swore that much!

The job horse's hooves clopped steadily over the cobbles, and outside the carriage she could hear the first hiss of rain. Exhausted, she closed her eyes, seeking to calm down, to cool the fever in her brain. A steady wit must ever prove master of the situation; she could not hope to achieve

21

anything as long as she stewed and simmered. She must think now, and think well. But, *peste*, it was a pretty tangle Milord had gotten them into this time. Because of his passion for the faro table a Frenchman might sit on the British throne before the end of summer; only time could tell what fortune she and her people might wring from it all. She gave a low, wry laugh. At least she could be assured her ennui would be dismissed for quite some time to come.

'Oh, Aunt, it was an uncommon scene I played tonight with Napoleon and General l'Intrépide! I wish you might have seen it.' Finishing her tale, Catherine seated herself upon a stool with one booted foot thrust out and one elbow poised negligently upon her aunt's dressing table. With more calm than her smoldering interior preferred to show, she lifted an eyebrow at Milady. 'Well, madame? Do we dance to Longboot's whistle, or do we play our own game?' She could not completely cover her temper with jauntiness, however, and clenched a fist. 'Surely you guess my own vote. *Sacredieu*, he will betray the bargain! We both know it!'

Milady sniffed and rearranged her elegant hands in her lap. 'Do not let your spirit make you a fool,' she said. Stung, Catherine started to speak but was forestalled. 'Yes, child, we none of us doubt your courage or your fire. But you have listened to too many of Robert's tales of derring-do. Prudence is sometimes more to the purpose than wild escapades. The trick is to learn when one will serve the better. We must do as Bonaparte demands.'

'But you place no trust in Armand?' asked Catherine impatiently. The memory of her interview boiled over her afresh, sending her up and pacing round the small confines of her aunt's chamber. 'And the very insult of –'

'Silence! We need no histrionics.' Milady's patrician nose curved downward in disapproval, and the glance she returned to Catherine's stormy one was damping. 'Yes, yes, if you were a hotheaded young man you might shoot someone and so relieve your spleen. But you are merely a hotheaded young lady and, as such, of no use to us whatsoever. Of course I trust Armand to do his best. But to place all my trust in him is to be stupid, and that I never am.' She paused as though to take Catherine's measure. 'I've seen your temper, but now let us see your mettle. Do you fear the task?'

Still struggling to accept the scold with composure, Catherine fought back the temptation to say she feared no devilry. 'I should be an idiot to say I do not,' she said flatly, hands shoved deep in her pockets although there was no need at this moment for boyish affections. Catherine sighed. 'In faith, Aunt, I don't know if I can kill a man I do not hate.'

'Such a distasteful business.' Milady's nostrils flared fastidiously, then she awarded Catherine a dry smile. 'We shall consider the question later. To bed with you. Tomorrow we must begin preparations for a journey I know will be fatiguing.'

Catherine faced her, seeking an answer. 'Then we are for England?'

'Oh, go to, child! Of course we are.' The dry amusement faded from Milady's face, leaving her delicate skin taut with purpose. 'I tell you I will leave nothing undone if it will free Robert. I will do anything to give him another day of life. Now go to bed. I must think and think and think.'

She turned her face toward the fire in dismissal. As erect and elegantly poised as ever in her chair, she seemed fragile, as though Milord's absence had robbed her of some vital spark. Still, there was indomitable strength to be read upon the high cheekbones and firm chin. Milady needed not sympathy but action. Catherine sighed and went out. To linger was to incur a scold for impudence.

Yawning, she took herself along the hall with its threadbare carpet and entered her own chamber, where a tiny fire in the grate flickered up in greeting. Undressing by firelight, she started to roll her male clothes in a heap for Aglaé to clear away on the morrow, then checked herself and put them in her clothes-chest. Who knew when Jacques-Pierre might be required again? It might prove to be necessary to make a token appearance now and then to satisfy Bonaparte's spies. To her surprise the thought did not please her, and she paused to study her faint reflection in the looking-glass. She had gone off on her adventure as lark-hearted as any lad. What was wrong with her now that she must cling to her femininity as though it were to be wrested from her at any moment?

But the face frowning back at her seemed almost not her own. She shook her head. 'Gad, but I am weary,' she murmured aloud. 'I am thinking myself two people.'

That, of course, was nonsense. She was no poor halfwit so confused by her rôles she thought they were reality. But who *was* she becoming? Troubled, she fingered her cheekbones until the chill of the room drove her to the warmth of her curtained bed. In it and shut away from the rest of the world, she still reclined awake against her pillows. What she had greeted as a half-serious escapade had changed into a far too deadly intrigue. She did not like being Bonaparte's pawn; no, nor a tool of Aunt Eustacie's. Not when it involved such grim stakes.

She put her hands to her face, frowning. Could she murder in cold blood? Oh, aye, it seemed she must, but *could* she? In rejection of a question too large for comfort, she threw herself down and pulled the pillow over her head. It availed her nothing, however, and in a moment she sat up again, wide-eyed in the darkness. The whole crux of the matter was not could she, but *would* she. *Peste*, how easy to say yes and not mean it. Still, she dared not try to fool herself. She must make up her mind or she could go no further. In her perilous life to try and survive in a state of indecision meant disaster.

24

Well, then, how much did Milord mean to her? In his magnificent presence there would have been no need for such a question. But he was far away, locked up in a cell brimming with damp and disease. She smiled involuntarily at the thought of him grimacing over his linen, and all at once had her answer. Oh, she had made up her mind once tonight and changed it again. But this time she rested her decision on no childish confidence. The prospect of what might prove necessary terrified her, but she would not fail Milord.

Settling herself down for sleep with an apprehension too great to control, she whispered while clutching her pillow hard against her cheek, 'God keep us,' and said it again several days later when she stood at the rail of a packet boat which was leaving France's shore behind.

Milady inclined her head, the fresh breeze threatening to strip away the single plume upon her bonnet. 'What did you say, child?'

Catherine eyed the horizon as she stood shivering in her twilled stuff gown and thin pelisse. 'I said, God keep us, for there's no one else to wish it for our sakes.' She glanced briefly at her aunt without meaning to be defiant. 'Is there?'

Milady's face softened a fraction, and she placed her hand over Catherine's. 'No,' she said with a tiny shake of her head. 'But I pray you will never have to become used to it, as I have done. Years ago, when I married Robert, it was because he was rich and witty, and I loved him with all my heart. And then the Revolution came and took away all the happy times. But while his friends fled or were killed, Robert survived. He taught me to survive, though I did not wish to become so ruthless. And when your father was beheaded and your mother died, we saw that you learned to survive as well. We took a hard, bold life because to stay with the easy meant death. And now a bad hour is upon us again, but we will survive it too because we are strong and do not fail at what we do. *Pour Milord*, shall be our motto in these days. I pray God will keep him more than us.' Her lips tightened too abruptly, and she pulled Catherine's hand away from the rail. 'Come, no more mooning. We must make sure our letters of introduction are in order, and from now on you must speak to me in the English Robert has taught you. Come.'

She stepped away with a brisk rustle of taffeta, but Catherine lingered yet another moment at the rail. There was nothing to encourage or dissuade her there, however; nothing but the vast pewter sea heaving them along regardless of their presence upon its back. Sighing, she picked her way across the littered deck after her aunt. She was committed altogether now; she must not falter. She must not look back.

CHAPTER TWO

'So you desire to come under my aegis, do you?' said the small-boned woman with her dark gray eyes boring straight into Catherine.

Catherine performed a graceful curtsy and stood in silence, certain she must err if she did not let Milady act as their spokesman.

'Madame, I –' began Milady, but Lady Thorne raised one soft hand – still well-shaped and pretty despite her advanced years – to achieve silence.

'My good woman, be so considerate as not to interrupt. I am speaking to your niece, if you please.'

Milady stiffened, her chin rising. Despite the importance of the moment, Catherine's lips quivered into a smile she at once smothered behind her handkerchief. To be caught laughing would be an error of manners, but in truth it was diverting to see her aunt addressed in such crushing accents.

'Good heavens, girl, are you deaf as well as dumb?' said Lady Thorne. 'I don't fancy being kept waiting for answers to my questions. If you cannot employ our language to better effect, you would be much advised to return to Paris without delay!'

The rebuke brought Catherine out of her amusement. *Peste*, she thought, schooling her features, Lady Thorne had the tongue of a wasp! Lifting her brows to show she was not cowed by these *grande dame* manners, Catherine made her low voice as pleasant as possible. 'If my manners are not pleasing, I beg madame to forgive them. *Oui*, I do wish to be sponsored in society. You were highly recommended to us by Mrs. Bathcombe, who –'

'Highly recommended, indeed,' said Lady Thorne with a sniff. 'I cannot say I like being discussed in terms befitting a servant. No girl, I do not think –'

'Lady Thorne!' broke in Catherine with the sharpness of desperation. Letters of introduction to three other ladies of the *ton* had met with refusal; no one, it seemed, possessed the inclination to lead two French ladies into the pink circles. If Lady Thorne was also permitted to deny them, they might as well give up any hope of seeing Milord alive again. A blaze of scorn stiffened Catherine. It seemed Bonaparte had failed to consider the haughtiness of Englishwomen when he formed his plan. But she would succeed. She must! Standing on their best behaviour had served them nothing; Catherine now gave her frustration rein as she had not dared to do since setting foot on this wretched island.

'Lady Thorne, if you do not wish to be described as a servant, *I* do not wish to be addressed as one. I am Mademoiselle de Bleu, *not* "girl".'

A bit of pink tinged Lady Thorne's cheeks, and she sniffed as she raised her lorgnette. 'Hoity-toity.'

'Let us not descend to name-calling, shall we?' said Catherine with one of her sweetly sinister smiles. 'If you do not like us, that is your prerogative, but personal opinion need not enter into this matter. We are of some means. We are not the scruff of the gutter. Nor are we French nationals. I have resided in almost every capital of Europe. Now I desire to see London. And I wish to do it properly – as my rank and position demand – and not as some bourgeois citizen you call, I think, mushrooms.'

'*Bon*,' murmured Aunt Eustacie.

Catherine drew a deep breath. *Dieu*, but she felt better for having given that setdown!

'Catherine,' said Milady, one thin hand closing over

Catherine's wrist, 'we shall go. One could not bear this company long –'

'Fiddlesticks!' said Lady Thorne, looking at them in rather sharp surprise. 'Do not assume your dismissal before I have given it. Sit down, Comtesse. And you, mademoiselle, you may ring for tea.'

Milady glanced at Catherine with her brows uplifted, then seated herself upon a narrow chair and arranged her stiff taffeta skirts with a grace only she could achieve. Catherine grimaced to herself as she turned away to pull the bell. She preferred a glass of claret to the acrid brown stuff these English adored so, but she would drink anything if it meant success. Finding a chair for herself, she laid her reticule in her lap and took advantage of this opportunity to study the drawing room and its particulars. Sheraton and Hepplewhite dominated the furniture, a finely aged parquet floor peeped coyly from beneath the fringe of an Aubusson carpet, and a completely incongruous breakfast table fashioned by Elfe of Charleston filled the corner near the window. Catherine could not fathom the reason for the little table's presence, but she dismissed the consideration as trifling and looked up to find Lady Thorne glaring at her in a hard manner.

'Already sizing up my possessions, are you? Pray take note of the mantel candlesticks fashioned of German silver. It requires a stalwart footman to carry them.'

Nettled by this sarcasm, Catherine decided her hostess did not merit the gentle treatement usually accorded one possessed of snowy hair and a cane. '*Voyons*, what a suspicious senile!' she said to herself, conscious she trod brittle ground, but irritated enough not to care. The part of a mouse did not suit her at all, and though she had clung to it for the past fortnight, now she abandoned it altogether. 'I was informed that English demoiselles are expected to be demure, timid creatures, but if this means submitting to unjust waspishness and tyrannical vapors, then a pox upon it!' She lifted her chin, sensing she had quite taken her hostess aback, and shook off the hand of caution Aunt Eustacie placed on her arm. 'Madame, I was merely of a curiosity as to how came a table of American manufacture in your drawing room. You need not suspect me of evil designs. Milady, we should take our leave, *d'accord*?'

'Of a certainty,' said Milady, picking up her gloves and sending an ironical glance in Lady Thorne's direction. 'If we may have our *congé*?'

'You are a very knowledgeable young lady to recognize that table,' was all Lady Thorne said, however. 'My son brought it home with him from a visit to America.' She frowned a bit, and despite her vexation Catherine was quick to sense a change in the elderly woman's mood. But almost instantly the pensiveness was gone as Lady Thorne gestured. 'He has a passion for incongruities; I wish he would keep the piece in his own house. But what type of season do you have in mind? Do you want entry to a few functions, or do you aspire to the highest circles?'

'Madness,' breathed Milady. "Catherine, let us –'

But Catherine paid no attention. She eyed Lady Thorne and began to see through the Tartar façade. 'Why, madame, the best of course.'

Lady Thorne frowned. 'I am an old woman, but . . . yes, very well.' She nodded. 'I like spirit. I like *your* spirit. As long as you don't simper at me, we shall get on.'

It was enough. Catherine smiled in relief and stood up, not daring to dawdle in accepting this assistance, lest it be withdrawn at her ladyship's next whim. 'Thank you, madame. We are grateful to have your favor.'

Aunt Eustacie swept an awesome curtsy, her lips still very compressed. 'Thank you. Come, Catherine. We are late for other appointments.'

But Catherine, though she was equally ready to be gone, caught a glimpse of something in Lady Thorne's expression and waited to see what might come of it. On impulse she smiled when Lady Thorne's gaze flickered to her, realizing, rather to her own surprise, she had enjoyed their sparring match.

'Please stay for tea,' said Lady Thorne, touching the silver tray which had been set before her by an unobtrusive servant, then looking down as she fiddled with the lace on her sleeve. 'My sons spare little time to call, and my acquaintance is naught but a bevy of jaded idiots and gossip-mongers.'

It was easy to hear the note of loneliness in her voice. Puzzled, for it was odd to hear such a note of dissatisfaction in one who gave every appearance of having spent her life exactly as she wished, Catherine hesitated and wondered which way to go. Was it sufficiently worthwhile to make friends with an old she-dragon? In faith, why not? They needed all the help they could get to play this game.

'*Oui*, but of course we are pleased to linger,' said Milady suddenly. She steeled herself – a bit obviously, Catherine thought – and retook her seat. Then she sent a sharp glance Catherine's way. 'Take your ease, child. We will shop tomorrow for your ribbon.'

Catherine obeyed and silently accepted the cup which Lady Thorne filled and thrust at her. Sipping slowly to hide her grimace of revulsion, Catherine studied her aunt through her lashes. Yes, Milady was vexed by the cavalier treatment she'd just been dealt, but the easing of her tightened lips told Catherine she was pleased by their success in the face of what had at first seemed certain failure. Catherine smiled to herself and took a biscuit to quieten a pang of hunger. In truth, she'd brought this off neatly enough. Now, *s'il plaît à Dieu*, if only Lady Thorne had sufficient weight in society circles to carry them forward. They had so little time to achieve so much. She had yet to even catch a glimpse of the Prince Regent.

'One more thing,' said Lady Thorne loudly, startling

Catherine from her thoughts. 'I have lost my hired companion. The poor fool fancies she can do better raising pullets in Warwickshire.' Lady Thorne snorted. 'Since I cannot live alone with the servants, and my son has thus far failed to find anyone who suits me, I desire you to come and stay here. Don't look surprised; I make up my mind quickly. Now. I have my faults. I cheat at whist and backgammon, but you shan't mind as long as you are fed and housed comfortably –'

'*Non*.' Firmly, Milady put down her cup. 'I do not wish to be rude or appear ungrateful, madame, but we are possessed of excellent lodgings, which we like.'

As equally set upon refusal as her aunt, Catherine leaned forward with her hazel eyes intent. To think, when everything seemed perfect, they had stumbled into yet another pitfall! One must ever be on guard, for here they now sat with no plausible excuse prepared. She was furious with herself.

Lady Thorne's countenance hardened, and she brought up her lorgnette to stare at them. 'Rented lodgings are never excellent. This show of stubborn pride is quite ridiculous.'

Milady drew herself up. 'As long as we are satisfied, you need not –'

'Drivel!' Lady Thorne gestured curtly. 'You'll get nowhere with the *beau monde* as long as you give an hotel for your address. And besides, I've taken a fancy to your niece, impudent though she is. I want her here to talk to.'

'We must refuse,' said Milady, quite stiff.

Clinging to caution, Catherine neither breathed nor moved lest she be noticed and drawn into the conflict. If only Aunt Eustacie's dignity could crush Lady Thorne! But already it was plain Lady Thorne could not be easily routed from any position she chose to take. Perhaps, however, she might be led round.

'Then go!' snapped Lady Thorne, pink-faced. Her lorgnette was tapping a furious rat-tat upon the tea-table.

'But I promise you, Comtesse de Chalier, you shall not receive one invitation from my hand. No, and I shall see you cut from every assembly!'

Quelle horreur! In alarm Catherine saw they must fall into the greater evil if they persisted in clinging to prudence. Lady Thorne, small and old as she might be, was plainly not a person of empty threats. But, *bon sang de bon sang!* It would be bad for them to live here where their freedom would be at once curtailed. But how much worse to find themselves blackballed because of an old woman's pique! Catherine saw that caution must be flung to perdition, and she hoped her aunt did, too.

'Aunt!' she cried, leaping into a pout as rapidly as she rose from her chair. 'You must not provoke Lady Thorne into taking such a measure. I mind not at all to come here, and you must agree it is an offer of handsomeness.'

Milady stared at her as though she were a changeling. Catherine tried to put as much warning into her gaze as could be crammed there. But when Milady's dark eyes merely glared back in a smolder of fury, Catherine could have struck something in her frustration. It was plain Aunt Eustacie could not see past her dislike of this frightful woman, but must she let all other considerations go to the devil? It was so unlike her! So stupid!

'You are impertinent, Catherine,' said Milady at last in accents that would have frozen a pool of water.

Lady Thorne snorted. 'Comtesse, the girl's got more sense in her noodle than you have. Stop being such a hen-wit and send for your things. It's high time this household was plagued by a flibbertigibbet of a young miss.' Lady Thorne lifted her lorgnette to survey Milady, who was standing pale and tense and unmoved. 'I need a girl here. One shall attract others, and I want this house filled with hustle-bustle.'

'Why?' asked Catherine, sensing a blunt question would not go amiss.

Lady Thorne's dry laughter crackled out. 'Because I have

33

an ulterior aim – grandchildren. And I cannot acquire any until I persuade my eldest son to marry and set up his nursery. Good heavens, the man is on the verge of middle age!'

'I hope you do not have Catherine in mind,' said Milady icily. But she was no longer as pale as before, and Catherine hoped she had seen her error.

'Certainly not,' said Lady Thorne in a derisive tone Catherine could hardly find flattering. 'But she'll do as an excuse to have an assembly. Provided you don't intend to be an idiot by refusing to come here. I warn you I have known most of the patronesses of Almack's since their leading-string days, and my influence against you would not be inconsiderable if I chose to so direct it.'

'I detest blackmail,' said Milady, causing Catherine to cast another glance her way. 'I detest it as much as I hate to beg for help. But I have no choice other than to submit. Very well.' And there was a quiver of strain to submit. Very well.' And there was a quiver of strain beneath the chill in her voice. 'We will stay.'

'Good.' Lady Thorne turned her piercing gray eyes upon Catherine, who was drawing a long breath of relief. 'Have you a ball gown? If you do, I shall take you to Lady Reginald Sperling's this evening. She is an old friend and shan't mind an extra pair of guests. Now send my butler in to me so I may direct him to prepare rooms for you.'

Catherine inclined her head and went away to do as she was bid, her brows lifting in cool wryness as soon as her back was safely turned. Milord always said one must be as flexible as a cat when dealing with people, and indeed it was true. Who would guess the lady would take such an instant fancy to her and bring her into the house? *Probablement*, it was because no one else had stood up to her in years.

Realizing Lady Thorne desired a private word with Milady, or else she would not have sent Catherine outside the room, Catherine dallied in the hall and studied the Jacobean hall chairs covered in royal-blue velvet and the graceful proportions of the staircase. Her mind, however, was not on her new surroundings.

Reflectively she began to tap her chin with one slender finger. It seemed, if one played one's cards with a bold hand, that Lady Thorne could be put to good use. Indeed, her favor would assure a rapid rise in the approval of the *beau monde*. Very well then, it was a good thing to come here, and she must hope any spy surveying their activities would possess the intelligence to realize she was doing what she should be doing. Only, *peste!* The creatures were nearly always great stupids. Still, it could not be helped, and while she chaffed at the loss of independence this move entailed, she betrayed no frustration and was even able to gasp in genuine delight when shown to her new chamber an hour later.

The bed was canopied in lace with a blue coverlet and a step at the side. Dainty chairs done in rose-colored satin set before a mantel of veined marble. Upon it reposed a gilded clock between vases of lilies whose fragrance filled the room. Fingering the delicate lace curtains and gazing out one spacious window which overlooked the street, Catherine – who had always prided herself as being a resourceful individual untouched by sentiment – now knew a sudden longing to stay here forever.

It was such a charming, pretty place she could not help but adore it. At Fenton's Hotel one was free to come and go as one pleased in whatever guise one found necessary, but one was also obliged to hold a glass under the sheets to check for dampness and keep a chair under the door-knob to make sure the lock held throughout the night. Here there was comfort and a sense of security. She wondered who had once used this room. Surely it had not always been saved for an occasional guest! But it was hers now for a space, and she was transfixed enough by its spell to cast off her doubts and give herself over to the simple joy of being in it.

'Catherine?' It was Milady who entered with a soft rustle of skirts. Catherine smiled to see her glance round with widened eyes, and ran forward to clasp her hand.

'Aunt! Is it not *charmante?* Lady Thorne is kind to place me here.'

Milady's nose curved down. 'Yes, it is *belle*, provided it does not trap you. But I think madame our hostess more selfish than kind.'

Catherine moved away with a frown she did not trouble to conceal. '*Vraiment*, does it matter? She will be useful.' Catherine paused, suddenly weary of her life and the way she lived it. Was there never to be a change? Was she never to be permitted to consider people for their own worth rather than for what use they might be put to? She sighed. 'Her ladyship is lonely.'

'Of course,' agreed Milady dryly. Catherine's head came up, but her aunt spoke first. 'Child, be wary of yourself and her. We do not need the complications she will thrust upon us.'

'We need her help. You must grant that. And if I must read to her and drink that ipecac they call tea, what of it?' Catherine said, determined to remain here no matter what the difficult. Milord had taught her a vast respect for deep hunches; she would not ignore the urge to stay. 'Companionship is tedious, *sans doute*, but an easy thing.'

'If she tries to wed you to her son, it will not be easy,' said Milady, her hands clenched.

Catherine was surprised into a laugh. 'Why, madame! She vowed such was not her intention. And the son cannot be that desperate.'

Lady Thorne would swear upon her honor and still betray you if it suited her.' Milady seemed about to say more, then she sighed. 'Some day I want you wed and safely

36

away from these dangerous games. But, child, we cannot afford the distraction of an unwanted romance now when –'

'Romance is the chief pursuit of the *ton*,' said Catherine in quiet rebuke, marveling at her aunt's confusion of purpose. 'Do not fear I shall lose my head. The game shan't be lost because of a middle-aged bachelor.'

Milady regarded Catherine a moment, then she nodded. '*Eh bien.* I am wrong to encourage these misgivings. Robert would not like them.' She patted Catherine's hand. 'Child, I trust your judgment. But be cautious. We dare not underestimate these persons. No one is ever as he seems.'

Catherine inclined her head in agreement, while thinking of how excessive caution could so easily undo one. 'But we will stay here.'

'Yes.' Milady tried to smile, then suddenly clenched her fists with a little gasp. 'But I do not like this woman! I cannot! You think me a fool,' she said, pressing one hand to her trembling lips, and turned away as Catherine started to reach out to her. 'Perhaps I am, a little. I have no taste left for this life. If Robert survives this, we must give it up. Oh, *Dieu!*' She buried her face in her hands.

Concerned, Catherine took her aunt in her arms. 'Milady, he will come back to you. Do not fear.'

Milady stiffened and pulled away, haughty beneath the tears glistening on her cheeks. 'When Aglaé comes with our things, send her to me with a soothing draught from my dressing case. I need rest.' Without another word, she went out.

Catherine softly closed the door and lingered there before shaking her head of cropped golden curls and removing her hand from the smooth panels. It would do no good to go after her aunt. Milady was a solitary person; as long as she must endure separation from Milord, she wanted no one else. It had always been this way through the years when

Milady had raised Catherine as her own child. Even Armand had known very early that his *maman* would always think first of Milord and then of him. She was not a soft or a sentimental woman, but her every fiber belonged to her husband. If he died, it would kill her.

Thoughtfully Catherine sat down by the fire. Gad, but devotion was an odd creature. Would she ever hold a man that dear? It was doubtful. She was not cut of ordinary cloth, and she had not been raised in the ordinary way. A proper mate would be hard to find, providing she was ever given the leisure to look.

She yawned, showing a glimmer of white teeth, and stretched out her long body. She, too, needed rest if she were to attend a full-dress ball this evening. *Merde*, but the old woman was quick in her decisions. And tonight no gaffes dared Catherine permit herself. She cocked her head to one side, considering the choice of charming the English *ton* at once or letting them come gradually to her. Ah, if time was not in the way! But she would keep her nerves steady and let them come to her. It was best.

Excitement stirred within her. This merry occasion promised to be the real beginning of her task, and a challenge which she looked forward to taking on for Milord's sake. Ah, *oui*, for Milord.

CHAPTER THREE

Silence hushed the narrow dressing room, silence maintained strictly to preserve Sir Giles Thorne, Bart., from distraction of any sort. He stood – tall, lean, and rather rangy – before a cabrioled looking-glass in his shirt, silk breeches of powder blue, and stocking feet, his chin pointed toward the ceiling, where cupids cavorted among painted flowers. Intent upon winding a starched neckcloth round his throat, he spared no glance for the underfootman who was hunched on the floor and polishing his master's dancing shoes as though his life depended upon producing a mirror gleam from them, nor did he appear to notice the somberly clad valet – a scrap of a fellow with a pinched face and thinning hair – who was hovering about in a state of suppressed anxiety with six fresh neckcloths over one arm. Three ruined ones hung across his other arm. Sir Giles leaned forward, frowned in a moment of hestitation which made the valet bite his lip, then tied the neckcloth with two quick, deft movements of his hands. By studied and infinitely skillful degrees which had the underfootman gaping in admiration, Sir Giles lowered his square, somewhat bony chin, and, in so doing, formed precise folds in the starched muslin. He paused again, rolling one of his cold blue eyes to survey his reflection.

'Well, Creed?' he asked.

The valet started forward with a delicate clearing of his throat. 'If I might venture to suggest it, sir ... not, er, quite.'

'Ah.' Sir Giles turned back to the glass with a tightening

of his firm mouth. Must he stand here all night tying starchers? Accepting the square of fine linen which Creed put into his hand, he began to perfect the sharp creases in his cravat with rapid delicacy, not looking at the brief note written on elegant, hot-pressed paper now lying atop his dressing-table, though it was uppermost in his mind nonetheless. Why the devil must she take the bit in her teeth? It was addlepated of her to drag in a brace of unknown females with as much nonchalance as one might adopt a stray cat or mongrel.

He threw down the finishing cloth, which the underfootman hastened to snatch up, and snapped his fingers. 'My waistcoat, if you please.'

Creed presented him with the desired article, a creation of marvelously fine satin in a blue as pale as Sir Giles's nether garments. Sir Giles examined his cuffs, still undecided as to whether the length of the ruffles was exactly right. Thunder take her! How could a man think clearly about anything with such a tangle before him? He had little doubt she'd done this just to plague him, and it was his notion to make her rue she'd ever entertained the fancy.

Stepping into his gleaming shoes, Sir Giles gave his thick tawny hair a particularly savage brushing. 'Thank you, that is well,' he said to the boy, then, impatiently, for he was in a fever to be gone to this cursed ball and put a flea in his mama's ear, he snapped his fingers once more. 'I am ready, Creed.'

The underfootman sprang to attention and quivered there like a young hunting dog at point. A reverent hush fell over the room once more as Creed brought forth the long-tailed coat with its short waist and magnificent shoulders, fashioned in dark blue superfine by the hands of Weston of Bond Street. It required both Creed and the underfootman to fit Sir Giles into the coat, so closely was it molded to his

40

figure. He surveyed himself one last time before the looking-glass, grimaced in satisfaction, and accepted his chapeau bras, snuffbox, and handkerchief from Creed.

'Thank you both,' he said in his curt, dispassionate fashion and took up the letter between his fingers as he strode out of the room into his bedchamber, which was kept as sparsely elegant as the rest of his life.

'Giles! I thought you would never come out!'

Sir Giles paused in mid-stride to eye his younger brother, who was perched astride the carved eagle foot of his bed and munching upon an apple with the smug air of a cat filled with cream. 'If you are conspiring with Mama, Willy, I am going to be vexed with you.'

Willy lowered his apple. 'Lord, you're in a regular blue fit. What's she done this time?'

Sir Giles tossed him the letter. 'That will provide enough explanation. I am in a hurry.'

Willy waved the sheet of paper idly, his green eyes bright beneath a mass of tousled brown locks. 'You, in a hurry? What fustian! You are only afraid I'm here to dun you.'

'Aren't you?' Impatient as he was, Sir Giles supposed he must spend at least a moment with the lad, and sighed as he prepared himself for a bout of bantering. '*Aren't* you?' he repeated.

'No, of course I'm not, so you may as well stop looking martyred.' Willy grinned, with a show of teeth dazzling against his swarthy complexion, and took another bite of his apple with a great crunch. 'Felicitate me, sir,' he said, swallowing, 'for I have made a conquest in the art of love.'

That did take Sir Giles's thoughts from his mother's latest start. 'You alarm me,' he said in his blandest accents, and drew out his watch to check the time. 'Who is the, er, delight?'

'Ah.' With another brilliant smile Willy cast his apple core unerringly into the grate across the room, sending up a

41

shower of sparks. 'The Divine Harriette, no less.'

'Good God!' Jolted, Sir Giles groped for his sangfroid. 'Rather above your touch, I should have thought.'

'Well, so did I,' admitted Willy ingenuously. 'But I've been permitted to join her circle of acquaintances when they all call in the afternoons. It's prodigiously dull, if I may say so, with tea cakes and a sip of claret, but she does let me come, though I am the youngest of the group and with the smallest expectations. Surely she would not do so if she didn't care for me. I mean, *really* care for me.'

Sir Giles realized at once her reasons were far different than Willy supposed. Harriette Wilson was as shrewd as she was comely, and it was obvious she saw Willy as but a means to Sir Giles's purse. Willy was a blithe individual, yet if this matter was not nipped in the bud it would leave its scars. But to protect the boy from a woman of that stamp would be difficult. He could not bear much frankness at his age.

Sir Giles sighed. 'My dear Will, with all due congratulation, I do not think you can afford to give Miss Wilson carte blanche. Have you considered the strain this would put on your quarterly allowance?'

'Giles!' cried Willy, red-faced. He clambered off his perch. 'How can you be so devoid of understanding? I desire to marry her! She is a divine creature, so beautiful one's breath is quite snatched away –'

'Nonsense!' retorted Sir Giles in alarm. 'She is nothing at all out of the common way. Besides, you cannot go marrying the queen of the Fashionable Impures, even if she would agree to it . . . which I doubt.'

'Not at all! Devil take it, she will agree, because, given time, I mean to make myself indispensable to her peace of mind. Oh, yes, I know what she is, but that can be changed. It isn't as though she'll be providing the heirs to the baronetcy.'

Sir Giles winced at that shaft and eyed Willy darkly. 'As you say, William.' Going to the bed, he picked up the letter, crumpled it, and tossed it into the fire.

'I say!' Willy stepped forward. 'You asked me to read that, remember?'

'I do.' Sir Giles subjected him to an arctic stare. 'But the rose clouds at present in your brain would not permit you to give the consideration at hand full justice. Excuse me. We will talk of your ... plans later.' With a glint in his blue eyes Sir Giles left the house and climbed into the sedan chair waiting at the steps for him. Only then, in the privacy of that darkness, did he allow his fist to clench and strike his knee. How perfectly damnable of Willy to come along with need of having his head rescrewed just when their parent showed every evidence of going out of hers! If there was anything he detested, it was the need to be in two places at once. His lips tightened as he tried to force his tensed muscles to relax to the sway of the chair. Very well, he would give Willy time to come out of this coil on his own. Failing that, Sir Giles would deal with the modern Aspasia himself, and if Willy got a trifle burnt in the process, perhaps he would learn something. As for these females who had insinuated themselves into his mother's household ... let them learn to regret it! Whatever Lady Thorne chose to say, he intended to turn them out in the street as soon as possible.

The Sperling residence blazed light between its Palladian columns. Paying off the chairmen and linkboy, Sir Giles left his conveyance to approach the entrance on foot, thus sparing himself the annoyance of having to sit in a hopeless jumble of carriages jockeying for position at the steps.

'Sir Giles!' The voice was rich and full as a plume-adorned head with masses of luxurious curls appeared in a landau window.

Sir Giles bowed over the perfumed fingers extended to

him, murmured something, and slipped away before the lady could claim him as an escort. He had no intention of wasting the evening as a cavalier. Striding up the grand staircase with its scarlet carpet and festooned banisters, Sir Giles entered the ballroom with a purposeful step. Consciously he paused just short of the receiving line and glanced round. At once he saw his parent, dressed in a purple silk gown and turban, and holding court upon a gilded settee. A young woman of queenly lines and admirable shoulders was at her side. His gaze narrowed in a moment's speculation before he turned his attention to his hostess and executed a bow.

'Sir Giles, how good of you to grace my party.' Lady Reginald Sperling, who had once been attractive in a mild way, gave him her gentle smile. 'And this is my niece, Augusta Lyndon. I believe your mama will have mentioned her.'

Gazing at Lady Reginald's arched brows, Sir Giles felt a deeper frustration stab him. She really was not clever at conveying significances, but that hardly mattered when here he stood confronted at last by the miss his mother had been rhapsodizing over for the past three months in hopes of arousing his interest. Miss Lyndon had her fair share of looks, but one glance at her blushing face told him nearly everything he could care to know about her. She appeared to be generous and kind to a fault, a frequent blusher, and someone who probably adored kittens. He guessed her years to be seventeen, which in comparison to his own made him wonder once again about the state of his parent's mind. Miss Lyndon looked frightened of him, an absurd attitude which annoyed him further, but which he could understand. One need hardly guess what she had been told to persuade her to favor him! And the fact that she was alarmed rather than eager to join the pursuit decided him to show her kindness.

He bowed. 'Charmed, Miss Lyndon.' She murmured a

confused acknowledgment, and he promptly forgot her as his eyes strayed again to his mother.

'Is that not the dearest girl Lady Thorne has brought?' asked Lady Reginald. 'I must point her out to you ... no, she is not in sight. But how silly of me! I suppose you know all about her. Not quite in the common way, is she?'

'I fear I cannot say, never having met the, er, young lady,' he said in a silken voice. The effrontery of it, dragging one of those females here and claiming her before one and all! It would appear his mother had taken complete leave of her senses after all, for she would not perform her histrionics before the world merely to plague him. For a moment he toyed with the thought that the unknown pair might not be mushrooms at all, only to at once dismiss the notion as niggling. No one with the least amount of proper breeding or intentions would go to a stranger and ask to be taken in. The very idea was extraordinary. He frowned, then recalled himself enough to do what was polite and request Miss Lyndon to save one of her dances for him.

'You are most gracious, sir,' she said, looking more dismayed than ever. 'I ... I should be honored.'

'Thank you,' he replied. And his doting parent desired him to wed this child, who had more hair than wit and not the least conversation to recommend her! He could imagine no worse fate. With another bow he moved on.

A matron with a brace of daughters signaled to him, but at that moment he spied Lord Reginald Sperling, who likewise indicated a desire for his presence with a small motion of his balding head. With some relief Sir Giles threaded his way through the crush of guests, pausing only to lift an eyebrow at one of the musicians, a youthful fellow whose attention was trained more on the female guest than upon his fiddle-scraping.

'Good evening, my lord,' he said, coming up to his host and giving his hand.

Lord Reginald clasped it warmly. 'My dear boy, you're

45

looking unaccountably grim this evening.'

'So are you.' Sir Giles was quick to note that Lord Reginald's frown did not clear away. In fact, Lord Reginald, who was on the downhill side of fifty and keenly good-natured, betrayed a tenseness which was not at all like him. Sir Giles sent him a swift look. 'What is wrong?'

'Nothing... yet.' Lord Reginald sighed. 'Come. Let us slip away where we can have a brief talk.'

'Of course.' Refusing to throw his mind open to useless conjecture, Sir Giles followed him away to a spacious library that smelled strongly of leather armchairs and tobacco. While Lord Reginald locked the door behind them and stuffed his handkerchief into the keyhole Sir Giles stood studying the room with approval. A wine-colored rug was tossed across a floor of mahogany parquet, and a brass dragon guarded the dark-hued mantel. Two large maps dominated one wall; one was of England, the other of France and its neighbors – which, in view of the war and Lord Reginald's close acquaintance with half the members of the Foreign Office, was hardly surprising. Tiny colored flags marked the positions, presumably, of Napoleon's armies across Europe; it was not a reassuring sight. Near the door a watercolor sketch of a liver spaniel struck an incongruous note.

'Well!' Lord Reginald crossed the room to throw his key onto the littered desk. 'Sit down, my boy, unless you've a fear of creasing those splendid breeches. I'm dashed how you can be such a clotheshorse and still come out all right. Would you care for a cigar? I have some of those clever French matches about –'

'My lord,' interrupted Sir Giles with one of his gentler smiles. 'You are shilly-shallying. Let's cut line, shall we?'

Lord Reginald sighed and nodded. 'I can't say I'm eager to face this business.' He handed over a slim cigar from an ironbound box and a bottle of sulfuric acid. 'You know, it's

46

decidedly queer, not to mention dirty.' Digging out a box of splints from beneath a pile of papers, he leaned back in his chair, grasping his lapel with a frown. 'Devilishly dirty. It concerns the Prince Regent.'

'Good God.' Selecting one of the splints, Sir Giles gestured with it in exasperation. 'If that is all –'

'There is a plot out to murder him!' said Lord Reginald sharply. 'You know I do not hang upon court gossip.'

Sir Giles nodded an apology, his brows drawing together as he plunged the splint into the bottle, then drew it out to watch it ignite with a small puff of flame. 'Who has set it about?' he asked, drawing gently on his cigar before tossing the match into the cold grate, where it went out beneath a small swirl of ashes. He let the acrid smoke rise about him, his every sense and thought alert. 'The princess of Wales?'

'No.' Lord Reginald did not smile at the joke. 'The Emperor of France.'

Startled, Sir Giles drew too sharply and filled his lungs with the bitter smoke. 'Napoleon Bonaparte?' he asked, coughing, and grimaced at the cigar. 'Good God, is this Spanish?'

'Italian,' replied Lord Reginald. 'Vile, isn't it? Yes, it's Napoleon. The man has the effrontery of Satan.'

'Granted.' Sir Giles threw the cigar away. 'And?'

'I think you can understand the consequences if this assassination plan should succeed,' said Lord Reginald with a grave look.

'There would be confusion –'

'My boy,' laughed Lord Reginald, 'you have a gift for understatement. State mourning would have to be observed, crippling our military forces – especially the navy. A new regent would have to be named, following a fresh examination of the king. I'm not at all certain the Royal Family would consent to having York in that position, no matter what the line of succession may be.

There would most certainly be another confrontation with Queen Charlotte. But in any case there would be more concern over these matters than over what the French might be up to.' Lord Reginald frowned. 'Napoleon has begun fitting out a new fleet of warships and troop-carrying frigates. To my mind this all spells invasion.'

Sir Giles nodded. He did not consider himself the military type; certainly he had never experienced any desire to purchase his colors and follow Wellesley about Spain, but that did not prevent him from being able to grasp matters such as these, or to be concerned about them. 'And this all hinges on a royal assassination. How then, do we save Prinny from murder?' His lips curled slightly. 'Shall I volunteer to play watchdog over him?'

'No, there are others for that.' Now at last Lord Reginald did smile, although thinly. He rubbed one sagging jowl. 'We would prefer His Highness not to know of this danger to his person. It might alarm him into leaving London, and he can be better protected here. You see, our informant at the Tuileries – actually he is the lackey who opens the door to Napoleon's audience chamber – has sent us specific information concerning the plot. Do you know, by chance, one Jacques-Pierre de Bleu?'

'We think he arrived in England perhaps a fortnight ago, but we cannot be sure. He's staying very well hidden. But we do know his sister and aunt are here. In fact, they are among this gathering tonight.' Lord Reginald placed his fingertips together, one by one, and kept his gaze intently upon his guest. 'Giles, you are a handsome figure. If you were to seek out the girl –'

'No, my lord,' said Sir Giles in quick refusal. 'What good would my seducing her do for us? She is not the killer.'

'Of course not, but she will know of Jacques-Pierre's whereabouts. She can lead us to him.' Lord Reginald leaned forward. 'I know you're not much in the petticoat

48

line, but, pray, do reconsider this, Giles! There are not many men in this realm whom I would trust with what I've told you this evening.'

Sir Giles smiled thinly in acknowledgment. 'Your confidence overwhelms me, sir. But again, no. I doubt I would be very convincing.' Lord Reginald's snort brought up his gaze, and he shook his head. 'I am sorry. I would willingly serve my country in any way but this.' His brows drew together. 'In fact, it's an intolerable suggestion.'

'So is the murder of our prince!'

A tense moment stretched between them, Sir Giles very much on the verge of anger and Lord Reginald looking hard pressed to hold his in check. 'Very well,' said Lord Reginald, and rose. 'I see I was wrong in coming to you.' He gave a little bow. 'Forgive me. It can be done by anyone, I daresay, although... Giles, I merely thought you had the best means of striking up an acquaintanceship with the girl.'

'Why should I?' asked Sir Giles, brows high. 'I don't know her, and I hardly think a French adventuress has access to any circle I move in.'

'Well, she does.' Lord Reginald gave him a rather peculiar look over his shoulder as he crossed the room to unlock the door. 'She's your mother's new protégée after all.'

'What?' Sheer astonishment struck Sir Giles, leaving him rather stunned. Then the combined exasperations of the evening boiled up into wrath, sending him to his feet. Almost he protested the coincidence but did not, realizing with a lash of cold fury that it all fit together very neatly. 'Good God, so that is where they have come from!' He hardly noticed he spoke aloud; he knew only that these matters could not be left untended a moment longer. With a curt glance at his host he said, 'I should like to see this girl, if I may.'

'Why, yes. Do you mean you haven't met her?' With a blink Lord Reginald hastened to accompany him back to the ballroom, where noise and stuffy warmth rolled over them like an oppressive wave. After the comparative dimness of the corridor, the blaze of the chandeliers – nine of them, in fact – almost blinded Sir Giles. Narrowing his eyes, he permitted his host to lead him to a vantage point.

'There she is, still sitting with your mother. I don't believe she's danced yet. Not the type that immediately takes a gentleman's fancy, I expect.'

Studying the girl, Sir Giles scarcely paid him heed. Yes, good God, yes, that tall girl with the guinea-gold curls cut ridiculously short, the girl whose shoulders he had previously admired, she was the encroaching mushroom he had meant to turn out into the street! It was intolerable that she should be taking advantage of his mother and more so that she should dare plot against his ruler and his country. He could not permit it; by heaven, he would not!

Curbing his rage, he said in a cool manner, 'I believe I was too quick in refusing you, my lord. You may depend upon me to do all that is necessary.' And his voice deepened as he thought of the longer and more satisfying treatment which could be dealt this audacious doxy; one might even call it revenge for making his mother a dupe.

'My dear boy! Giles, you take such a weight from my mind!' Seizing his hand, Lord Reginald wrung it warmly.

Sir Giles winced. 'What did you say her name is?'

'Catherine de Bleu.' Lord Reginald beamed and gave him a pat on the shoulder. 'Thank you, thank you ever so much. And now I've got to get back to my guests before I raise Amelia's temper.'

Letting him go, Sir Giles stood aloof from the guests a moment longer, savoring the name beneath his breath. 'Catherine de Bleu.' There was an obvious falseness about it he did not care for. She looked a cool piece at this

50

distance, and if she was not dancing, that would soon be mended. Not caring to hesitate longer, he moved forward in her direction. *And now, Mademoiselle de Bleu,* he thought with a savage sort of anticipation. *And now your troubles begin.*

At closer glance, she was more striking of feature than she had first appeared. Ignoring his mother's acerbic comments of greeting and introduction, he took his time in appraising that direct face with its wide, firm mouth, open brow, and fiercely acquiline nose, all fashioned in skin as delicate and as pure as porcelain. He vastly disliked her short hair, but its golden color was acceptable to his standards of beauty. Her hands were shapely but strong for a woman, and the firm chin hinted at determination of purpose. But it was her eyes which seized his attention, even distracted it. As open and direct as the rest of her countenance, their cool green depths held the hint of a challenge – of what nature he did not care to guess – but he disliked that quality, too. Her voice, when she spoke in response to their introduction, was low and pleasing in tone. She did not simper.

'I have been misled, madame,' she said at once with a plainly fluent grasp of English. 'You told me your son was in his declining years, and he is not.'

Piqued, Sir Giles frowned.

Her ladyship merely shrugged, however, in response to his ironical glance. 'You honor me, Giles, by bestirring yourself so soon to meet my protégée.'

Her tone was deliberately provoking, as was the gaze of her dark gray eyes, and he derived dry satisfaction in taking the wind out of her sails. Ah, and what she would say when eventually told what sort of little charmer she had taken to her bosom! 'You appear to expect my disapproval,' he said, pulling out his snuffbox to examine it, but not missing Mlle de Bleu's lift of her brows and smile, as though she enjoyed watching the battle lines being drawn. At once he took warning. Any other chit would have been supremely uncomfortable; it seemed he faced a devilish little intriguer. He must remember not to underestimate the jade. 'But, my dear ma'am,' he continued smoothly to his frowning parent. 'I fail to understand your attitude. I am delighted you have found a companion who suits you.' He permitted the faint gleam to fade from his chilly gaze as he lifted a minute pinch of snuff to each nostril. 'She is a trifle young perhaps, but –'

'Coxcomb.' Lady Thorne rapped her ebony-handled lorgnette across his hand. 'Madame de Chalier serves for that.'

'My aunt,' put in Mlle de Bleu helpfully. Her green eyes appraised him in a manner he found disquieting.

Irritated at having his measure taken so coolly, he bowed. 'And where is she?' he inquired at his most attentive, proffering the snuffbox. 'Do you dip, mademoiselle?'

'Thank you.' She helped herself to the blend with an elegant turn of wrist he found arresting in spite of himself. 'Milady is not present. She is laid down with the sick headache.' Mlle de Bleu dusted the crumbs of snuff from her fingers and leaned back upon one elbow, one green slipper swinging gently beneath the hem of her white gown. 'We regret it.'

'Poppycock,' said Lady Thorne with a sniff. 'Sheer lack of discipline, *I* call it. Mollycoddlers have no place in my sympathies –'

But he was not listening. Again speculation narrowed his gaze. The girl bore herself like a princess; she could be no common adventuress! He began to look forward with more interest to the prospect of thwarting her and her unknown brother. Abruptly he executed a bow. 'Mademoiselle, balls are for dancing, I believe you'll agree.' He proffered his arm. 'May I have the honor?'

A genuine smile of amusement lit her face, and the cold green of her gaze melted into golden hazel. '*Peste*,' she said with a ripple of laughter in her low voice. 'At last I am presented with a dancing partner. Gad, sir, but I am honored indeed.'

The suspicion that her mirth was for some reason directed at him, coupled with his annoyance at his mother's open expression of surprise, left him hard put to keep his sangfroid as he escorted Mlle de Bleu onto the floor to join a country set. He supposed his parent had come to considered him totally incapable of gallantry and had already been instructing her charge to that effect. How he detested being an object of gossip!

'Forgive me,' he said with something of a snap. 'Perhaps you are not acquainted with our country dances –'

'You are too kind, monsieur.' Her thick, dark lashes veiled the amused eyes, and the blaze of candlelight sparked a thousand highlights from her golden curls as she cocked her head at him. 'But I am well versed in the accomplishments.'

At that point the music struck up, and she skipped away down the line, graceful and light on her feet despite her height. He caught a glimpse of neatly turned ankles beneath a flash of her skirts before he was obliged to give attention to his own capering.

But what a sight she presented, a straight, graceful figure in her simple gown, queenly in her manner but rather dashing in her boyish curls, and moving through the steps with such supple ease he realized she had not spent her formative years confined to a stool and a lapful of needlework. She was no beauty, but as Lady Reginald had remarked, she *was* a cut above the ordinary. And he was quite aware of how her laughing features and dazzling complexion was attracting the notice of the guests, who had chosen to snub her earlier. Now she could not be ignored, and to take advantage of this fact, he asked her to stand up with him again as soon as the dance ended.

She regarded him a moment, twinkling, but breathing more lightly than he. Yet for all her manner of the *bon enfant*, he noticed her cool calculation was still present. 'You, sir, wish to make me a byword,' she said in light accusation, and he was intrigued that she had yet to blush. 'But, faith, why should I fail to take my chance at pleasure? You are a superb partner, Sir Giles.'

A hush fell over the ballroom, for it was to be the grand minuet. As Sir Giles took his place in the line with her he was not unappreciative of the picture they presented – both fair, he in blue and she in white. A rather grim smile touched his firm lips as the stately music began. It pleased him to think his sudden show of favor toward this unknown would raise her status in society. She would be sought after now, and the more distractions for her, the easier for him to trick her.

He glanced sidewise at her and blinked to see the complete change in her manner. Who would have thought to see the merry sprite of a moment ago now as stately as the music, her elegance of carriage and movement unsurpassed by any other damsel present? She was like a chameleon, and he realized with some pique he had yet to take her measure as she had, apparently, taken his. When they finished, she swept him a magnificent curtsy to the floor, head high, and her eyes cool and green again.

'I thank you, Sir Giles,' she said in obvious dismissal and accepted the arm of a young cousin of Sefton's who had appeared out of the crowd.

Sir Giles found himself abandoned as callously as though he were no more than a schoolboy. Such treatment had not been dealt him in years. He did not find it a pleasant sensation, and as he rather abruptly left the floor his promise to undo the adventuress burned inside him as a coal of determination. Now free of the girl's admittedly distracting presence, he marveled at her composure. For surely she must know of her brother's commission, and if so.... Sir Giles lifted his brows and thought he must have just danced with the devil's female. Well, she would not harm his mother or destroy England while he stood in the way!

Concealing his thoughts behind an icy exterior, he stood up with Miss Lyndon – who was as vapid as cloth after the bewitching mademoiselle – then with Princess Esterhazy, who flirted so enchantingly he lingered at her side until she began her usual tedious game of trying to make a pet of him.

Lady Thorne was deep in conversation with a zealously corseted matron when he took his leave, so he did not go to her side, reflecting with a wry twist of his lips that she would not care to interrupt her discussion for him unless she had discovered yet another damsel to throw at his head. But the following morning when he emerged from his imposing residence in splendid buckskins, top-boots of soft brown, and a corded riding coat of Bath cloth to mount a sorrel hack, he turned his direction toward Half-Moon Street and dismounted there a half-hour later to stride inside with an idle swing of his riding whip. From Hartleby, the butler, he learned his mama had not yet left her boudoir, and, arrogantly tossing his hat onto the hall table, he passed up the curved stairs to that formidable chamber, where the combined scents of jasmine, hartshorn, lavender water, and hot chocolate, plus the yapping of a bit of fluff he assumed was a dog, assailed him like a blow the moment he opened the door.

'Ah, Giles! Do come in.' Lady Thorne measured him with her eagle gaze as she set down her cup and a handful of invitations. 'I was just having my chocolate. Would you like some?'

'Please,' he said and sat down on an overstuffed chair, at his ease in a room that had never put him at a disadvantage, no matter how many feminine trimmings she crammed into it. He watched her fill a cup for him, as conscious as she that he had succeeded in surprising her with this early visit. 'That's a fetching cap,' he said merely to distract her.

She put an involuntary hand to it before pulling down the corners of her mouth. 'You did not come here just to flummery me.'

'Suspicion will make you bilious,' he chided, accepting the cup she thrust at him. Its smooth porcelain warmed his fingers, which had become chilled during the brisk ride there. 'I thought you might be glad of a visit.'

'Fiddlesticks!' She sniffed and groped across a cluttered occasional table near her chair for her lorgnette. 'You've come to read me a scold. Only I won't endure one, so you may as well finish your chocolate and be off again.'

He paused, curbing his annoyance until he could be sure of the coolness in his voice. 'I protest this unkindness, ma'am. You persist in your notion that I never spare time for you, yet when I appear to remedy this fault –'

'Very well!' she broke in with a snap. 'For heaven's sake, do stop prosing on like Chesby Sperling. You may talk until you're blue about the eyes, but I know very well you've come to take Catherine from me.'

'I certainly intend to,' he said and almost smiled at her gasp. 'In my curricle. Do you think she would like a drive about the park this afternoon?'

Lady Thorne dropped her lorgnette. 'Giles! You insidious man, what are you up to? If you mean to entice the girl out merely to buy her off –'

'Good God,' he said with some irritation, 'I should like to see her again. Why you must begin ringing a peal about my ears, I have no idea.' Going a bit on his hauteur, he rose. 'I did not realize she is a candidate for a nunnery and never to be conversed with or taken on outings. Goodbye, Mama. I shall come again when you are in a better humor.'

To his vexation she said nothing but sat there gripping her cup with her eyes narrowed and hard. He was at the door before she stirred in her chair.

'Giles, I'm sure I don't know where you get these toplofty quirks of yours. No one said you could not take Catherine out driving if she wants to go. I shall ask her later.'

Sir Giles turned slowly back from the door with the urge to give her a good shaking. He bowed with an ironical gleam in his eyes. 'Thank you.' It was impossible to tamely resume his seat, and instead he propped his shoulders against a flower-strewn mantel, wrinkling his nostrils at the sharp scent of crushed greenery and nudging the fluff's black button nose away before it could mar the polish of his boot.

'But never say you've taken a fancy to her,' continued Lady Thorne, snapping her fingers at the dog, which bounced to her feet like a furry India-rubber ball. She peered at him with an air of speculation that made him long to cast in the towel and flee this entire business, but since it was out of the question to take her into his confidence as long as she remained besotted with the girl, he forced himself to stand fast and endure her bristly eccentricities.

'Is such a thing so unlikely, Mama?' he retorted with unfeigned impatience. 'Good God, I'm a full-blooded man, you know –'

'Let us not discuss your various bits of muslin.'

He snorted. 'We are not discussing them. I simply found this girl beyond the usual. She's French, isn't she? And not taking well, from what I could see last night.'

'Stuff!' Lady Thorne shook a finger at him. 'I should have guessed at once it was not interest but merely more of

57

your moonshine madness you persist in calling acts of kindness. Fiddle-faddle with you! You're as hopeless a case as ever!'

He all but lost his temper then. Really, mother or not, she had no right to be throwing such loose reproaches in his teeth. 'I think we need not venture into the past,' he said through stiffened lips, distaste at this whole affair bitter within him. Why the devil had he let a moment's desire for revenge embroil him in this? But he'd be damned if he'd back out! He let his steely eyes narrow. 'Who are this girl and her aunt? Have you learned their background? I hope someone suitable provided their recommendation to you.'

'Yes, yes, I've had all that checked.' Lady Thorne scooped up her lapdog with a sniff. 'I did not cut my eyeteeth yesterday, you know. They are displaced aristocrats, of course, but hardly beggars if they are accustomed to jaunting about the Continent at their leisure. I would not give you a brass farthing for that uppity Milady de Chalier. Such airs as she does put on; I think she could rival a royal duchess. But the girl's all right. I like her because she stood up to me with no nonsense about it. That's why I made up my mind to have them stay. Someone needs to take the chit in hand besides that bundle of nerves she's got for an aunt.'

Sir Giles concealed his alert interest behind a dry smile. 'I've no doubt they jumped at the invitation. You were rather precipitate, weren't you, ma'am?'

'If you mean I should have consulted you first, no, I do not think so.' Lady Thorne's soft hands fondled the dog, which yapped in shrill contentment and squirmed about in a fawning manner Sir Giles found repuslive. 'I told you I like the girl, and I've never needed you to tell me how to make up my mind. And, *no,* you dreadfully cynical creature, they were not eager in the least to stay here. I cannot abide misplaced pride, or I should have left them to their nasty hotel. Stay at Fenton's indeed.' She sniffed.

'Whoever heard of such a peagoose notion?'

'Fenton's is very fashionable, ma'am,' he replied in a calm voice which gave no hint of his satisfaction at this piece of information. So the intriguer had lost her chance to come and go as she pleased, but still he thought she had gained a great many advantages by the move. 'I have eaten a very tolerable beefsteak there. And perhaps these ladies are hesitant to place themselves in such dependency on you.'

Lady Thorne frowned. 'I believe you have gone cock-a-hoop over the girl. Are you taking her side of the matter? Don't be a dolt. This may not be Thorne House, but it is far more suitable an abode for a genteel young lady than any common travelers' lodging. And so I have told them.'

Sir Giles affected a yawn. 'My dear ma'am, must we wrangle over a matter that seems to be settled?'

'You are quite right.' Lady Thorne seemed almost to hesitate for a moment, then clutched her lorgnette. 'Giles, I have a favor to ask of you.'

'Oh?' Coolly he lifted his brows.

'I wish to give an assembly of some kind. A ball perhaps.'

'But of course,' he said, thinking more of what he was to say to the adventuress this afternoon than of what her ladyship was speaking of. 'If the preparations shan't prove too fatiguing for you.'

'Well!' she said, visible unbending and putting out a hand which he was obliged to kiss, despite its having just stroked the dog. 'I did not hope you would be so obliging as to give me Thorne House –'

'One moment,' he said with the alarm of having been tricked. 'I did not agree to –'

'Block! How may I have a ball without a ballroom?' Scornfully she pushed the dog from her lap. 'I want to do something in style for Catherine and –'

'What? That –' He stopped himself just in time and stood

tight-lipped for a moment before continuing more calmly. 'If you think you will escape becoming an on-dit for this, by all means proceed. Do you mean to adopt her as well?'

'That tone is not one which you may use to me, sir!' she snapped, in equally high dudgeon. Sparks of crimson began to fly in her cheeks. 'Lady Reginald has a niece, Augusta, who is a very good, biddable girl. I mean to pair the girls, and there will be no reason for anyone to find exception in that. Can't you recall her? You danced with her last night.'

He gestured in frustration, beginning to lose direction in the tangled web of her attack. 'A vapid damsel with nothing more than fluff and stars between her ears?' His expression hardened. 'Pray, do not begin more of your matchmaking! I shall not endure such humiliation again.'

'*Who* endured the humiliation?' retorted his parent just as sharply. 'You jilted poor Alice at the very altar, leaving her prostrate before the scandal –'

'So cut up with misery she managed to wed a marquess with one foot in the grave and more wealth than sense,' said Sir Giles in icy disdain. 'And I did not jilt her, Mama. She spoke first of breaking off the engagement.'

'Yes, and in honor what else could she do?'

'Was it honorable of her to deceive me as she did about –' Abruptly, as though cold water had been dashed over him, he checked himself and turned away, his eyes bleak. 'In any case,' he said quite softly, 'I beg you will not drag forth this Sperling girl –'

'She is not a Sperling but a Lyndon,' broke in Lady Thorne, as hard-eyed as he. 'And she has every quality a young wife ought to possess, no matter what your opinion may be of her mental powers. I shall do something for her, no matter what you say. Yes, even if I must drag out all the furniture from my own drawing room and attempt a rout which shall bore everyone unmercifully.'

He sighed, still unwilling to give way. Good God, if his parent were permitted to go forward with her schemes to put Catherine in the public eye, who would not think Lady Thorne a giddy old fool once Catherine was denounced as a minion of the enemy? And now that the conversation had taken so bitterly personal a turn, he could not hope to cajole his mother out of the idea. Damn! But there was nothing to do but give way.

'Yes, very well, you may have Thorne House.' He eyed his parent in no friendly manner. 'Next, I daresay, you will be throwing the mademoiselle at me.'

'It is you who came here mooning after her,' said Lady Thorne even more sharply, and gave no sign acknowledging her triumph. 'No, I do not want her for you at all. No foreign, *brassy* ways will ever rule at Thorne House if I have my say in the matter!'

He could not resist the temptation to be provoking. 'I thought you liked the girl,' he said, taking snuff.

'I do.' Her ladyship glared at him. 'She is very well in her own way and amuses one for a time. But I expect someone more complacement in a wife for you, once you cease doing as you please with no thought to be obliging toward others.'

His lips curled as he bowed. 'I thank you for your frankness. But be advised, ma'am, that I shall never oblige your matrimonial schemes! Use them upon Willy, if you must, but kindly leave me alone.'

'Willy is much too young for such a consideration,' she said with a sniff.

Almost he retorted to that, but his conscience would not condone telling her of her youngest child's fresh-conceived *tendre* for a barque of frailty. No, that was too low for her hearing, and he held back with tightened lips. 'I think,' he said shortly, 'we have no more to say to each other today. I shall be by at half-past four. If Miss de Bleu desires to go

61

out, please ask her to be ready at that time.' He swept an icy bow. 'Good day, ma'am!'

Striding out, he shut the door with a forceful snap and left the house with thunder on his brow. Devil take every female and her wiles! Vaulting into the saddle, he sprang his mount to a canter, vowing as he did so to make short work of his devilry with the fair Catherine's heart. He would woo her in the teeth of his mother's displeasure, charm her out of every secret, and abandon her as he had once abandoned his prospective bride. His brow darkened further at the thought of that piece of disaster. It seemed no one would ever let it lie forgotten. But Alice Mayfield was in the past. Now, he meant to see Catherine de Bleu pay well and dearly for her effrontery. Let the Frenchwoman beware! He would laugh to see her fall in the tangles of her own intriguing, and perhaps Lady Thorne would learn some prudence in the process of it all.

CHAPTER FOUR

A stray beam of sunlight peeped through the bed curtains, then leaped forward to skip across Catherine's face in a thousand impossibly quick pirouettes. Blinking against its sunny dazzlement, she awoke with a yawn, putting out one hand to tug at the bell, then snuggling deeper among her snowy pillows. What heaven, this luxury! Lazily she watched the maid enter to draw back the curtains, build a fire to dispel the lingering traces of a chilly spring night, and whisk away the white ball gown, which had been flung over a chair in the small hours of the morning. A kitchen-maid in a starched cap knocked and ventured inside with a breakfast tray of rolls and steaming chocolate. Catherine smiled to herself as this was set across her knees. She liked the English and their notions of how to be comfortable, but, gad, one dared not forget Milord or his desperate straits!

A frown appeared between her brows and she polished off her breakfast in a haste. Catching up a dressing gown of lace-covered silk, she swathed it about her slender figure and made her way to her aunt's room. Despite Lady Thorne's claims to have little use for Milady, she had assigned her guest apartments which could only be labeled magnificent. Catherine still had not learned not to catch her breath whenever she entered. Constructed along especially spacious lines, the bedchamber possessed an enormous canopied bed of rosewood. The walls were hung in celery-colored silk, threaded through with gold, and a vast picture of some wild American lake and forest was affixed above a Grecian fireplace. The sitting room never failed to delight Catherine, for it was oval in shape and done in the French style, with scarlet-and-cream-striped silk on the walls and chair cushions.

Here upon a settee reposed Milady, thin and dark and regal in draperies of burnished gold satin. Seeing Catherine, she waved dismissal to Aglaé, who was attending her, and looked up with a certain bleakness in her gaze. 'The glow in your face tells me you were a success at the ball. *Bon.*' Then she sighed. 'I fear already you grow too enchanted with this island. Remember, *s'il vous plaît*, who you are!'

'I never forget,' retorted Catherine, but without a rise in her tone. She gestured. 'How I adore this room! It is clever, don't you think?'

Milady shut her eyes. 'It makes me dizzy. Sit down and tell me of last night.'

'In faith, there's little enough to say.' Catherine perched upon the window seat. 'I made nothing of an impression. People are little interested in a *jeune fille* of foreign extraction.' Pensive, she studied the broidered toe of one slipper. 'I think the English are bored perhaps with the *émigrés.*'

'We are not *émigrés!*' snapped Milady. '*Mon Dieu*, those cowards! If they had thought less of their own skins and more of France, we –'

'Aunt,' rebuked Catherine with a lift of her brows. 'We are discussing the future, not the past.'

'Of course. *Oui*,' Milady's indignant eyes fell and she plucked at the pillow beneath her elbow. 'I am sorry. So you achieved no notice?'

'None.' Catherine nibbled at one slim finger with a frown. 'I think the dress was too simple. It is a garment for someone having seventeen years instead of four and twenty. I have learned this lesson.' She waved one hand. 'And I did not dance, no, not at all, until this one gentleman came striding up.' Cocking her gold head to one side, Catherine considered the faint thrill his approach had given her, and which even yet lingered. What sort of man was he to stir her in this odd way? It was almost as though...

'Catherine!' said Milady, jerking her from her thoughts. 'Continue, please. How rude you become, leaving yourself unfinished.'

'*Pardon.*' Catherine shifted in discomfiture both at Aunt Eustacie's rebuke and her own fit of daydreaming. *Peste,* it was unlike her to go off into the clouds! 'I... he was arrogant, Aunt, and held himself so.' She threw up her chin for emphasis. 'I do not think it was all the cravat, as with some. And such attire!' Her voice deepened with appreciation. 'Milord would have admired the coat.'

'Never mind his coat,' said Milady, with the corners of her mouth pulled down. 'Who is he? Has he position?'

'Oh, yes.' Catherine smiled. 'He is Sir Giles Thorne.'

'Bah!' Milady sat upright, her dark eyes snapping. 'I knew it was a mistake to come here. She –'

'Madame, you flatter me,' interrupted Catherine, impatient with this persistent suspicion. 'Lady Thorne does not want me for her son. She desires to see Miss Lyndon in that rôle and has herself told me this. I am to help her, and I do not think I mind. He needs a wife to soften those hard eyes. *Peste*, how cold and blue they are!' She affected a shiver. 'Like steel.'

'A pox upon his eyes,' snapped Milady, with her hands gripped so tightly together they showed white. 'Do you forget why you are here? We have no time to waste upon local affairs of the heart.'

'I think it would be wise to do so,' said Catherine, her eyes growing hard. 'Miss Lyndon is the niece of Lady

Reginald Sperling – a lady of high standing. And Sir Giles is himself of the Regent's acquaintance.' She nodded at Milady's faint gasp. 'I am never so foolish, Aunt, as to forget my purpose. Sir Giles stood up twice with me, out of kindness perhaps, although he does not look to be a kind man, and afterwards I did not lack for a partner.' She smiled with wry scorn, trying – for all her usual lack of feminine sensibilities – to ignore the pique such insulting behavior had wrought upon her. To be a wallflower one moment and toadied to the next was not at all to her liking! 'It was not pleasant,' she said simply enough, her eyes blazing green in contempt, 'but it was useful. I think we begin to make progress.'

'I hope so.' Milady leaned back and seemed to soften. 'Very well, child. Perhaps you should inveigle yourself into the good graces of this Sir Giles. We must use everyone we can, and never mind my fidgets. At least you are keeping your head.' She sighed. 'If only I could be sure Joseph has reached Armand...'

Catherine started to speak reassurance when a light knock on the door interrupted. Bidden to enter, the butler, Hartleby, stepped inside with a bow.

Excuse my interruption, madam,' he said to Milady before turning to Catherine. 'Her ladyship wishes you to know, miss, that Sir Giles called earlier with the desire to drive you through the park this afternoon. He will return at half-past four to learn of your pleasure.'

'Oh?' Rather pleased, Catherine lifted her brows. 'Thank you.'

He bowed himself out, and Milady sent her a curious glance. 'You will go, of course.'

'*Naturellement*.' Catherine smiled, then jumped to her feet. 'But it is past noon! *Mon Dieu*, I must decide upon my dress and then –' Swiftly she glanced at her aunt. 'What part shall I play? Oh, gad, how best to make good of his favor?' Frowning, she began to pace rapidly about. 'Last night I was very cool, very sophisticated. It piqued him. I think he did not know what to make of me, and yet sometimes it seemed almost as though he saw through this façade.' She halted with her frown deepening to a scowl. 'But I could not guess his measure at all. And now I need to know it. *Quelle horreur*, this uncertainty!' She faced Milady, who was in her own thoughts. 'He is terribly clever, one who can notice everything and guess more. He is also high in the instep, so I cannot dare to dazzle him with flirtation –'

'Catherine!'

Catherine tossed her head. 'I said I will not –'

'Do not even consider such things,' said her aunt, outraged. 'We have committed many scandalous acts, but we have never been *low*. Milord would be bery angry.' Having quelled Catherine, she nodded. 'I think in this instance you might be wiser simply to be yourself and not play any part.'

'But –'

'Protests?' Milady swept her into silence with a commanding gesture. 'If he is as you say –'

'Lady Thorne says he never acts but to please himself,' put in Catherine, most dubious about this notion of her aunt's. Be herself? Bah, she had been so many things for such a length of years she did not know herself at all.

'Then it is better not to try to enslave his usefulness,' said Milady in a voice of strengthening conviction. 'If he noticed you last night of his own volition, you must continue to let him assist you socially of his own free will.'

'Or else make him think it is his own idea,' said Catherine slowly, unable to help rising to this newest challenge. 'This will be difficult.'

'I depend upon you,' said Milady.

Shortly afterwards a thoughtful Catherine returned to

her room to dress in fawn cambric and then seek out Lady Thorne to thank her prettily for her efforts the previous evening.

'Flummery!' snapped her ladyship, looking pleased. 'I thought you would lie abed all day. Here.' She thrust a slim volume into Catherine's hands. 'You may read to me from that for a half hour, and then you may be excused to dress for your outing.'

It seemed Lady Thorne was giving commands. Although she intended to go out, Catherine lifted her golden head somewhat sharply from the opening line of Scott's *Marmion*. 'Do you think I should accept Sir Giles's invitation, ma'am?' she asked with disarming sweetness, the light of half-kindled anger in her fine eyes. 'I would not wish you to think I am . . . I am throwing my bonnet at him.'

'The expression is throwing your *cap*, girl,' corrected Lady Thorne with a sniff. 'And I know very well you haven't any such designs, and little good they would do you if you did. No one could *like* such a provoking wretch; he tries my patience sorely, you know.' But Catherine thought she heard a note of complacency beneath the sharpness in Lady Thorne's voice. Indeed, the old lady seemed unaccountably smug today, as though she had some matter going very much her way. 'By all means go with him. You're no milk-and-water miss to be shrinking in fear from his tempers. Gussie Lyndon is another matter, drat the girl. But get on with the book.' She put up her lorgnette as though to listen the better to Catherine's low, clear voice.

In a quarter of an hour two callers arrived, both gentlemen, and within five minutes of each other. Catherine found herself introduced to the Honorable William Thorne, my lady's youngest and something of an imp if his youthful features were any indication. Next, she met Lord Chesby Sperling, a portly man of middle years who peeped at her through his fingers, turned crimson beneath her astonished gaze, and apologized for having failed to meet her earlier.

'For I was in the throes of poetic inspiration, you see,' he added, leaning toward her so that she could see the ink stain upon one of his shirt points. His brown hair had a look of being perpetually damp and tousled, and his features were fleshy and soft. 'And so I failed to attend my sister's-by-law assembly.' He cleared his throat and for a moment seemed not to know what to do with his broad but well shaped hands. 'Er, wish I'd gone. You're devilishly inspiring.' And he crimsoned all over again.

He should have been coarse with this bumbling of speech and manner, his bulk and redness, and his large hands and feet, but there was an essential quality to him that made him seem not at all offensive. Catherine chose to laugh.

'Lord Chesby styles himself a poet,' explained Mr. Thorne, his grin all but blinding her. She gave him a swift look, the better to carry out one of her lightning appraisals, and was at once satisfied. Here was nothing but a boy, hey-go-mad as a sprite and one who would not hesitate to stake his all at the snap of the fingers. There was no guile in him, nor cunning; people who lived for the moment posed no danger to her.

But Lord Chesby was gasping in hurt reproach. '*Styles* myself? My dear Willy, I –'

'Never mind your fiddle-faddle,' said Lady Thorne. 'Catherine, you are forgetting the time.'

'Yes, I am.' With a blink Catherine withdrew her fascinated gaze from the scene before her and rose with a murmur to each gentleman. A startling pang of regret made her pause halfway up the stairs, however, and glance back over her shoulder at the drawing room door. In faith, she had enjoyed this afternoon and these people who had no more thought of anything than their circle of pleasure-filled life. To have such an existence was to have merriment and comfort, as well as being spared wondering of when a slip was to bring betrayal and the thrust of a knife in a dark street. And though she dreaded summoning up her talents for Sir Giles, she was eager, too, and could skip on up the stairs with a smile upon her lips. At least he was handsome and certainly well made!

For an instant a half-formed dream caught away her breath, then she threw her fingers to her lips in startlement. *Dieu*, it was absurd to indulge in a passion of creampot love with a man one was pledged to deceive and make a puppet of. She would not be so stupid! Tearing at the fastenings of her dress, she stepped out of it and kicked it across the floor. It was very well, this pretty room and this pretty life, but if she let it enchant her, she would have none but herself to blame when nemesis chopped their hopes asunder. She must prove impervious to company amusement; she must not be swayed by longings to nibble cake at dull little parties and dance at balls, especially when before such things had always bored her. She must not even acknowledge love for the lavender tree groaning at her window beneath its burden of fragrance and bursting blooms. She must remain cold as Milady and Milord had taught her to be cold; she must keep cool wits at hand, for the game was hardly begun and it would not do to wander in thought while in Sir Giles's company. There was no use hoping his aloof eye denoted more than an interest in his own vanity. From the first she had sensed a certain quality about him which could prove ruthless should he ever expect she was not the mere miss she played. Every appearance told her he was simply a gentleman to be used to gain access to the Regent, but she had not trusted appearances for years.

Still, there was a clearness of heart here in England which was new to her. She was drawn to it as though a pitcher brimming with spring water had been handed to her

70

after years of thirst. Pausing with her comb in midair, she gazed into the looking-glass at her part boyish, part woman, part nothing at all reflection. It was well to know her breeding and well to remember the legacy of her ancestors, but *parbleu!* She wanted something different than the small satisfaction that she was who she was no matter if none else ever knew it. Milord and Milady could never change now, and it was not fair to make them. Living as they did with schemes and intrigues and masquerades, however, was not life; it was as empty as a career upon the boards. She wanted more; yes, though Aunt Eustacie might throw up her hands in horror, there must be more! Catherine wanted a house that would stand over the next centuries, growing old slowly and steadily and gracefully beneath its tendrils of warm ivy, growing smaller beneath yews and oaks. She wanted a garden of flowers which she could plant and tend, and which after her some other lean girl would watch over, and after her another. ...

Catherine came to herself with a start and dropped her comb with a clatter upon an enameled box of rice powder. Gad, was she standing here dreaming of her grandchildren? Madness had surely struck her! She began to bustle about again, hurrying the finishing touches of her toilette as though to scold herself for falling into daydreams. But deep within her nestled a new resolution. This game she would finish, for she owed as much and more to her aunt and uncle. But more she would not do, not again, ever. She was finished with this half-life. When Milord was free, she would leave them and find a place for herself in the real world. The years had been too long; she could no longer accept their dream but must reach out to find her own.

Precisely at half-past the hour Aglaé, who had been hovering near the stairs, signaled, and Catherine sailed down the staircase in full view of Sir Giles, who was in the act of surrendering his hat to Hartleby in the hall. He glanced up, his eyes widening ever so slightly, and her chin lifted in satisfaction. She never intended to dress so simply again that she at once escaped the memory, and with this aim in mind had donned a bronze-green carriage dress with long sleeves puffed and drawn tight with innumerable tiny buttons. A pelisse trimmed at the throat with dark ermine protected her from the chill of a brisk spring day, and besides a poke bonnet adorned with a plume and tied with bronze ribbons beneath her chin, she carried a frilled sunshade to protect her fair complexion from the sun. Drawing on York tan gloves as she finished her descent, she gave him one of her cool glances.

'*Bonjour*, Sir Giles,' she said, speaking first, and made a slight gesture. 'As you see, I have delight to be accompanying you. Is it an honor much given'

'No,' he said, awarding her a bow. She noted his eyes were gray instead of blue at this moment and was disappointed, for she much preferred the other color. 'Shall we go?' he asked, proffering his arm and accepting his headgear back again from Hartleby. 'I am glad it is your habit to be punctual, for I do not like to keep my horses standing long in a wind as sharp as this.'

On the whole it was a provoking first moment. At once on her mettle, Catherine determined to be equally cutting if necessary. She said nothing as he led her outside to a pair of spirited chestnuts standing in the traces of a blue-and-cream-striped curricle but merely let her eye run over the animals' lines.

'Well?' he asked after he had handed her up to the box, covered her with a rug, and set them off at a high-stepping pace. 'Do you approve of my blood-cattle, Miss de Bleu?'

She sent him a serene smile. 'Sweet-goers, monsieur, but from the action of the left one, I think you should consider changing his bit.' Having delivered this shaft, she calmly

72

gazed at the sights of the street they were traversing.

'We changed it but yesterday to a Buxton,' Sir Giles said in a more bearish tone than ever, making her wonder if his valet had not put vinegar in his bathing water to make him so cross today.

'Oh?' Amused at having him already off his balance, she permitted him to see her smile. 'It was obviously the wrong choice. A snaffle, *peut-être*?' And she dared lift up her brows at him.

He took his gaze from his driving to glare at her. 'The horse is done with that aspect of his training.'

'You must still go back to it,' she said without hesitation, having been taught that the best way to carry off audacity was with a high hand. 'Now, knowing this new bit is not at all to his liking, the horse will be thankful to have his snaffle again, and perhaps may not mind so much as before when it pinches his tongue.'

Though she had her face turned straight ahead, she still managed to catch the faintest quiver at the corner of his firm lips. Inside she gave a little sigh. *Dieu*, how dull it was after all, to charm this gentleman round her little finger.

'It would appear,' he said finally, 'that I am in the lauded company of an expert.' He lifted a brow at her with such mockery she was piqued anew and wondered why either of them were bothering with one another. 'Would you care to take the ribbons? With effort the brutes can be kept well up to their bits.'

An ill-suppressed grunt from the scrawny tiger perched behind them made her hesitate and quickly reconsider taking up his offer. *Peste* and *peste* and *peste*, but would she never remember to be careful? He knew she was gammoning him about the bit, and while it was rude of him to challenge her, she would be an *imbécile* to take the bait. She was no longer a scamp in boy's clothes when every dare had to be met; she was now a demoiselle and must remain upon her dignity. But, oh, *diantre*, if she declined, it would be an admission of weakness. How best, then, to sting him to chagrin?

She turned to him with an expression of cold surprise. '*Comment?* Sir Giles, I think you forget we are in town.' Up went her chin. '*I* do not drive save in the privacy of the country where I am secluded from stares of the curious.' Pretending to unbend as his brow darkened, she added with an air of kind condescension, 'You are kind to make this offer. And if I am so old-fashioned as to be more nice in my notions of seemly excursions than your English ladies, I beg your indulgence.'

Abruptly he began to laugh. '*Touché*, miss,' he said, taking one hand from the reins to accord her a little salute. 'We seem to have begun on the wrong foot today. But tell me, have you made the Promenade before?'

'*Non.* It is very exciting,' she answered at once, but thought, Ah, monsieur, you are not yet deft enough in your command of useful conversation. Almost immediately, however, she blazed scorn at herself for thinking he had an intrigue in his sleeve. How had she come to suspect every person she met was filled with duplicity? Was it because she was so full of it herself? He had merely not appreciated her criticism of his choice of harness, and was now attempting to channel their topics into a more aggreeable area. She must stay wary, yes, but she need not distrust him so ferociously. *Bon Dieu*, if she continued to make these mistakes, she must soon fold her cards and give up this game to save Milord, for once one lost touch, one could not regain it, no, and not for all the desperation in the world.

'So exciting, in fact,' he said with a dryness that broke through her thoughts, 'you cannot help but pull a Friday face.'

'No!' she cried in protest, discomfitted. 'Is it?'

'Decidedly long.'

She pulled off one glove and slowly fitted it on again, taking note as they swept through the imposing gates of Hyde Park with Sir Giles's whip thong streaming out over their heads, but leaving the frown in place between her brows. He must be answered, now that she had been so preoccupied as to arouse his curiosity, and the best reply seemed to be the truth. Glancing up in a little confusion, her cheeks lightly tinged with warmth, she said quickly, 'Oh, it is a nothing. A passing thought of family troubles which you need not regard, for I do not mean to speak of them.'

'You relieve me,' he said, annoying her to such an extent she commanded the curricle be stopped. 'Why?' he asked with frank surprise.

'Because I have seen jonquils in that grove there beneath the trees.' She pointed with the tip of her sunshade. 'I wish to pick some for the room of your *maman*.'

She thought she heard him sigh; certainly his gaze did shift to several passing carriages as though he was reluctant to do anything beyond joining the slow procession circling the park's confines. But he said nothing as he nodded for his tiger to jump to the horses' heads and climbed down himself to help her descend.

'You think me a great bother, Sir Giles?' she asked, gazing at him in her cool fashion as she accepted his arm for assistance in crossing the uneven ground. 'I know it is silly to make your horses stand while I pick flowers –'

'Not at all.' He had become detached again, even bored. 'It merely occurs to me that my mother's rooms are filled to overflowing with hothouse flowers.'

'Then these blooms will please her with their uncultivated freshness.' Catherine ducked beneath a low branch and began plucking her selections. 'Simple pleasures can sometimes unjade the palate, *d'accord*? I think I should adore living in a mossy stone cottage nestled in a corner of a wood, with a brook by the door and flowers in the window boxes.' She avoided a knobby root growing atop the ground and glanced at him. 'Does that not sound like an enchanting pastoral scene, Sir Giles?'

His powder-blue eyes glinted. 'It sounds uncomfortably damp. You would take a chill in your lungs and be carried off by consumption before a week is out.'

She stood upright in suspicion and then began to laugh. 'Delightful! So you *do* have a sense of humor. I am glad. It makes you much more bearable.'

'Good God, who is laughing at whom?' he demanded, with such a snap that her genuine amusement seemed suddenly to be stupid and out of place. 'You were not a vapid widgeon last night, Miss de Bleu. What has persuaded you to become one today?'

Her fists clenched, and she could have struck him down for his presumption. No other gentleman would have dared give her back an even basketful of what she'd been dishing him this afternoon. And somehow that fact dashed away her anger, leaving her... well, leaving her far more uncertain of her ground than she cared to be. She flung down her bouquet.

'I had hoped to be a companion of charm, but since you are determined to be rude and disagreeable, I think we must abandon this outing as a failure and cease plaguing one another. We are neither one of us enjoying ourselves –'

'I fear you are much too forthright to successfully enact tragedies,' he broke in without compunction. 'Who taught you such excellent English?'

'Milord,' she snapped, not at all appreciating this attempt to confound her. Obviously she and Aunt Eustacie had erred in their hope of relying on his help. He was of no use whatsoever, and she could be better spending her time with a more obliging gentleman, such as Lord Chesby Sperling, who would be simplicity itself to manipulate.

'My lord *what*?' asked Sir Giles, gathering up her

scattered flowers and handing them to her anyhow.

She straightened the crumpled blooms, determined not to let him push her into one of her rages, for she had far too many irons in the fire at present to require yet another complication. 'Milord de Chalier, of course,' she replied at her most distant, and began making her way unaided back to the curricle. 'My uncle by adoption,' she added, speaking over her shoulder. 'He is a *grand seigneur*, one who has seen and done everything.'

'What good fortune.' Unimpressed, Sir Giles handed her up onto the box while she tried not to seethe and thus lose her coolness of head she required at all times. 'Who else do you have in your family?' he went on, shaking out his whip with a smart flick of the wrist. 'Sisters? Brothers?'

'I have a cousin, Armand,' she replied, admiring, despite herself, the smooth manner in which he coaxed the horses to a trot. She also noticed they were joining the other carriages instead of turning back, and she boiled with impatience to be rid of this man. But it would be a foolish breach of manners to insist he take her home, and so she kept silent and wished she had not let herself fall into a moonstruck fancy for his arrogant figure last night when everyone else was so cold-shouldered.

'It would appear you do not like this cousin.' Sir Giles had pursued her once again into the midst of her thoughts while she all but pulled the jonquils to shreds in vexation at her own dream-headedness. She was making a fine mull of this, *sans aucune doute!*

'No, how can you think so?' she asked, forcing her mind back to the conversation at hand. 'Armand is like a brother to me. *Peste*, but we had a merry childhood together!' She smiled involuntarily at the memory. 'I am an orphan, you see, and have been rasied all my life by my aunt and uncle. If I had other relations, they are insignificant to me, for they make no attempt to know me.'

'You are an only child, then?' he asked, lifting one brow.

'Why, yes!' She had resigned herself to this tedious discussion.

'How fortunate for you!' He was smiling now, with rather more warmth than he had exhibited all day, but she was struck by how bleak his eyes had become. Their gaze struck a faint shiver through her, but there was nothing alarming in his next words: 'I am possessed of a younger brother, who is nothing short of a trial at times. He . . .'

But she heard nothing more, having caught the note of triumphant hostility in his voice. It was as though – parbleu! – as though he had caught her at something. Her brain threatened to spin, but with an iron will she brought her wits to order. Then, with a certainty so sudden it caught her breath, she saw the trap she had fallen into. Fool! Imbécile! How could she have been so stupid, so blind, so trusting? It was all clear. Lady Thorne had expected him to disapprove of her guests, and had evinced much astonishment when he made no protest. But Catherine could see now he had merely been waiting for his moment. No doubt he had sought out an information merchant, one of those beggarly curs who haunted the less savory streets of every city with one ill-shod foot in the doors of half the émigrés still struggling for existence and one hand in a pocket armed to strike at any moment with blackmail. Spies, some people called them, and it was just vaguely possible – although damnably incredible – that her creation of Jacques-Pierre had filtered through the tiny routes of whispers and become a fact in someone's mind.

Sir Giles must be sounding out her credibility; why else would he have sought out her company today when he was so plainly bored past all endurance? He thought he had caught her in a lie, and although she could not for any reason see how the existence, or nonexistence, of Jacques-Pierre could help him be rid of her, she determined, with the lightning reflexes of a cornered cat, that he would not catch her so easily.

Leaning back, she twirled her sunshade, having to grip it hard to keep from cracking it down across his head. None of her fury showed in her face or her manner. '*Voyons*, Sir Giles,' she said with a sigh broken by rueful laughter. 'I am deceiving you, and it is too bad of me, *je suppose,* although I would rather stangle than admit it.'

'Why, my dear Miss de Bleu, you alarm me,' he said, perfectly bland.

'I am sorry,' she said in her sweetest tones, and longed for a pistol in her reticule to shoot him with. 'It is very wrong for me to lie and say I have no brother when in truth I do have one. His name is Jacques-Pierre, and he is very bad, so . . .' – she appeared to search for a word – 'so . . . *méchant*. We prefer to forget he exists.'

'Has he committed any criminal act, or is he merely depraved?' asked Sir Giles, relaxing visibly. For a moment she was again baffled, but he seemed reassured enough to make her give up the puzzle and be thankful she had caught the danger in time. Still, it made no sense.

She laughed. 'Sir Giles, how impertinent, but I suppose we must choose depraved, for he has not yet dared commit highway robbery. Aunt Eustacie cannot bear the thought of him.' Which, of course, was true. 'And she does not let Milord give him any money. We do not see him often.'

'I seem to have called up a pungent memory.' Sir Giles tipped his hat to a most handsome lady passing them in a stylish barouche whose wheels were painted to match the velvet squabs. One glance told Catherine's practiced eye she was not a lady at all but rather a highflyer of superb quality. 'Willy is not as dreadful as that,' said Sir Giles. 'Of course he is forever falling into the most tiresome scrapes at Oxford and being sent down. Apparently his dean has no liking for a peddlar's donkey dressed in a waistcoat and installed overnight in his study.'

Catherine laughed. 'Ah, *très bien*, this prank! I met your

brother this afternoon. Now I see I must pay him more attention.'

Sir Giles gave her one of his dry little smiles. 'It's to be hoped he shan't run into your brother and the two hatch up some real devilment.'

'Oh, no!' she said quickly. Almost too quickly, she thought, and frowned. 'Jacques-Pierre is not in London. At least I do not think so,' she amended and pretended annoyance. 'If he dares follow us here to vex us, I shall scratch out his eyes!'

'Good God, what an unwholesome suggestion,' murmured someone who was *not* Sir Giles.

Nonplussed, Catherine turned quickly to find an unknown gentleman riding even with her astride a long-legged gelding of showy proportions. The man was dark, pleasant-faced without any particularly remarkable feature, and slight of build. Looking past her, he nodded a greeting at Sir Giles.

'Hallo, Giles. I'm back at last from Suffolk.'

'I beg you to meet Mr. Barclay, mademoiselle,' said Sir Giles, at his most courteous. 'We endured the miseries of Harrow together, and if it had not been for this fellow, I should have failed Latin altogether. Frank, this is Miss de Bleu, who is staying with my mother for the season.'

'Charmed,' said Mr. Barclay to Catherine, lifting his hat and exhibiting a well-bred lack of curiosity about her. 'Do you come from Paris, mademoiselle? I am ever so delighted to welcome you to London.'

'Thank you.' She deigned to give him her hand. 'You are too kind ... such a pretty speech.'

He promised to call and expressed the hope of someday introducing his sister to her; Catherine expressed herself all willingness, and after Sir Giles had accepted an invitation to share Mr. Barclay's beefsteak that evening, the curricle drove on. For several minutes nothing was said between her and Sir Giles, Catherine studying the streaming multitude of carriages and riders on a wide range of horseflesh – everything, in fact, from firmly bred hunters to showy hacks with more flash then flesh. As the afternoon progressed she was introduced to no less than two patronesses of Almack's – whose haughty manners impressed her of their insecurity of breeding – to Mr. Byng, driving an equipage all bang up to the nines with his poodle on the box, pink tongue and curly ears streaming in the breeze, to Lords Sefton and Alvanley, to Lady Pembroke, and to Her Grace, the Duchess of Devonshire, who spoke to Catherine in a charming manner. Pointed out to her from afar were several other notables, including the notorious Mrs. Fitzherbert, very ample and attractive still, and apparently out of favor with the Prince Regent, whose chariot dashed through the park at such a careening clip it all but grazed the wheels of Lord Barrymore's racing curricle.

Catherine gasped and snapped shut her sunsahde. 'That was the Regent?' she asked, staring, as was, after all, most everyone else. 'That fat, ugly man?' At once she could have bitten through her tongue for having taken the risk of giving offense, but she could not easily bottle her repugnance. *Pour l'amour de Dieu!* Was this pop-eyed German the one she must charm?

Sir Giles's laugh, though dry, was perfectly placid. 'Yes, it was him. And you are dying to meet him, no doubt. I am not sure the Queen will hold her drawing room this year.' Sir Giles frowned. 'What a pity your graceless brother is not about. From what you tell me he would fit Prinny's set to perfection. If he were here, I'd take him to White's where he might come to royal notice and thus wrangle you and your aunt an invitation to a Carlton House dinner party.'

Catherine tensed so, she could have been felled with a feather, and did not spare one thought for this extraordinary offer from a man who appeared to care not a snap for her. Rallying, she tossed her head in seeming unconcern. 'I would not let Jacques-Pierre do any favor for me. He would never let me forget it. Besides, he is in Switzerland, or Austria. I do not remember the location of his school.'

'What a pity,' repeated Sir Giles and after another half-hour of bedazzling her with the company of the *crème de la crème*, drove her home, on his most urbane behavior. She was glad to take her leave of him, and indeed could scarcely conceal her impatience to bolt up the stairs for a private word with Milady.

'Well?' asked her aunt, who was found instead in the library with a book and the lapdog for company.

Casting off her bonnet, Catherine flung herself into a chair. 'Aunt, he is the vilest creature ever made by God's hand! And Jacques-Pierre must reappear, or we shall find ourselves undone.'

'*Non!*' Milady came straight up, white to the lips, and paying no heed to the yapping dog she spilled from her lap. 'Catherine, you are mad.'

'Am I?' Catherine laughed. 'Sir Giles is useless to us. Lady Thorne was right when she said he serves only his own pleasure. But with Jacques-Pierre, we do not need him.' Catherine's hazel eyes glowed a piercing green. 'My *brother* can enter the men's clubs and gain admittance to the acquaintance of the Regent himself.' The idea was so perfect, so ideal, she broke off with a gasp and gestured imploringly. 'It is the quickest and surest way. And quickness is what we need. Milord –'

'Yes,' agreed Milady, plainly torn. 'But I do not think you can keep your guise intact in London. The pitfalls are too many. And if you appeared once, you would have to do so again.' She shook her dark head. 'No, child, we dare not risk it.'

'I say we must!' Catherine gestured. 'It is futile to coquette with every gentleman in London –'

'*Imbécile.*' Milady's dark glance flashed. 'Do you think you can masquerade in two parts at once? Jacques-Pierre would be out, and Lady Thorne would ring for you to go to her. Then what would be done? If Sir Giles cannot be used, find another who can.' She turned her back before Catherine could utter another word of protest and pointed at the door. 'Go. We will discuss this no more.'

Cheeks burning, Catherine stood still a moment, then snatched up her hat and hurried out. Her aunt was wrong; Jacques-Pierre could succeed. She had brought him off before, and in the most dangerous circumstances; there was no reason why she could do so again. Running the rest of the way to her room, she bolted the door and leaned breathless against it for an instant before dragging out her battered trunk from beneath the high bed and ferreting to the bottom of it. Breeches she found, and the coat. They were so crumpled she held them up in dismay. If she asked Aglaé to press them, her intentions would be betrayed at once to Milady, for Aglaé permitted her loyalty to be shared but never divided. Bah! Catherine shrugged and tossed the garments onto the bed. It mattered not if they never saw the iron, for she did not mean to make her first appearance at White's. No, she would try a casual place for practice, and as long as she kept well muffled in her cloak, the state of her clothes would not matter.

Digging out the rest of the attire she would need, she closed the trunk with a thud of the lid and sat back on her heels to push it out of sight again beneath the bed. Then she stood up to smile her sweetly sinister expression into the looking-glass. 'Yes, Aunt Eustacie has closed the discussion, but she did not make me promise not to go out in the guise of a male.' Enjoying the effect of speaking aloud to herself, Catherine smiled wider, but there was no amusement in her heart as she suddenly clenched a fist. 'I shall never promise! I am the best! Even Milord has said so, and it is an insult to speak of failure to me!' Tight-lipped, she glared at herself one last time in the glass, then bundled the clothes into a hiding place at the rear of her wardrobe.

CHAPTER FIVE

Afterwards Catherine could only recall the rout that evening with an abhorrence bordering on the nightmarish. As a rule she made herself a patient creature, but from the moment she began the ascent of Lady Jersey's grand staircase till the late hour when Lady Thorne's carriage bore them all homeward again, faces, voices, and events seemed to rush and whirl about her, scarcely acknowledged by her pulsing senses. She longed to be out in the cold, fresh air, alone like a cat and searching for the opportunity to prove she could carry off as many rôles in this overcivilized country as in any other. Already she had decided to go to a cockfight; a bit of skilled eavesdropping upon the conversation between the footman and a drayman delivering flour that afternoon had gained her the knowledge of where such sporting events took place. She would show herself, make a wager or two, then perhaps drop in at one of the sporting saloons for a glass of daffy before returning to Lady Thorne's house. And in the morning she would confront her aunt with the disclosure of these doings as proof of her ability to gain the Regent's company in male guise.

Too strung with nerves to have any taste for the conversations eddying about her, she sat upon a settee, gowned in mushroom-colored satin embellished with rosettes and streamers of matching lace, and fanned herself with absorbed energy. The minutes crawled by like the ponderous turning of centuries. Murmurs of gossip and flirtatious laughter smothered her. She knew very well she ought to be up and stirring through the stuffy salons, enchanting all who crossed her path, but her mind and her being were not focused upon such trivialities and she made no effort to move from her positon.

Of course she was not oblivious to the scene about her. She felt curious side-glances and the occasional uplifted brow. More than one dandy ogled her through his quizzing glass, but she ignored such scrutiny, and no one ventured toward her. Turning her head, coiffed *à la muse*, she swept the select company for a glimpse of her aunt. Milady was holding an aloof little court in her corner. And Lady Thorne... bah, there *she* sat near the pianoforte some wretch was pounding upon. Diminutive and plump in rose sarsenet, her ladyship eyed the company with a gaze less needling than usual. Catherine caught her breath in curiosity. In faith, what was the *dame* up to, to look so smug?

Suddenly she realized Lady Thorne was beckoning to her. With a faint sigh Catherine obeyed and approached her ladyship, by whom now stood a damsel with soft brown locks and fawn eyes, a damsel called... ah, yes, the Miss Lyndon.

'Good heavens, girl, what are you thinking of, mooning about in a corner by yourself?' demanded Lady Thorne with a painful rap of her lorgnette across Catherine's wrist. 'I should think you'd be more grateful for my efforts on your behalf.'

'I crave your pardon.' Catherine dropped her eyes and curtsied, but she was too intent upon her anticipated adventure to exhibit much contrition. 'Perhaps if you are so displeased with me, I should take my *congé* now of Lady Jersey and go.'

'Go?' Lady Thorne sniffed. 'Don't be a gudgeon. There's no reason at all for you to go. You are stiff-rumped to a fault, my girl. Now take this child away.' She seized Miss Lyndon's soft hand and placed it atop Catherine's. 'Well, go on! I don't want to talk to the chit any longer.'

Miss Lyndon colored from the modest décolletage of her muslin gown to the roots of her gently waved hair and looked at first – to Catherine's severe eye – as though she were on the verge of tears. *Peste*, thought Catherine, appalled. Lady Thorne must be sinking into her dotage if she believed a miss like this could smite through Sir Giles's armor. One flicker of his brows would crush the pretty morsel into stammering confusion. Catherine's lips quirked in scornful amusement. If many matches such as this were made, little wonder the English were so cold. What had they to be warm about?

'Please.'

The whisper interrupted Catherine's thoughts, and she glanced down to find a pair of steady brown eyes, not at all misty with tears, regarding her.

'Yes?' said Catherine, a bit haughtily in surprise.

The soft hand tightened upon hers, pulling her away toward a secluded corner. There Miss Lyndon subsided upon a sofa in a cloud of pink while Catherine poised warily upon the edge with crisp, alert grace.

'I wish to talk to you about a particular matter which is troubling me,' began Miss Lyndon in a rush of diffidence. She put out a hand as Catherine gestured with involuntary distaste. 'Oh, no! I don't wish to make you suffer confidences here in this crush of people. It's so stuffy one could almost have the headache, and I'm sure I couldn't say anything properly.'

She paused, her eyes fastened upon Catherine's face with an expectancy that again caused Catherine to pull away. 'No, Miss Lyndon, I –'

'Please call me Gussie.' Miss Lyndon put one hand to her breast, heedlessly crushing the primroses pinned there. 'I have been used to turning to my sister Cordelia for advice on all matters, and I miss her and her good sense so. You see, my aunt could only bring one of us out and so I came because I am the prettier and have the better chance of contracting an advantageous match.'

'*Peste!*' said Catherine, astonished again.

Gussie laughed. 'There! I knew I should say everything in the most muddled way. You must think me a ninny, chattering on without coming to the point. It concerns Sir Giles Thorne.' Gussie paled and bit her lip. 'Please, please meet me for a stroll tomorrow morning. I know it's presuming of me to come to you in this way when we are barely acquainted, but . . . well, you seem so . . . so capable and good, and besides, Lady Thorne has expressed the wish of giving a ball in our joint honor, so we may as well begin by becoming friends.' She paused to take an anxious breath. 'Don't you agree?'

Catherine eyed her a moment, taking note of the blushes, the sudden pallors, the little agitated movements of the soft hands, and the worry in the gentle brown eyes. It was plain the chit had caught whiff of Lady Thorne's plans for her nuptials, or else Lady Thorne had already spoken frankly. It was a blundering manner in which to handle a girl of this stamp; suddenly Catherine melted a bit and put out her hand.

'Oh, very well. *Oui*, I shall meet you if you wish it. Where and at what time?'

'Thank you! Thank you!' Eyes shining, Gussie pressed Catherine's hands. 'You are too kind! I shall never forget how good you are. Tomorrow at eight o'clock, in the park. I must walk every morning for my constitutional and shall say you have consented to join me in my exercise.'

'*Dieu,*' breathed Catherine, eyes wide in consideration of the present advanced hour and all the things yet to be done before dawn. She shook her head. 'Eight is an hour of barbarism.'

'Nine, then, if you wish it,' said Gussie with ready generosity. 'And I think I shall burst before then, for I have so much advice to ask. Thank goodness, Sir Giles is not present tonight, or I should be dying of mortification. He looks at one in *such* a way. Oh! There is Mrs. Drummond Burrell trying to catch my eye. How cross she looks. Conversations with her always make me long to sink, but I must go. Good-bye, Catherine. Till tomorrow!'

And she was gone, in a flutter of pink muslin, leaving Catherine to lean against the back of the sofa in some pique. How could she have judged that chatterbox an insipid damsel with more blushes than words? And what had possessed her to take on the thankless task of confidante? She must be losing her wits, and rapidly, too. Could it be the English pudding? Ah, *peste*, no! She liked Gussie Lyndon and liked her squarely, and in the face of that rather new sensation she was glad she had not turned the girl off. Catherine frowned in consideration. She had never had a friend before – that is, not a bosom bow. This Gussie was all she had ever thought a girl of normal life was like, and it intrigued Catherine to take the chance of watching such a real miss more closely. After all, was it really so much better to sit on the needle-end of one's wits, and to play a greater multitude of parts, at the drop of a finger, than the famous Mrs. Siddons would ever know than to get in a flutter over the warmth of a gentleman's hand clasping hers? Bah! She was becoming maudlin.

'Mademoiselle?'

Blinking alert with a start, she found herself staring straight at the thinning spot of a gentleman's head. *'Mon Dieu!'* she said, repulsed.

The head came up with a grunt to show a face – quite red – and a portly, corseted figure stood before her. It was Lord Chesby Sperling, and he wore the astonishing attire of black knee breeches and a pink spangled coat.

Catherine could not help it; a laugh bubbled from her

lips and she snapped her fingers at the gentleman. *'Tiens, tiens!* It is my new cavalier.'

'My dear mademoiselle!' Redder than ever, Lord Chesby clasped her hand to his spangled breast and bowed so low she feared his stays would break under the strain. 'If I might dare believe you,' he said, coming up with a gasp and settling his bulk beside her. He frowned with some anxiety. 'Do you wish me to go away? I am not accomplished in polite company. I . . . you see, my work is –'

'Milord Chesby, I do not think you should go at all,' said Catherine firmly, though her lips quivered. Indeed, he was comical, but she felt well enough disposed toward him to accept his attentions. After all, was he not to be of use if she failed to reach the Regent by her own means?

So she chatted quite readily to him, and even endured a brief recitation of his newest work without wounding him with a display of her boredom.

'Miss de Bleu,' he said, finishing and cramming the paper back into his pocket. 'May I say . . . that is, I hope you will not take offense . . . but might I presume to ask you to accompany me to the park tomorrow afternoon? There is a bench set up amidst a charming circle of rose hedge. Would you consent to sit there while I write a poem inspired by you? I am sure it will be an instant success, and my most earnest desire is to have my verse published.' Clasping her hand again between his fat ones, he leaned so near she caught a whiff of tooth powder. 'Please?' And she could not bring herself to refuse.

Was she mad? she asked herself impatiently. What was all this kindness to serve her if she dispensed it? Gad, to imagine herself sitting in a bush! 'Yes, I will come to the park,' she said, then sighed. But it was said now, and Lord Chesby wandered happily away before she could change her mind.

Distracted, Catherine bestirred herself to be charming

and approached her hostess to deliver compliments on the success of the evening. Lady Jersey appeared not to hold her in much favor, but she did respond by seeing Catherine established in several persons' acquaintance. And then at last, merciful heaven, it was time to go. Milady leaned back against the squabs of the carriage with a sigh.

'I am too old,' she declared. 'These functions render me shattered. It becomes a strain to be serene.'

'Poppycock,' said Lady Thorne with a sniff. 'In my book, madam, serenity is merely a high-flown phrase for uppity, and I have no patience with it. You know very well you enjoyed yourself, snubbing everyone in the most illbred way. Little wonder the two of you sought my help in making your way into society.'

'Bah!' said Milady.

'Good heavens, that appalling expession! I hope, Catherine,' Lady Thorne said, reaching unerringly through the shadows in the carriage to rap her lorgnette across Catherine's hand, 'I shall never hear you utter it. So unbecoming.'

Catherine returned some answer, her thoughts far from the by now habitual squabbling between their ladyships. As soon as the carriage rolled to a halt before Lady Thorne's residence she climbed out and made a direct path to her chamber, pleading exhaustion when Lady Thorne would have fed her a light supper of cold meat and tea, and adding she must have her rest if she was to join Miss Lyndon on the morrow.

'Very well,' said Lady Thorne, and Aunt Eustacie gave Catherine's hand a squeeze.

'*Bonne nuit. Allex aux vos rêves,*' she whispered and sat down to partake of the tea.

Now! The fog and blur of the evening fell away. Catherine bolted heself into her room, put her chamber-stick upon the corner of the dressing-table, and began to divest herself of her finery with quick, expert movements. Just as swiftly, she shook out her male attire and donned it. Then there came a tap on the door and a query. She gasped and sent Aglaé away with a word delivered in sleepy accents. Letting out her breath, she flung herself before the looking-glass, yanking the ribbon from her curls, and brushed them into a style as close to the Brutus as they would lend themeselves. She pulled on the boots with the stuffing in the toes to make them fit and adjusted her hat to a rakish angle over one eye, which gleamed so roguishly she laughed aloud at the effect.

'Silence, ma sotte!' she adjured herself and swirled the dark cloak about her shoulders. *Bon*, everything was well. She caught up a handkerchief – too dainty for use, but she could affect to carry it as a lover's token – and a plain silver snuffbox which she slipped into a pocket. The cravat was poor, but at this hour no one would remark that. She was ready, yes, even to the pistol of Milord's she had not relinquished into her aunt's keeping. Its weight was comforting beneath her hand, for she knew very well she was not venturing into the most respectable quarters of the city. A qualm of nervousness shook her, then she pushed it aside with a snap of the fingers. *Voyons*, she was able to deal with most dangers, and the rest she could outrun. She sneered at herself in the looking-glass and prepared to make good her escape.

Since Lady Thorne was still no doubt lingering over her tray, it would be folly to hope she would not encounter any servants on the back stairs. Catherine did not waste time in indecision, but turned at once from her door to the window. Throwing it open, she looked to make sure the way was clear, then climbed out and down, using the stout ivy and drainpipe as her ladder. She smiled at the thought of how her reputation would lie in shreds if anyone should perceive her boyish person departing from her window.

'*Peste*,' she said somewhat breathlessly a moment later after surviving the final jump to the ground. Carefully she thumped the crown of her hat to make sure its angle had not been disturbed. 'The things I do.' And wrapping her cloak more tightly about her, she swaggered up the street to hail the first sedan-chair in sight.

In time she found herself set down in Birdcage Walk, where she looked keenly about her with an affected yawn and paid off the chairmen without pleasing to engage them to wait for her.

'It's like as not yer've missed the best of the matches, guv'nor,' said one, tipping his headgear at the generosity pressed into his callused palm. 'It's late, yer know.'

'Is it?' said Catherine with coolest ennui. 'How inconvenient.' And she sauntered her way through the hallowed portals of the Cockpit Royal.

Inside, she was struck with an assault of smoke, noise, and the reek of gin, and she had to battle the instant urge to take to her heels and flee back to the bounds of feminine respectability. Bah, she thought with a sneer at her cowardice. If she had been meant for respectability, would she have been born with a fleur-de-lis on her blanket and a price on her head? It was all the joke of fate. Drawing herself up, she advanced into the company, squeezing haughtily through the ranks of the rougher patrons jostling for standing room at the back, and picked her way through the tiers of benches until she found a space among a number of genteel fellows, half-foxed and eagerly claiming their wagers.

'You're late!' said one swarthy youth over his shoulder as he punched a fat gentleman with the tip of his stick. 'A monkey, my dear Wells. A monkey and not a guinea less.' Again he almost glanced at Catherine. 'Here, squeeze a seat with me. You've missed the best.' In a moment, having collected his money, he swayed and plumped down beside

93

Catherine with a grunt of satisfaction. 'There now, all is right and tight once again. I say, don't believe I know your . . . Good God!'

Staring full into the face of Mr. William Thorne with equal startlement, Catherine was suddenly overwhelmed by the closeness of the pit, with men crowding up so tightly there could be no escape from the trap she'd so blithely sailed into. The reek of sawdust, blood, and tobacco suffocated her; she was certain her face was as white as her ill-tied cravat, and her limbs seemed to have turned to water. For a hideously long moment they sat thus, gaping at each other. One last hope rose within her, but though his face showed the muddled signs of an evening spent warmly with drink, the recognition in his eyes was clear enough. In fact, it was growing clearer . . . *Dieu*, he was about to speak! She clenched her hands beneath the cloak. Turn, wits!

And they did so, recalling her into her rôle of the wicked Jacques-Pierre just in time. She raised her brows and achieved a sneer. 'At what do you stare, monsieur?'

'But –' Willy's glazed eyes blinked and attempted a better focus. 'No, by Jove, I . . . Miss de Bleu!' he gasped out at last with a sort of desperation.

Heart in her throat, Catherine jumped to her feet with a glare of fury. 'How dare you speak the name of my sister in this place public? *Sacredieu*, the manners of the English are not to be borne!'

'Sit down, Frenchie!' snarled a rough voice and someone shoved her down on the bench with force enough to bring tears to her eyes.

'Sister?' said Willy, attempting to pull himself together. The last match was starting up; the cocks were brought out of their bags and placed in the harshly lighted pit, and the yells of excitement from the crowd put their little problem in isolation. 'But Mama never mentioned a brother . . . oh, Lord!' His face suddenly crumpled and he buried it in his

94

hands. 'It's happened at last. Giles always swore I should rot my wits by drinking stark-naked, and – and it's happened! I'm mad. Oh, Jove, gone and lost to Bedlam!'

Catherine frowned at this maudlin turn and poked him sharply in the ribs. '*Sot.* Have you never seen twins? I am Jacques-Pierre de Bleu, Monsieur... ah, Monsieur...'

'Willy.'

'I am Jacques-Pierre de Bleu,' she repeated, ignoring so casual an introduction, 'and if you know my sister please do not bandy her name in these places!' She snapped her fingers under his nose. '*D'accord?*'

'Jack,' said Willy solemnly, after digesting all of that with a blink, 'you are my friend. You have saved me from Bedlam. I am – I am grateful, dashed fawningly so. Let's go home – tell Giles.' Carefully he stood, then plunged his way out, gripping Catherine's cloak to pull her along, regardless of the protests of those whose view of the fight was obstructed.

Emerging on the street, Catherine took advantage of Willy's pause to jerk in a breath of clean air. Her ribs ached where someone's elbow had jabbed them. Certain she would be left with a bruise, she pressed one hand to her side, rubbing her fingers over the soft brocade of her coat, and sought to slip from Willy's inattentive grasp.

'Here! Where're you going?' he asked, tightening his hold on her arm. 'That's the wrong way. Poor fellow, you don't know how to get about at all. We're going home. Giles has some grand cognac.' He brought his handsome, blurred face close to Catherine's and winked. 'Must celebrate meeting one another. A new friend must always be celebrated. Oh, Jove! No job carriage to be seen.'

He looked around wildly and swayed. Apparently the blow of fresh air had served to muddle him further. Catherine grimaced at the reek of spirits on his breath and steadied him.

'*Alors*, monsieur,' she said severely. 'We will wait until one comes by.'

'No.' Willy shook his head. 'It's not such a walk up to jolly old Fairmay! Besides, the exercise will clear my head. It's here somewhere. Handy, what? And devilish full. Come on.'

With the same unexpected strength he dragged Catherine forward. Frowning, she gave herself up to the situation and shook free her arm as she lengthened her stride to match his. On the whole, she thought, half-inclined to be amused, it could be worse. She had been a fool; she had made a mistake in a game where mistakes usually meant ruin. Only her good fortune in meeting no one other than a half-drunken boy had saved her this night from disaster. She ought to be thankful she was free of that hole of vice, but instead she knew exasperation. The youth was as quick in his judgment and as stubborn in keeping to it as any Thorne! If only she could shake free of him. God alone knew what he was chattering about; she was too shaken to listen. Think of it! If she had happened to have met Sir Giles tonight instead ... *diable!*

With a shudder she quickened her pace, ignoring the jar of the street cobbles through her boot soles. A pox upon Armand for letting his footgear wear so thin! How she wished she were home in the cozy chamber Lady Thorne had given her.

'No, no, my dear fellow,' said Willy, drawing to a halt as they came at last across Piccadilly and into the elegant Mayfair district. He plucked at Catherine's sleeve, pinching her arm through the fabric. 'Jack, my brother is a dull card. We don't want to go home yet! Why –' Willy frowned with an effort while Catherine fought to contain her impatience.

'Monsieur,' she said, eyeing the dark corner they were on with distrust. Some ruffian had broken the gas lamp, and the next was too far away to be more than a dim glow in the distance. 'Let us go on, if you please. It is cold.'

'Aha,' said Willy with illumination. 'That's it. You need a good glass of something to warm you up. Giles has the finest cognac, but, thunder take it, he'll but give us stout and put us to bed.'

A shiver not entirely due to the night air ran through Catherine, but she sternly reminded herself to put Sir Giles out of mind and stick to her rôle. Faith, what sort of young gentleman started at every word? She must act more the buck, or Willy's confused brain would never separate the Jacques-Pierre from the Catherine.

She tried a scornful laugh and threw up her head. 'Your brother sounds a paltry fellow.'

'Precisely,' said Willy, slurring the word. 'Not to say paltry. But devilish strict. Devilish...' He swayed and laughed. 'Let's turn about to White's. I don't belong, but someone will let us in.' He turned about and grinned, his white teeth a flash in the shadows. 'What say we visit Harriette? Much better idea.'

Peste! Catherine could have sworn aloud in frustration. Blast his eyes for seeing her tonight! She was not so strict with her acting that she would consent to escort him to the arms of his light o' love!

She seized him by the collar. 'Monsieur, we go to the house of your brother. *Immédiatement!'*

To her relief, he fell into step, but sulkily. 'I daresay she wouldn't let me in anyway,' he said, shoving his hands into his pockets and sinking his chin deep into his cravat. 'She don't take me seriously, though I've told Giles different. You should have seen his face!' Wrapping one arm around Catherine's neck, he began to giggle.

She stopped, bent beneath his weight. If he fell on his face in the gutter, it would mean disaster. She could not hope to drag him home by one foot. Then in surprise she

97

caught her thoughts. Was she mad? Had she forgotten every teaching of Milord's? It did not matter what befell this young fool. She should have deserted him long ago. He was only a hindrance and a danger. 'Willy –' she began, pulling away, then hissed in her breath as her ear caught a faint, odd sound in the shadows behind them.

At once her mouth went dry. Was it possible? Gad, but of course she knew the rasp of a furtive footstep when she heard it! Swiftly she swung around to get her back against the iron paling protecting the row of houses and dragged Willy with her. The move saved them, for a club glanced off her arm instead of her head.

'What?' cried Willy and struggled to disentangle himself from her. 'Damn it, Jack, and I've nothing but my stick –' He broke off with a grunt as another footpad sprang to knock him flat.

Breathless, Catherine paid no heed to Willy's struggles or the ache in her own forearm. She whipped her pistol from the folds of her cloak and fired it, point-blank, at the thief coming at her. The report deafened her, a puff of wind blew the smells of powder and fresh blood back into her face, and she stepped aside as the footpad crumpled at her feet. With a oath the other one ripped the jewel from Willy's cravat and fled, lost among the shadows in an instant. Overhead a window flew open and someone shouted, but Catherine ignored everything as she knelt beside Willy and helped him to a sitting position. Her hand brushed his forehead and touched blood.

'Peste!' Her eyes widened. 'He did hit you.'

Willy put a cautious finger to the rising lump and gasped. 'Burn it, he did. And got my diamond too!'

'A stone – bah! You are alive, and we care for nothing else. Get up.' Catherine strained and managed with his not very successful help to get him on his feet. He staggered a bit, and she slipped her shoulder under his arm, her own senses swimming at the struggle to support him. 'You must walk!' she said into his ear, fierce with desperation. Her breath was still coming too harsh and short. 'I am not an ox to carry you. Walk!'

Shakily Willy did so. 'We aren't far,' he said in a faint but more sober voice. 'Dash it, but you're the coolest shot I've seen. Care to wager you've killed the fellow?'

Catherine tossed her head in anger. Always betting, these English! '*Non.* He is dead.'

Willy swore, his admiration plain. 'You saved me, you know. I hadn't a weapon on me. Don't affect them, and my stick broke at the first blow. There, the white door is Giles's. I've got to let him thank you properly.'

'I was pleased to rid the world of one more vermin,' said Catherine. She saw a hackney carriage approaching and dumped Willy on the steps. '*Pardon.* I must go.'

'Yes, but wait! I mean, you can't just dash off! Jack! Jack, don't –'

But Catherine had already leaped inside the carriage. She slammed the door, not looking back at the youth fainting on the steps. 'Driver!' she snapped, and the carriage surged on, leaving her free at last to pull off her hat and wipe her perspiring brow. *Mon Dieu*, how she was shaking! Oh, *peste*, she did not dare cry here . . .

CHAPTER SIX

The following morning Catherine dressed and reluctantly set out for her rendezvous with Gussie Lyndon. Surely London was at its most charming at this early hour; there shone a soft freshness in the air. The fashionable avenues were quiet; it seemed a city of the imagination.

She sighed, regarding her surroundings with a jaded eye. In faith, she did not wish to be cynical on such an exquisite morning, but her inner wellspring had gone dry. She felt flat and devoid of all energy. No amount of self-persuasion could make her look forward to an hour of chatter with Gussie.

It was not her bruises or lack of sleep or exhaustion which had drained her, for she had known such things many times before in her life. No, it was shame which dulled her step. Never had she been so dispirited. She had failed last night. But, oh, *bon sang!* There had been failures before. Then, one had shrugged and gone on. Now she knew she could not. The worst possible thing had happened. She had not failed because of a faulty plan or because of inadequate preparation. No, she had failed because she lost her grasp of the rôle she was playing. She lost it the moment she entered the cockpit; otherwise she would never have committed such a string of faux pas.

She had forgotten one did not multiply one's basic rôles. Her aunt was right in saying she could not bring off two parts of such importance. If she had not let pride blind her, she would never have attempted such foolhardiness. But that aside, she had attempted it. And she should have deserted Willy at the first opportunity. Now a character which should not exist was no doubt imprinted upon his muddled recollections of the evening. He would remember Jacques-Pierre, and he would speak of him. She could but hope he would forget the name, although Milord had taught her never to trust to hope. It was too undependable, promising much and frequently delivering nothing.

Catherine clenched her fists, hardly noticing they were already to the park gates. Why had she persisted in playing the hero? Willy would have forgotten her otherwise. But instead she had let compassion rule her; she had been too squeamish to permit a drunken boy find his own way home, and never mind that if she had deserted him he would probably have been killed by those footpads, or else left robbed and stripped in the gutter.

With a shivery sense of discomfort she recalled herself at nine years, when she had been at the height of her career of deception. Milord had grasped her chin with his thin white hand and looked straight into her eyes with that piercing stare he could assume at will.

'My child,' he said with a solemnity which echoed even now through her mind, 'you shall never be a true rogue. It is not in you.'

At the time she had been insulted and succeeded for many years afterwards to prove him mistaken. But now she considered the old statement and knew a chill of foreboding.

'Gad,' she whispered to herself so that Aglaé would not hear. 'I've changed. *Quelle horreur!*' And she knew as she spoke that Jacques-Pierre was dead and finished, never to be revived again. From now on her intrigues must be from a feminine direction. She dared not trust herself to try more.

'Catherine!'

The call came from Gussie, already waiting with her abigail at the tall gates. She skipped forward, throwing out both mittened hands in greeting. 'Is it not a splendid morning? The air makes me feel as though I am at home with the cherry blossoms blowing down about me. Do come on. I promised you I should be bursting with talk and so I am.'

Linking her arm with Catherine's, she set off at a gay pace. Behind them their two servants fell correctly into step just out of earshot.

'And yes?' said Catherine. She must end this interview as quickly as possible in order to get back to her thoughts. 'Let us speak direct to the point. I have not, I fear, a mood wonderful.'

'No?' Gussie hesitated a moment to look at her, the huge brown eyes searching. Then she continued on with a grimace. 'I am sorry. You *are* pale, aren't you? But the exercise will do you good. And I shall be direct in my speaking.' Almost at once, however, a blush stained her face, and she bit her lip. 'Do you know Sir Giles Thorne well?'

Catherine shrugged. '*Non.* He is haughty.'

'Well, yes, he is,' said Gussie as though she hadn't expected such a reply. 'Though I wouldn't think that would discomfit *you.* But can you think of any reason why I should marry him?'

'*Nom de nom!*' Now it was Catherine who halted. Her brows lifted at this child. 'A thousand.'

Gussie shook her head. 'No, no, I do not speak of the obvious. Oh, I was sure you would understand –'

'If you mean you thought I would understand that he and you are of temperaments unmatched, *oui,* of course I do,' said Catherine. '*Enfin,* am I blind? The ages, the interests – *pouf!*' She snapped her fingers. 'There is nothing in common.'

'Yes, that is exactly it,' said Gussie eagerly. 'My aunt and Lady Thorne have been dicussing the possibility of a match for some time, and by the time I arrived in London it was almost settled. Only –' She wrinkled up her nose, her eyes a deep, unreadable brown. 'Sir Giles has said nothing nor given any sign, and I am glad. I mean, I am not unaware of his position and his wealth. He isn't coarse or ugly. But –' She seemed to cast about for words, her distress as evident as it had been the previous evening. 'He is so cold, so stern! I feel like a stupid child every time I am in his presence, and since that is true I do not think it could be very comfortable being married to him.'

'It would seem not,' agreed Catherine, diverted from her own problems in spite of herself.

'Besides, he is so *old*,' said Gussie. 'My aunt says that ought not to weigh against him, for at least I may be sure he is settled out of any wild habits. But whatever she means, it sounds like a silly argument. And I do not feel at all equal to overcoming the *disappointment* he suffered in his past.'

'Oh?' Catherine realized she was starting to enjoy the conversation. Indeed, when had she ever been granted the leisure to discuss a gentleman in such a way? The novelty of it intrigued her, and suddenly her failings no longer seemed of such pressing importance. 'But go on! You make me curious.'

'It is very well known, but few people besides Lady Thorne dare bring it up,' said Gussie, breathless at the chance to recount the tale. 'Five years ago he was to have married a young lady named Alice Mayfield. But on the eve of the wedding her father was found cheating at cards in White's and shot himself from the shame of it. Miss Mayfield gave Sir Giles the chance to break the engagement, and he took it.'

'*Peste!*'

'I know! Mama says he could not have been as

104

enamoured of Miss Mayfield as had been claimed, to take so *easy* a course. I daresay not. A true love would stand through anything.' Gussie lifted her eyes to Catherine. 'Don't you think so?'

Considering the difficulties and strain involved in braving scandal, Catherine was not so sure. 'Sir Giles is a practical man.'

'Oh, pooh! You're hedging. But he went away to America for two years, and by the time he returned, Miss Mayfield had become the Marchioness of Gleburn and people did not look askance at him anymore. I think he could have at least worn his heart upon his sleeve a little.'

Catherine thought the man had shown an unexpectedly dramatic turn in going away as he had. But she merely laughed. 'Bah! Are you not stirred by the tragedy of his past? Do you not yearn to comfort and heal the old wound? No wonder he is so stiff, with such a mockery in his shadow.'

'I do not want to marry him,' said Gussie, still taking the matter seriously. 'I know it is my duty to marry well, for Papa has not been at all clever at providing my sisters and me with good dowries. That's why I have tried to consider every side of the matter.' She sent Catherine a swift, shy glance. 'And you are so much wiser and more perceptive than I. That's why I dared ask you for your opinion. Because if I am just being silly, I should like to be told so before I make a mistake and drive him away.'

'Voyons,' said Catherine with a cool shrug that hid her pleasure at Gussie's compliments. 'Who can say?' She began to feel a little sorry for the gentleman – could he like being the intended prize of every matchmaking scheme when his one willing step into the circle had proved so disastrous? 'He does not appear to be too close.'

'No, but although I don't wish to flatter myself, I think he will eventually offer for me,' said Gussie. She stepped over

105

a tree root which had been carelessly left to grow up through the path. 'He looks so tired. Men of his age frequently do. And his mama and my aunt can be persistent enough to win him over to the idea.'

Catherine frowned at this reasoning. 'You talk as though he has seventy years!'

'He is six and thirty, and I am seventeen,' said Gussie. 'That makes him old enough to be my father. But if it is my duty, I –'

'Fie on this duty!' Catherine snapped her fingers. 'You talk like a spinster, *mon amie*. At seventeen one should think of love and dancing and handsome young soldiers. That is correct, *non?*'

Gussie blushed from the throat of her dress. 'As a matter of fact, I do sometimes . . . only it is quite impossible! He's a younger son, and very irresponsible, and besides, he never notices me at all.'

'And who is this *parti?*' asked Catherine, laughing. 'We must consider his eligibility.'

Gussie's blush deepened from pink to crimson. 'Willy Thorne. And my aunt would send me home at once if she guessed.'

Catherine drew in a breath at the name and glanced down at Gussie, who, childlike, had knelt to pick a handful of flowers growing beside the path. Catherine felt irritation. What had induced this child to trust her on an instant's acquaintance? Such innocence was dangerous.

'Gussie,' she said and waited until the fawn eyes were turned up to hers.

Gussie laughed a bit selfconciously and buried her face against her bouquet. 'Am I silly, to feel for someone I've never been introduced to?' she asked, inhaling deeply. 'Oh, Catherine!'

'Don't vapor. It is not yet the time,' said Catherine, then laid her hand upon Gussie's arm. 'Why do you trust me?

How do you know I should hear what you've told me today. Sometimes, Gussie, it is not good to take someone at the value of their face. You must be more careful.'

The brown eyes widened; Gussie shook her head. 'What questions! Why, Catherine, who could fail to see at once how good and honest you are? Of course I know I can trust you not to betray my secrets.'

'Bah!' said Catherine, alarmed. 'I am – I am haughty to a fault.'

'No, no! Never say it.' Earnestness shone in Gussie's face. 'You are like a princess. No, it is Sir Giles who is haughty, and cold, and far too proud. He isn't good like you are. And like his brother is.' She blushed again. 'He is an iceberg, and I wish very much that you would tell me how I may dissuade him from making an offer for me – providing he ever decides to do so!'

It was impossible to go on being grim. Catherine threw back her head with a laugh. '*Mon amie,* I wish I were one who is wed, so I could speak to you of how men should be handled. But I have no advice.'

Gussie smiled. 'Never mind. It does me good just to converse with one who is sympathetic. My aunt simply will not comprehend my doubts, and Uncle Reginald is too busy with foreign affairs to heed me. But, Catherine,' she went on shyly, her eyes intent upon the flowers she held, 'there is a favor you could do for me.'

Rashness! warned a voice within Catherine, but she ignored it to press the child's hand. 'Of course. What is it?'

'Would you please introduce me to Willy Thorne? Don't think me brassy! I –'

'*Tais-toi,*' said Catherine with a quirk of a smile upon her lips. The very mention of that young man reminded her of an evening's work she much preferred to forget. But avoiding him would serve nothing. She must cling to the boldness which never failed to serve her. 'Yes, I shall when the chance arises. He does not much go to the soirées, but he visits his *maman* often and perhaps there...' She gave Gussie a nod.

'Thank you.' Gussie turned her head quickly away and pressed one hand to her lips. 'I fear I am a dreadful, *scheming* creature.' But she looked radiant for the rest of the morning.

'And now, how is this? *The sun shone bright upon the curl so fair/ I stood amazed before this star.* Eh? It's so difficult to describe radiance when the plaguey word won't fit the meter.' Lord Chesby, sitting upon a bright tartan rug spread over the ground, pulled out his handkerchief and mopped his brow.

Catherine readjusted the angle of her sunshade and fought the urge to jump up and walk away. She was well trained to commanding patience, but she had not known verse took so long to write. *Peste*, but this was tedious!

She sighed. 'Milord, I fear the lines are not of the same length. You must try again.'

He snatched up his paper and read the lines again. 'No, they aren't. Bother! We've scarcely one stanza done.'

'Only one?' Catherine could not keep the dismay from her voice. She was stifling. 'How many does milord plan?'

'Five.' He pursed his lips and sent an unhappy glance over the crumpled heap of discarded efforts littering the grass around him. 'I must say, being at the foot of nature is not as comfortable as I had imagined. I should have brought a lap desk.' He sighed and scratched his head with his pen still between his fingers, so that a drop of ink was left smudged upon the point of his shirt. 'If only the ants would cease marching across the page at an angle, I am sure I could get it done in a –'

'Ants!' Catherine pulled her skirts away from the ground, her patience gone. If she did not do something at once to complete this poem, she would never be able to distract Lord Chesby into speaking of the Regent. 'Milord, I fear we –'

'Miss de Bleu,' broke in a masterful, unhurried voice. 'I did not think you were so fond of the out-of-doors.'

Startled, Catherine turned to see Sir Giles approaching, his rangy powerful form moving easily. In the bright light his tawny hair glinted a bit above his molded cheekbones and jaw. He paused as her gaze met his, and bowed.

'Your servant, Sperling,' he said with a hint of amusement in his voice. 'No, no, my good fellow, don't bother to get up on my account.'

'As a matter of fact,' said Lord Chesby, growing redfaced after a brief struggle between his bulk and the law of gravity, 'I don't think I can. My foot has gone to sleep.' Flustered, he waved at Catherine. 'Your pardon, miss.'

'Pas du tout,' she said coolly and took the chance to stand up and extend one hand to Sir Giles. She had not achieved much today with Lord Chesby, but it was good to turn aside to a man who was so admirable in form and manner. She almost smiled. 'You know Milord Chesby well, *non,* monsieur?'

'Yes,' said Sir Giles with an equally cool flicker of his eyes. They were blue today, a rather intense blue above his superbly tailored coat of the same color, and they moved beyond her to soften upon Lord Chesby. 'Look here, Chesby, it's much too warm for concentration. You would feel revived if you went home for a while and took a nap.' Lord Chesby blinked and gulped in some gratitude at the suggestion, and Sir Giles glanced once more at Catherine. A faint line appeared between his brows. 'Have you been sitting here long? Surely the day is unsuitable for this project. May I buy you an ice, Miss de Bleu?'

She hesitated but only for an instant. A man who wore buff colors and arranged his linen to such perfection would not distract her by requiring simpers and missishness. She had failed with him before, but that was because she had been seeking his use. Now she might discard that and relax into her own forthrightness. 'In faith, I am parched, monsieur,' she admitted, and deserted Lord Chesby, who seemed relieved after all to be giving it up.

'Good God,' said Sir Giles as soon as they were at his curricle. 'I never expected *you* to be taken in by his ploys. He's not got the least shred of talent.'

'*Oui*, I know.' Catherine arranged her skirts upon the box, making sure they were not in her companion's way, and brought up her sunshade as he coaxed his showy chestnuts into a trot. The breeze was marvelous against her face. 'But as it pleases you to be kind to him, so does it please me. He is a harmless one.'

'That's rather well said of you,' he said after a pause, surprising her. 'Very few take the trouble to be kind, especially females of your cut.'

Her hazel eyes grew cool. 'Oh? Do you compliment me, monsieur? I am not sure of the remark.'

He skirted a slower carriage and swung them out between the park gates and into the traffic before glancing at her. But when he did so it was with a smile. 'You have an agile tongue, miss.'

'You are not pleasant,' she snapped. 'If I were not dying with the thirst, nowhere would I go with you.'

'The snub is wasted,' he replied, drawing up before a confectioner's. His tiger dashed to the horses' heads, and Sir Giles held out his hand to her. 'Gunter's is tolerably good at solving these problems. If we may declare a truce, I would be delighted to introduce you to one of his fruited ices.'

He looked like the sort of man who was rarely delighted by anything. *Dieu*, she thought in irritation, he bears himself *comme le roi du monde*. But all the same, she placed her hand in his, liking the strong clasp of it, and permitted him to help her down. And as she entered the establishment on his arm, her nose assailed at once by the mingled smells of oranges and sugar cakes, with cinnamon topping the fragrances, it pleased her to be escorted by someone so much a man.

Indeed, he had a bearing of magnificence. Silent, he commanded the eye, and his wits were as rapier-sharp as her own behind the stiff mask he wore. Even her uncle could not play the *grand seigneur* better. And Armand, athletic as he was, gave off no such air of powerful strength.

Sir Giles found a table for them and glanced at her with raised brows. 'What is making you look so pleased?'

Her estimation of him raised another notch. So he was observant, too, and she had betrayed nothing. How thankful she was for her training never to blush! 'I am not often in the company of gentlemen equal to my uncle and cousin,' she replied. 'It is a novelty of experience.' Then on a whim she relented, not because of what Gussie had told her that morning, for a man such as this could deal with scandal upon his name, but because she now had the freedom to say what she pleased to him and that freedom was heady.

She gave him a genuine smile and a slight nod of her head. 'Thank you, monsieur, for making a rescue. I was very tired of the poetry.'

'You are welcome.' Their ices were brought, and he cleared his throat. 'By now you must surely know I did not approve of my mother's decision to sponsor you. Not, of course, for any reason concerning you personally, but because at her age she ought not to attack life quite as forcefully as she has done in the past. Lady Thorne thrives on a challenge, however, and she is very much enjoying the attempt to bring you out successfully.'

'But still you do not approve,' said Catherine, digging

111

into her ice and sighing as the treat cooled her throat.

Sir Giles lowered his head so that his eyes glittered at her from beneath his brows. His hair grew thick and very full, yet was perfectly controlled. She liked the way it was streaked with gold and brown. 'No,' he said, aware of her covert scrutiny but unheeding of it. 'But I find myself in your family's debt.'

'*Comment?*' Surprised, she frowned.

'Had you not heard?' It was his turn to look surprised. 'A pair of ruffians set upon Willy last night, almost within sight of Thorne House.'

It was a dangerous subject, which caught her breath, but at least it gave her the chance she had been seeking to ask about Willy's injuries. '*Mon Dieu!* That is *barbare!* He is not hurt? *Oui?* Oh, I am so sorry. Is it bad?'

'No, not really. Merely a stiff clout on the head. At least it will keep him out of mischief for a few days. He was very much shaken by it.'

Catherine gave an emphatic nod. 'I should think so! The crime in Paris is bad, too. Did he lose all his money?'

'No, only a jewel.' Sir Giles frowned, his square chin uncompromising and hard. 'Thank God he was with a friend ... your brother, as a matter of fact.'

'No!' It took no acting to wring that denial from her.

'Why, yes, Willy was most particular on that point. He would not rest today until I consented to seek out this young fellow and give him Willy's appreciation. I should like to thank him myself.' Sir Giles's eyes had changed to a shade somewhere between blue and gray, a shade like steel, and somehow ominous; they were square upon her, making it almost impossible for her to think of the right reaction to display. 'He shot one of the footpads and frightened the other one away, or else I should now be in mourning.' And still the eyes were steady upon her. 'I am very fond of Willy. I –' Now the gaze did falter, and one of his hands gripped the table, but almost at once Sir Giles regained his self-possession. 'I should be very grateful for your brother's address.'

Catherine abruptly realized she was shaking. At once she put her hands in her lap, lest they betray her. *Bon sang de bon sang*, but she deserved this problem! How was she to dissuade Sir Giles? She had vowed never to revive that troublesome twin of hers, and, besides, Jacques-Pierre would not fool this man, who discerned so much and betrayed so little. *Peste*, how she was glad she did not face him as an enemy.

'But Jacques-Pierre is not in London,' she said in an unsteady voice she did not have to feign. 'He cannot be. We have heard nothing from him in weeks.'

Irritation brought a spark of gold to her eyes. Curse the man for watching her so closely!

He leaned forward, his ice melting unheeded in its cup. 'Then he has arrived without informing you. I see. Willy met him at the cockpit, quite by chance. You know how quickly lads strike up friendships. Willy isn't too clear on all his points, but he is certain it was your brother. He said the resemblance to you was remarkable.'

'We are twins,' she said, the reluctance of that admission plain. Oh, she had been a fool!

Sir Giles lifted his brows. 'Ah,' he said after a moment, to her further irritation. 'You really do dislike him, don't you?'

'He is an *imbécile*,' she snapped. 'And he must have been drunk because otherwise he would not have helped your brother home, *non*, not even lift a finger to save him from attack. I have told you he is wicked. And now, I wish to go home. If you please, monsieur!'

'Of course.' Frowning, he rose at once to lead her out. 'You're trembling,' he said as though unable to believe she could be so distraught. 'I am sorry if I upset you. I merely wished to –'

'Oh, *oui*.' She hardly knew what she was saying. The

113

wretch had demolished her sangfroid, her cool wits, everything she was! It took all of her willpower not to burst into tears, and, worse, she did not understand why she must cry at all. It was madness. Tears were no solution. She had never faced a difficulty with them before. Oh, what was wrong with her? '*Pardon*, Sir Giles. I am not myself. The sun, the shock, *peut-être*...'

'I'll take you home at once,' he said in concern.

She was thankful he remained silent during the short drive to Lady Thorne's house in Half-Moon Street, for indeed if he had said another word she did not know how she could have stood the alarm. Everything was going wrong, most of all herself. How she longed for her uncle at that moment! But he was stuck away in a French prison, his life awaiting the whim of Napoleon, and if she did not cease creating mistakes with her every move, he would soon be dead.

To her horror Sir Giles insisted on escorting her straight to the presence of her aunt, who was helping Lady Thorne sort colors for a new piece of needlework they planned to start. At the sight of them Milady stood up, the skeins tumbling from her lap.

'Catherine! You are pale enough to faint.'

'Lead her to the sofa, Giles,' said Lady Thorne, her sharp gaze narrowing. 'What has happened?'

He replied while Aunt Eustacie began chaffing Catherine's limp hands. 'Lord Cheby Sperling kept her too much in the sun, and then I shocked her by telling her Jacques-Pierre was here in London –'

'*Mon Dieu!*' Milady jerked away from Catherine as though burnt. 'Child, no!'

Catherine flinched. Now her aunt knew of her disobedience, and her rage would be great.

'Giles, you are making no sense,' said Lady Thorne, rapping her lorgnette upon the chair arm to gain his attention. 'Who is this man you are speaking of?'

'Miss de Bleu's twin,' said Sir Giles. 'He saved –'

'Bah! Catherine, I cannot believe this has been done.' Her lips a thin line, Milady raked Catherine with a single, furious glance. 'I leave this to you.' And she swept from the room with an angry rustle of her dark blue taffeta.

'Don't mind her,' said Lady Thorne to Sir Giles. 'The comtesse enacts frequent tragedies. Now do cut line and tell me what this is all about. I so hate to be burst in upon in this scattered manner and then not told anything. Catherine! Get hold of yourself. Why didn't you tell me you had a brother? Surely you have more affection for him than to fly into hysterics whenever his name is mentioned.'

The scold brought Catherine back to herself. She drew a deep breath and managed an apology, but her thoughts were on Aunt Eustacie's wrath waiting for her once she left this room. Milord and Milady could bear anything but stupidity and mistakes. She had failed their training and their expectations of her. She had no excuse to offer.

Calmly Sir Giles told his mother of Willy's mishap. Catherine expected Lady Thorne to demand to be taken to her ailing son at once, but though she grew pale she did not become upset.

'Willy is an idiot, and you may tell him so,' she said, her soft hands gripping her lorgnette. 'I hope a cracked skull shall let in a glimmer of reason. What must he expect when he persists in strolling about unsafe streets? Let him know he mayn't expect me to come and soothe him. He ought to be caned.' But then she paused and looked up at Sir Giles. 'Is he truly all right?'

'Yes.' Sir Giles bowed, his eyes glinting blue with amusement. 'It will be my pleasure to inform him of your sentiments, madam. As for Miss de Bleu's brother I feel we owe him our gratitude, providing he can be found.'

Catherine winced, her hand clenched upon a silk

cushion. They were looking at her again, and, in faith, she had no desire to go on spinning lies. Why did they force her to deceive them? Somehow she found the strength to shrug. 'Jacques-Pierre is no hero. It is probable he killed the footpad not to save your Willy but because it pleased him to take a worthless life.' She stood up, carrying her head well. 'If he comes here, my aunt and I will not receive him.' She shook Sir Giles's hand, not daring to meet his eyes. 'Thank you, sir, for the ice. Excuse me now. I have the fatigue.'

Escaping, she forced herself to go to her bedchamber. But Milady was not waiting there, nor did she send Aglaé with a summons. After a few minutes Catherine shrugged and busied herself in putting away her bonnet and sunshade. Milady could not face her then; the disappointment was too great. *Eh bien*. Catherine nodded to herself and stretched out across the bed. *Dieu*, but she had bungled it and well! From now on she must be careful, or everything would be lost.

CHAPTER SEVEN

For a few moments after Catherine had left the room, silence hung in the air. Then Lady Thorne sighed. 'Giles, that child has a *past*.'

He came out of his thoughts with a start and raised his brows. 'Yes, I believe she does.' For a moment it was tempting to warn his mother against the girl, to warn her not to bring Catherine de Bleu into the circle of the Regent, but caution bade him be patient. Bonaparte had sent clever tools to England; they would not be easily caught, and anything could alert them to a waiting trap.

Taking his mother's hand, he kissed it, glad the lapdog was not in evidence today. 'Mama, do not pry.'

'Why not?' she demanded, drawing herself straighter in the Louis XIV chair she favored. The skeins of thread still lay jumbled in a bright heap upon the floor where the Comtesse de Chalier had dropped them. Disliking the mess, he rang for a servant, gaining time for an answer that would satisfy his parent.

'Giles,' she said with added sharpness, 'I believe the girl begins to take your eye. And if that's true I have the right to know everything about her. This brother she abhors so –'

Sir Giles frowned, not entirely at being forced to keep his mother deceived. 'Not another scheme of matchmaking, Mama, I beg! Have you dismissed the Lyndon chit so quickly?'

'No. And she is eminently more suitable for you.' Lady Thorne sniffed. 'At least you may be sure *she* will lay no scandals at your feet. No, Giles, you cannot have it both ways. You rejected a young lady of spirit. You must take your choice among the ones of a more vapid bent. When may I begin decorating your ballroom?'

He relaxed a bit in satisfaction at having successfully changed the subject. 'Any time you like. I must be going. There's a concoction from the apothecary I must get for Willy.'

She held out her hand. 'I will visit him tomorrow morning. Do see if you can't persuade him to act more sensibly in the future. We should have sent him back to Oxford after all.'

Sir Giles shook his head with a wry smile. 'He will settle down in time, ma'am.'

'Yes,' she retorted, 'but he may not live that long. Good-bye.'

Springing onto the box of his curricle, Sir Giles drove himself straight to the Palladian residence of the Sperlings, a rather grand edifice rising above an uncompleted square of new construction, and caught Lord Reginald in the act of descending his front steps. Sir Giles drew rein sharply.

'Good day, my lord. Are you much occupied? I've a rather fortunate event to report.'

Lord Reginald nodded at the significance Sir Giles put in his voice and pulled off the gloves he had just donned. 'Yes, of course. come in! I was to meet Alvanley at my club, but if you'll wait a moment I'll dash off a note with my excuses. It's not a pressing appointment.'

Sir Giles followed him inside and permitted himself to be conducted to Lord Reginald's library. There once again he found himself surrounded by maps and books and mahogany. Sir Giles smiled, liking the strong odors of tobacco and leather. No female touch invaded here; it smelled just as the room of a man should.

In a moment the door opened, and Lord Reginald

118

entered. His fringe of graying hair was ruffled as though he had yanked off his hat in haste, which indeed he had. He looked eager; his eyes were fairly snapping, and Sir Giles made an effort to put his thoughts in clear order.

'My dear boy, one moment.' Lord Reginald locked the door and deftly fitted a plug into the keyhole. 'Now we may speak freely. You've come about the De Bleu affair, of course.'

Sir Giles bowed, affected by the older man's eagerness. Of course Lord Reginald would have heard of Jacques-Pierre's appearance in London by now, but perhaps he did not know of Willy's part in it.

'Events have almost played into our hands,' he said, not one to amble round the point. 'As you know, Jacques-Pierre de Bleu is in London.'

He expected Lord Reginald to nod in confirmation, but instead the man paled and sat down heavily.

'Good Lord, Giles! I didn't know. When? How long has he been here?'

'God knows.' Sir Giles seated himself slowly to mask his astonishment. He had supposed Lord Reginald possessed a better system of information than this. To find out otherwise was not reassuring. 'He appeared last night in Willy's company.'

When the story had been recounted, Lord Reginald mopped his brow and the bald spot on his head. 'What good fortune you stumbled across this! I must say, I'm appalled to think of how the scoundrel slipped by us. He didn't come in through the ports. At least, no one thinks so. We have the most paltry description imaginable of him.'

Sir Giles traced a long finger across the arm of his chair where the leather was growing worn. 'He is an identical twin to his sister,' he said with one eyebrow lifted at Lord Reginald. He was not sure he liked knowing more about the matter than his host. The giving of this information smacked of common spying, which, while fair enough in wartime, nevertheless was distasteful in this domestic crisis. But he forced himself to continue. 'In fact, Willy said at first he thought it was Miss de Bleu in boy's clothing. That, of course, proved to be quite wrong.'

'Yes, it would be a shock,' agreed Lord Reginald.

In sudden impatience to be done, Sir Giles leaned forward and rested his arm upon Lord Reginald's cluttered desk. 'I thought sure I could have him today. Willy's mishap gave me the perfect excuse to seek him out.'

'You went to the girl?' Lord Reginald's voice had grown harder. He put away his handkerchief.

'Yes. There's something odd there.' Sir Giles remembered the horror on her face. She must know Jacques-Pierre meant to murder the Regent; how could she be his tool and not know? Sir Giles frowned. To see her stricken today made it hard to hate her. 'I think she may be acting under duress,' he said slowly, rubbing his jaw. 'There's no love lost between her and her brother.'

'Then all the more reason to woo her!' Lord Reginald stood and began to pace, his face flushed. 'Gain her confidence and persuade her to betray him!'

The feeling of distaste within Sir Giles deepened. He rose to his feet. 'This grows a bit vulgar, does it not?'

Lord Reginald whirled with a vehement gesture. 'So does the assassination of our prince! Don't be squeamish, Giles. For the sake of England you mustn't. Remember she is no lady, but merely a skilled actress in the business of intrigue. She's got even Chesby trapped in her coils. He'd do anything she asked.'

'And if I do persuade her?' asked Sir Giles, his lips very thin. No man need explain to him who was a lady and who was not. Catherine might be many dishonorable things, but she *was* quality.

Lord Reginald met his gaze squarely. 'If you talk her into

betraying France, France will try to kill her. She made her choice, my boy, when she came here. You cannot permit your gentlemanly instincts to affect what you know to do!'

Sir Giles hesitated, knowing his host had expected him to flinch at that sharp speaking. Well, he had not, nor was he likely to. When it came down to the matter of seeing England invaded by the pestilence that was Bonaparte's army, no young woman, regardless of queenly ways and spirit, could be permitted to bring it about. She had seemed almost glad to see him today. He would make sure there became no doubt of her pleasure in his company. Lord Reginald was right; she had made her choice when she set foot on English soil.

Sir Giles held out his hand. 'You may depend upon me, my lord.'

In Paris spring bloomed and the balmy air invited hundreds to promenade the *trottoirs*. But in the office of Napoleon Bonaparte the draperies were half-drawn against the sunshine, leaving the room in shadow. Napoleon leaned back in his chair, fingers pinching the bridge of his nose. *Dieu*, how his eyes ached! And already, though it was but late morning, he could feel the twinges which warned him one of his agonizing stomachaches was coming. He sighed.

The droning voice of the secretary faltered. 'Does Your Majesty desire me to –'

Napoleon leaned forward, bring his face almost out of the shadows. 'Continue.'

The droning resumed, and he leaned back in his chair, forgetting weariness and discomfort as his mind left the mundane matters his secretary was relating to run over the plan once again. It was flawless! He knew every point and every list of ships by heart, but it quickened the blood in his veins to think of them. All was ready. His new fleet waited poised, aimed toward Portugal to confound the spies of that long-nosed Wellesley, and as soon as the word came, the fleet would strike. But the target would be England, not Portugal. The little nation of shopkeepers would be ground beneath the heel of his boot. No one would be left to defy him. Even Russia would kneel, once her upstart little ally was crushed. He would rule the world!

He did not smile, but a gleam quickened in his dark eyes, intensifying their gaze. One last, glorious war, one last swift conquest, and then he would lay aside sword for crown and rule his empire. He would not be Napoleon the general, but Napoleon the administrator. He would mold these stubborn peoples into a new Rome. No Caesar could rule more justly, or establish better laws. Men would wonder why they had ever defied him, and he would devote himself to the sons his new bride would bear...

The secretary finished and waited in awkward silence. There was a knock at the door.

'*Entrez!*' barked Napoleon, noting the secretary's jump with a slight curl of his lips.

A flunkey appeared. 'Monsieur Savary awaits without, Majesty.'

Napoleon nodded to the secretary, who vanished, and leaned forward to rest his elbows upon the desk. Now it was time to deal with the crux of his plan. Its simplicity must be preserved; complications must be swept aside.

'Well?' he demanded as his chief of police entered. 'What have your men learned?'

Savary took a chair and raised his brows, but beneath these little actions he was as keen as Napoleon. 'It is confirmed. Armand de Chalier is in Paris. We even know the address of his lodgings.'

Napoleon frowned. 'Such is not important.'

Savary inclined his head. 'We have proof he is here to

effect his father's escape. A message to the comte was intercepted. These rogues would betray Your Majesty.'

Napoleon's brows drew together. He did not look at the letter Savary was proffering. 'Arrest Armand. Now. Forge his writing and send word to the women he plans an escape for their comte but is not yet successful. That will hold back their impatience to betray me.'

An appreciative smile spread over Savary's dark face. 'Your Majesty knows I only live to rid the world of these scattered Bourbons.'

'Silence! Do not even speak the name.' Napoleon got to his feet and began to pace. Was he always to be served by fools? 'If the populace got even a hint of the girl's existence we would have trouble.'

'Minor flares. The royalists are cowards,' said Savary with a sneer.

'Yes, but I will not have such a distraction at this time. My plans are in a delicate balance.' Napoleon glared at Savary, well aware the chief of police would sell his soul to the devil to learn the full extent of those plans. Let him sell it! He would learn nothing here other than what he was supposed to. 'Listen well. Send the letter to England. The girl must be reassured, but made to understand she is to continue. The instant we hear she has killed the Regent, you will begin the trial of the Comte de Chalier.'

'Ah!' Savary's eyes gleamed.

'He has been too long a thorn in the side of France, although at least he has kept the girl's existence a secret, knowing she can recover nothing of the old regime. And he has taught her well; I am sure she has the mettle to do what few other women could.' Napoleon's eyes stabbed at Savary. 'As for the other one, the girl's brother –'

'There is no such brother,' said Savary with a blink. 'I would know it.'

123

'Yes?' Napoleon's voice grew soft. 'Then explain why the young gentleman faced me a few weeks ago in this very chamber.'

Savary was shaken visibly, as he should be. He took out a handkerchief to mop his brows, and Napoleon smiled to himself without amusement. It did this ferret good to be reminded he was not omniscient.

'If this boy, this Jacques-Pierre, should get in the way, kill him,' said Napoleon harshly into the silence. 'I will permit no interference.'

Savary recovered himself, even smiled a bit. 'And the girl? When she has done her work?' He licked his lips, to Napoleon's disgust. 'After all, she is the one of importance.'

'Precisely.' Napoleon flung out a hand. 'Send men to England to watch her. As soon as she accomplishes her *petit assassinat*, bring her to France. Unharmed. There is always a use for a Bourbon.'

Savary bowed. 'It will be done.' He went to the door, then did not quite place his hand upon the knob before he glanced back. 'One last thing, Majesty.'

Napoleon's mind had already dismissed him and raced on to the next matter at hand. With reluctance he dragged back his attention. 'Yes?'

'The lackey who attends this door.' Savary stared at the doorknob with his lips pursed. 'He is in the employ of the English. Have I your leave to arrest him?'

Napoleon regarded him for a moment of silence which masked his fury. Savary was growing too arrogant with these little scenes of drama. 'Why,' asked the Emperor, 'have you waited so long? You grow slack, monsieur. *Allez!*'

The door closed hastily behind Savary, and the matter of England was dealt with for the day. That island had but a few unsuspecting days left to it. Even if the lackey had sent out a warning, it was too late. The English liked to form

124

committees and give lengthy speeches. They would never make a move in time. Gazing out the window, Napoleon nodded to himself in satisfaction and turned his thoughts to the Austrians.

CHAPTER EIGHT

'*Mon Dieu!* The day is of a loveliness fine!' Flinging open the window, Catherine leaned so impetuously over the sill that Aglaé clutched at the hem of her nightdress.

'Mademoiselle! You are not clothed –'

'Bah!' Turning, Catherine snapped her fingers with a laugh. 'It is a day to be mad. The fairies designed it. Has not Sir Giles promised to bring horses for my pleasure? Ah, *Dieu*, to gallop the hours away... I cannot wait! Has he come?' Again she ran to the window, only to be pulled back by Aglaé.

'*Méchante.*' Aglaé shook her head severely at Catherine, her fat cheeks quivering. '*Voyons,* you must dress. Now.'

Drawing in a long breath, Catherine halted in the center of the room long enough for Aglaé to attire her in the new riding habit. It was of dark green velvet shot with bronze. The bodice was fitted tight and frogged in the Polish style, and the long sleeves were puffed at the shoulder and slashed. Lace frothed at her throat and wrists. She permitted herself one jewel, a topaz which she pinned upon the lace. Then she stepped back and curtsied to her reflection in the looking-glass.

'*C'est très bien, non?* Aglaé!' Catherine frowned at the sigh which answered her.

'Mademoiselle is *magnifique*, as always,' replied Aglaé and sighed again.

Catherine drew a slow, deep breath, pulling in the air to the furthest reaches of her lungs. Thus far, these past three days, it had served as a good trick to quell her anger. But three days of magnificent self-control was enough for anyone. Milady was acting like a child. She had not vouchsafed a single voluntary word to Catherine since the final performance of Jacques-Pierre, and she transformed herself into a stone each time Catherine entered her presence. Conversely she had unbent in her manner toward Lady Thorne.

Such behavior had soon destroyed Catherine's sense of guilt. How could she desire to make amends when Milady acted in this unreasonable manner? At first Catherine felt hurt; for this was the first time in her life Milady had used ostracism against her. Then she became increasingly furious, her pride affronted. Yes, she had erred; her judgment had been at fault. But the mistake had not destroyed Milord's precarious safety. Aunt Eustacie need not continue treating her like a naughty child, to be rejected because of disobedience.

Catherine thought, I am grown to years. No more am I a child looking to Milord and Milady for my survival. I stay with them because it is my choice, not my obligation. They must learn this.

Abruptly she turned to Aglaé and did not bother to keep the crispness from her voice. 'I am going out now, but I shall expect a private meeting with my aunt directly after luncheon.'

Aglaé curtsied as she handed Catherine her hat. It was mannish in shape, fashioned of beaver with a curled brim and short veil. '*Oui*, I shall inform Milady of mademoiselle's wishes.'

Catherine turned so quickly the hat was knocked to the floor. '*Non!*' she snapped, the anger jabbing beneath her ribs. Had they all forgotten who she was? Her eyes blazed green at Aglaé, whose complacency had paled. 'I do not leave the interview to my aunt's desires, Aglaé. *Comprenez?*

128

Slowly Aglaé recovered the hat, smoothed the crimp in the veil, and proffered it once again. Outside the window a bird warbled in a sharp break in the silence.

Aglaé curtsied, more deeply this time. 'Milady will be told, mademoiselle.'

With a short nod Catherine turned back to the looking-glass and arranged her hat. It was useless, now that she herself had ordered the confrontation, to waste this time by thinking of what was to be said to her aunt. This time had already been reserved for Sir Giles and his horses. She would keep her mind on that.

She continued to dawdle over her dressing-table, although by now every detail of her appearance was perfect, nay, superb. Her eyes narrowed at the looking-glass. No beauty reflected itself, but, *alors*, she was striking enough. And her golden curls were growing into a length of less severity. Still, they and the mannish hat were enough to hint at the wicked Jacques-Pierre. Was it dangerous to attire herself so? Abruptly she laughed, undaunted.

The knock she had been waiting for sounded at last upon her door. It was Lady Thorne's footman come to inform her of Sir Giles's arrival.

'Bon,' said Catherine, with a little rush of excitement she concealed by sweeping the train of her habit over her left arm. With her free hand she took up her crop from the dressing-table and sailed down the stairs, smiling when she saw Sir Giles again awaiting her in the hall and thus able to see the full effect of her entrance.

He bowed over her hand. 'Miss de Bleu, I begin to believe you are at your best coming down stairs.'

She smiled, permitting him to retain his hold of her hand. 'Monsieur is too kind. And shall I say he is at his best in riding dress?'

Ah, indeed, this man did look to advantage in white buckskins and a blue double-breasted coat. His topboots gleamed and were well broken in, his thighs showed themselves muscular through the supple leather of his breeches, and his clasp was strong and as firm as always. A man of action, yes, and, yes, but a man of the fashion as well. Regard the cravat!

His tawny hair was well-brushed, his eyes blue with amusement as he permitted himself a slight smile. 'Thank you. Now let us see if I have brought a mount you will like.'

She lifted her brows as they went outside. 'But I am sure monsieur has an excellent judgment of –' With a gasp she broke off at the sight before her.

Two grooms in livery stood smartly in the street. One was holding Sir Giles's chestnut stallion. The second groom stood between two horses, one small of bone and cream-colored, the other a raking blooded bay, marred by a Roman nose but otherwise possessing a conformation unequaled by any animal she had ever seen. A lady's saddle rested on the cobbles at the groom's feet. Catherine perceived she had a choice; how delightful!

She cast a look at Sir Giles from beneath her lashes. 'Monsieur does me great honor. These are not the job horses you said you would bring.'

Now at last he did give her a complete smile. The charm of it rocked her. 'I could find no hacks which seemed suitable for you, so I had these brought up from my estate. The mare is short of bone, but superbly gaited.'

'And the bay?' Catherine ran her eyes over the horses again. The mare was arching her neck and being coy, but the bay stood stolidly, his wide brown eyes half-closed. 'He would carry a fence well, I think.'

'Yes,' agreed Sir Giles. 'Although there aren't many fences in London for you to try.'

Letting down her train, Catherine walked forward and put out her hand to let the mare nibble at her glove. 'She is *très belle*. To ride her would be to make all the ladies have

130

envy.' She gave the mare a pat and turned to the bay gelding, stroking his neck and laughing at the grave eye which rolled back to appraise her. '*Peste*, this one is too wise. I must ride him, Sir Giles. I saw so at the first instant.'

'Yes I know.' Sir Giles nodded, and one of his grooms hurried to saddle the bay, which snorted forcefully then gave Catherine a push with his nose. She laughed and returned the overture. 'Ah, mine ugly. What is he called, monsieur?'

'Romulus,' said Sir Giles, accepting the reins of his own horse.

Catherine's brows raised. 'I see the wit,' she said, tickling Romulus's long nose. '*Alors, ma bête,* you are a king. And we will not laugh at you.' Placing her foot in the groom's hand, she mounted with easy grace and arranged her full skirts. Looking up, she thought she saw Lady Thorne at one of the windows and waved.

They set off up the street at a gentle pace, the cream-colored mare nickering after them. Catherine glanced at Sir Giles. 'At last we are of the same height.'

His blue eyes flashed to hers. 'Yes. I am glad you favor a tall horse, Miss de Bleu. Most ladies of my acquaintance do not, and I end up with a sore neck from gazing down to speak with them.'

'Prettily said,' she returned, but her attention was more on her mount as they trotted up the sloping rise to Hyde Park. '*Maintenant*, this Romulus should have a long stride. Let us see.' With no more warning than that, she touched her crop to the big bay's hindquarters, and he responded at once by shooting through the marble gates of the park at a gallop.

She heard an oath and glanced recklessly over her shoulder to see Sir Giles still holding his fretting chestnut to a canter. Her eyes narrowed. So he still thought of her as a mere miss of society, an adornment to be gazed upon and spoiled, but not to be considered seriously. He knew she had come today for brisk exercise and not just to trot prettily about to show off her habit. And the sensible part of him had provided her with this big horse that could ably carry a general. Ah, but he still did not quite see her as she was. He must be shown her mettle!

In excitement she leaned low over Romulus's neck, low enough to feel his mane whip her chin, and murmured encouragement to him to lengthen his stride still further. If Sir Giles wished to ride beside her, he must work to catch up. But she had sailed over a low rise and dip, scattering a group of spinsters sketching the scenery, before it became a race. For the disturbance she had caused she was sorry, but she did not slacken her daredevil speed. Her quick ears knew Sir Giles was closing.

And then he was alongside, his face set with concentration rather than anger as the two horses strained of their own accord A copse of beeches was just ahead. Catherine used her crop once more to make Romulus surge ahead to the spot, then she reined to a sudden stop, crying, 'Victory, monsieur! I claim it!' while Sir Giles swept helplessly on.

As she watched him bring his snorting mount to a halt and turn back to her, she wondered with amusement if anyone had dared do that to him before. Probably not. He looked as though his desire to laugh at her antics was battling his sterner self. Catherine chuckled, flushed to exhilaration. 'Condolences, Sir Giles,' she said, still daring to tease.

His amusement won, and he gave her a wry smile. 'Mademoiselle is a cheat.'

She laughed and held up one finger. 'Ah, but only with the things that do not matter. Do you never laugh?'

This time his smile came more easily. 'Sometimes. You're a bruising rider.'

She shrugged off the compliment. Such things were easy to say. 'It was Romulus who did the work.' She patted the sweaty shoulder beneath her knee. '*N'est-ce pas, ma bête?* You have good fortune, Sir Giles, to own such an animal.'

'He's yours.'

Her head jerked up. '*Comment?* Ah, thank you! Never have I received such – but, no, I must decline.' She could not keep the reluctance out of her words, but she made herself say them. 'It would not be fair. You see, if I am here but for the season, then I could not keep him always as I would wish to, and it would not be fair to take such a gift, only to turn about and sell it.'

'He's yours – only during your stay in England,' said Sir Giles, as though she had not spoken.

There was a pause, then Catherine gave him a little salute. '*Touché.* Thank you for the gift on such terms. I am delighted to accept.'

'You know,' he said with a faint frown, as though at a loss to understand her, 'anyone else would have stammered in confusion or flown into a miff. Instead, you salute me as though honored I could achieve a hit with verbal fencing.'

Catherine looked away, a demure smile on her face for his sake, but her eyes were serious now. After a moment she spoke. 'Because, Sir Giles, it is an honor to find an opponent worthy of my repartee. There are so few.'

'Good God,' he said as though startled, and fell silent.

They let their horses walk away from the trees. Catherine bit her lip, wondering if she had been too frank. It was growing natural to be plain with him. Ah, she thought, soon she would be stupid enough to fall into his arms. Only he did not look as though he would enjoy having her in them. In fact, he looked rather as though he had just bitten something sour, and that, she decided, ought to be sufficient to quell her own fantasies.

'How is Willy?' she asked. 'I hope he will be well enough to attend the ball of your *maman.*'

'He's fine. His cut has healed enough for him to be able to

wear a hat again, and he is back on his old rounds.' Sir Giles paused, and this time when he glanced at her his eyes were cooler than they had been for the last few days. 'But the ball is yours, Miss de Bleu. Yours and Miss Lyndon's.'

'Ah. I am reminded.' Again Catherine chose to change the subject. She did not like it when his eyes became gray in color. They looked too much like Lady Thorne's then, too sharp, too observant. And if she did not understand why he continued to seek her out when he did not really enjoy her company, at least she could recognize the approach toward tricky ground. She skirted it. 'Gussie is not at all ready to fall into your arms as your *maman* wishes.' Catherine cocked her head, taking note of his frown. So he had not been thinking of that. *Peste!* What, then? 'I believe it is but fair to warn you.'

His brows came up in a bored way. 'How did we get onto this subject?'

She smiled, undaunted by the slight flare of exasperation. 'Because I brought it up. I am fond of Gussie. She is too much an innocent, too much the romantic, but in some things she is very sensible. She fears you and she would not suit.'

'At the present the question does not concern me,' he said, his tone cooler than ever.

What a haughty one, thought Catherine. She lifted her brows. 'But it very much concerns *her*. Especially when she suspects there is one who would –'

'Did she send you to fob me off?' he broke in.

Now it was Catherine who cooled. 'Monsieur, I am never *sent*. It is beneath you to make this accusation *maladroite*.'

His eyes fell before hers. 'Forgive me,' he said after a moment. 'But I am impatient with the topic of marriage.'

'*Pardon,* but we do not speak of yours, Sir Giles,' she said with equal hauteur. 'But perhaps of – dare I say it? – yes, of Willy's.'

134

'Willy's!' He drew rein and stared at her. 'What do you know about that? There's nothing to his infatuation with the hussy. He'll find out today I have paid her off.'

'Oh, *Dieu*, I do not speak of his Harriette,' said Catherine, irritated by such a lack of comprehension. Did this man notice no other nose but his own? 'Gussie has a *tendre* for him, and if he will but come to the ball, then they can meet and perhaps –'

'How do you know about Harriette Wilson?' asked Sir Giles in an odd voice, again looking as though he had bitten into an underdone cabbage. 'Surely Willy is not such a club as to speak of her in your presence.'

For a dreadful instant Catherine sat frozen, wishing her tongue might be ripped from her head and chopped into a hundred pieces. *Diantre*, why had she let her goodwill drag her into the jaws of folly? Like a stupid she had let slip something only Jacques-Pierre could know, and now here sat Sir Giles with his stern eyes, looking through her as though he could read every thought of duplicity. What could she say? She was blank, as bereft of thought as an onion. Whenever he looked straight at her, every thought in her head vanished. She wished he would kiss her...

'Miss de Bleu!'

'Oh, *peste!*' she cried, turning red in a confusion that had never in her life beset her before. 'I do not know. What questions you ask me.' Furious at herself for losing sangfroid, she averted her face and began to think. '*Oui,* I recall it now. Gussie has heard her brothers mention a Harriette, and then there are rumors which one hears but does not always understand. Is this Mademoiselle Wilson a – a *fille publique?*'

'Quite,' he snapped.

'Then I have been improper in speaking of her,' said Catherine, breathless at her near escape, but glib again with her tongue. She must be; she dared not let him wonder

135

about anything. 'Still, I must wonder if it would not be best for his attentions to be taken by someone *comme* Gussie or Mademoiselle Douglas-Chilbert rather than –'

'I think it is something he will very shortly grow out of, something the ladies of your circle need not worry about,' said Sir Giles firmly. 'Are you always so frank-spoken, Miss de Bleu?'

'No,' she replied, meeting his gaze with spirit. 'Only when it suits my purpose.'

Their eyes locked for a moment longer, and then a smile quivered into place at the corner of Sir Giles's mouth. 'Mademoiselle, I begin to realize you are incorrigible.'

She inclined her head, relaxing. 'Is that a compliment from monsieur?'

'I'm not sure,' he said. 'Tell me who taught you to ride. Your seat is superb.'

Again she inclined her head. 'Now I know you are speaking flattery. My uncle taught me. He insists I do everything flawlessly, as becomes my position.'

'Which is?'

She smiled, a secret serene smile that told nothing. 'I come from a family which is very old and has much history in its generations. But I belong to just a little branch. *Poof.* Not much.'

'It would seem your uncle disagrees,' said Sir Giles dryly.

She snapped her fingers. 'Milord is a royalist. In France that can be a danger, even in these days.'

Sir Giles's hand reached out and covered hers in a gesture unexpected and surprisingly reassuring. 'Have you any hope he will soon be released?'

But now she did not need his clasp or the faint concern in his face. Pride brought her chin up, and her eyes met his squarely. 'Yes, Sir Giles, very soon. Given the slightest opportunity, he can escape.'

He paused a moment, his hand still upon hers. Then his blue eyes swept her face and he spoke low and seriously: 'Miss de Bleu, you are an admirable young woman. I realize the strain you are suffering – your uncle in prison, a brother you fear and despise holding you under some sort of coercion –'

'Monsieur!'

'I just wish to say that if you ever have need of assistance, I am willing to do all I can.' His eyes pierced her. 'You may trust me.'

Shaken, she drew her hand away and could not look at him. *Peste,* the man saw too much! Oh, why did she continue to bother with him when he served no use and came daily closer to the truth? It was maddening. She ought to snub him for such presumption. And yet . . . when he said she could trust him, she believed it. This man had nothing at all to do with the game she was playing. At some time in his presence she had betrayed the strain she was under, and he was interested enough to let it concern him. He did not suspect she was here to bring about the destruction of all he knew and held dear.

Abruptly she was stricken with distaste for herself and what she was. Sir Giles did not know he was showing kindness to an adder. Please God he never knew it.

She made herself meet his eyes then, and the sense of companionship between them vanished as she withdrew behind the barrier which had protected her all her life. No one must touch the affection, Milord had always cautioned, for it clouded the judgment. She sighed, the warnings swarming about her. Keep apart, keep aloof, take no affection and give none, trust no man . . . bah! Sir Giles was a man not of Milord's world. He could be trusted.

She sighed. 'Monsieur is very kind. I will remember what you have said.'

Sir Giles did not smile as she half-expected. 'I hope you will,' he said with a significance she could not fathom, and they rode on.

She arrived home ravenous and was obliged to eat her luncheon alone. Lady Thorne had gone out for a final fitting of her ball gown, and Milady did not eat at midday. Catherine finished her meal of squab and garden potatoes served in cream and summoned the footman as she rose from the table.

'Please inform my aunt I wish to see her in the music room.'

'Very good, miss.' He bowed and went at once.

Lady Thorne's music room was long and rather narrow, with tall windows overlooking the street, and a fireplace at each end. Porcelain blackamoors holding crystal bowls guarded the doorway, and a harp reposed in solitary grandeur in the opposite corner. Filled with people and music it was a merry place; silent and empty its gold satin walls and gilded furniture seemed a regal but neutral meeting ground. Not for a dozen jewels would Catherine have gone to her aunt's sitting room. That would place her at a disadvantage, and they must meet as equals if this quarrel was ever to be dissolved.

It was nearly twenty minutes before Milady came, and when she did so it was with haughty eyes and thinned lips, the rustling of her bronze-green silk faint about her. She advanced five steps into the room and stopped, her elegant head very high as Catherine ceased an aimless Italian tune upon the pianoforte and rose to meet her.

'You have sent for me, Catherine, and I have come.'

Catherine checked a flare of annoyance. 'It is time, Aunt, to cease this foolishness,' she said in a level voice and sat down. 'If we are divided, we will achieve nothing.'

Dull crimson raged on Milady's cheeks. She did not sit. 'It is you who have lost sight of everything. You prefer to play and make friends with these *Anglais* rather than save your uncle.'

The bitterness in those words took Catherine aback, but she did not permit this to show. Instead she gave her aunt a quick, measuring glance and was surprised at the changes to be seen since this intrigue had begun. Cold, resourceful Milady had become fretful and impatient. It was as though the separation from Milord had undone her, although in the past she had faced worse times with unwavering courage. She has lost her knack at the game, too, thought Catherine. She is becoming old, the years of danger have been too many, and she has come to the end of her strength.

Catherine's eyes came up, cold and proud. 'I have not lost my mettle, Aunt. Remember when you speak such reproach to me that it is I who must commit the murder, if murder is done.'

'Bah! Are you squeamish again?' Milady snapped her fingers. 'What is the life of a man for Robert's –'

'No!' Catherine jumped from her chair and grasped Milady hard by the arms. 'That is where you err! Not a man, a prince! *Mon Dieu*, madame, does it never sicken you, this irony that we – staunchest of the royalists – are sent to destroy royalty?'

'We are not permitted that consideration.' Milady's dark eyes blazed. 'You *do* fear the task. I can see it! After all Robert has done for you –'

'I think the day when I no longer fear murder is a day when someone ought to do away with me,' snapped Catherine. 'For once come out of the world of dreams Milord has made and see things as they are! To destroy a prince of the blood is a crime of no common magnitude! To even think of it is appalling. *Oui,* we are forced to it perhaps by a self-crowned dog, but that does not excuse the act.'

Milady had gone as white as the lace pinned upon her bosom. 'Then you refuse to save your uncle. You ingrate –'

'*Tais-toi!*' Catherine's eyes blazed, and she caught her aunt's wrist hard. 'Do not forget, madame, whom you address.'

Pulling away, Milady leaned against a chair for support. 'I do not forget. But Robert and I raised you against all odds –'

'*Oui*, and I am grateful.' Catherine's voice hardened. 'But I have paid the price. I do not complain of my life, but I see it for what it is. We are gamblers, adventurers, ruthless takers of what we can grasp. Years ago we could have made our escape and lived normally. But, *non!* We clothe ourselves in a self-deception of our blood and our birth, madame, but the fact remains that we do not act as befits our origins. If we did, Bonaparte could not touch us – not in this way. Think of it! *I* – blackmailed into murder! It broils me with rage. Daily I detest my position. Daily I pray for Armand's success in gaining Milord's release. But I make my preparations just in case he is not successful. I am no fool. What must be done will be done.' Catherine turned away, striving not to let her fury overwhelm her. 'Do not treat me as you have this week, or I will leave you to deal with the prince yourself.'

Milady gasped. 'Catherine!'

Catherine did not look at her as she headed for the door. 'No. I can stay no longer. We will talk again when we are more calm.'

But scarcely had she left the room than the footman brought her a letter. She glanced at her name scrawled upon it, and her heart stopped.

'Armand,' she breathed and whirled to hurry back to the music room. 'Aunt! Look at what has come!'

Milady was sitting in a chair, weeping, when Catherine burst in. She pulled out a handkerchief with haste, but Catherine paid no heed to the attempt to salvage pride.

'*Voyons*, Armand writes us at last. You must open it. My hands are trembling.'

Slowly Milady took the letter and kissed it. Then she broke the seal. 'Armand,' she whispered, color returning to her drawn face. 'He will save us.'

'*Vite!* Read it!' commanded Catherine.

Milady came to herself with a start and read, her dark eyes flying over the page. Then she closed her eyes and crumpled it against her breast. '*Grâce à Dieu*. He thinks he can save Robert.'

'Yes?' Catherine snatched the letter and read for herself, noting her cousin's hand was a bit unformed as though he had written in a great hurry. Ah, dear cousin! He was as daring and as resourceful as Milord. He had a plan, but matters were tricky and he must be slow. They must give Napoleon no cause for suspicion, but continue to do as he wished.

Catherine lowered the page with amusement lighting her face. 'Armand has learned caution. Perhaps his heiress in Vienna has taught him much we could not.'

'This is not a time to joke,' said Milady, but mildly. Then she smiled and hugged Catherine close. 'Forgive me, child. Now we can be happy.'

Catherine returned the embrace, not failing to notice how easily felt were her aunt's bones beneath the fine silk she wore. Milady was taking this too much to heart. A diversion must be planned.

'*Alors,*' said Catherine. 'We must celebrate. Remember Lady Thorne wished to attend the theater tonight? Why do we not go?'

Milady pulled back. 'But the theater is so *publique*, I –'

'Nonsense. It will be great fun. You will wear jewels and smile, because Armand has seen to it we have nothing to worry about. Our task is almost over.' Catherine laughed. '*Mon Dieu*, I feel like a person reborn. Let us make a real party of it. We will take Gussie –'

'No men?' asked Milady, beginning to relax, even to smile.

141

'*Quelle horreur!* But of course we will have men. Willy and –' Catherine hesitated in spite of herself. 'Oh, bah! Why not Sir Giles, too? That will please Lady Thorne, *non?* As soon as she returns I will convince her to agree.'

No persuasion, however, was necessary. Lady Thorne was delighted by this sudden animation in her guests, especially since it meant they were now willing to go along with her plans for the evening. She sent round an invitation at once to Miss Lyndon and a command to Willy. But as for Sir Giles her expression became dubious, and she shook her head.

'But why not?' asked Catherine in disappointment so great she squeezed her ladyship's lapdog, and he snapped at her.

'My dear child, nothing would give me greater pleasure than to be escorted to my box my by firstborn son.' Lady Thorne sighed and fished a sweetmeat from a silver box for the dog. 'But . . . oh, I suppose you may as well know. There has been a dust-up between him and Willy over some dreadful Cyprian Willy is enamored of.'

'Ah,' said Catherine, remembering her earlier conversation with Sir Giles.

'Indeed.' Lady Thorne sniffed. 'However one deplores it, there's no denying a young man's nature. Willy is bound to fall into the muslin company once in a while, and Giles has bought this newest creature off, with an ill-advised homily to Willy on top of it. I realize Giles means well, but he does tend to hold his brother on a tight rein.' Lady Thorne delved into the sweetmeats again. 'Sometimes I think Willy turns up his pranks just because Giles is so stiff. But there was a time when Giles himself was rather . . . well, never mind. Willy will probably be in the sulks, and as for Giles, he abhors the theater. An appearance there by him would bring the house down.'

'*Peste,*' said Catherine with a frown, then shrugged. '*Eh bien,* if it is so, it is so. The party will have odd numbers. And I do not know other gentlemen enough to invite –'

'Others? Nonsense,' snapped Lady Thorne, taking up her pen. 'I shall inform Giles I wish him with us, not that he'll take a moment's notice. And when he fails to attend, I shall have the perfect excuse to scold him on the morrow.'

Catherine's brows came up. 'Do you enjoy to scold?'

'Why, of course.' Lady Thorne smiled. 'Giles is so steeped in his own conceit that if I ever dared praise him it would mean his complete ruin. Now run along. I've things to do.'

The theater at Drury Lane was filled to capacity with people and noise. The boxes stirred with late arrivals and visitors for the entr'acte, the lobby and stairs swarmed with those in search of elusive refreshment and *tête-à-têtes,* and the pit still seethed with an ever growing number of blooded bucks full of wine and high spirits. One of these was standing upon his seat, reciting the scene which had just ended and flourishing his cane to the endangerment of his companions' hats. Another chubby fellow, with wilted shirt points and a spangled coat, had gone to sleep upon the stage and could not be wakened, to the manager's increasing distress. On one side the royal box groaned with a multitude of beautiful women and obsequious men, but it was the Dukes of York and Clarence who sat there tonight and not the Regent. A group of provincials occupied a place in the lower tiers, the gentleman scarlet, his wife's mouth open, the daughters flirting with a group of rakes they should not meet.

'Isn't it marvellous?' Gussie leaned over the edge of the box, her modest décolletage flushed with excitement. 'Catherine, don't you think so? I am having *such* a good time.'

Willy yawned and slouched deeper in his chair, his

143

swarthy young face bored. 'Tolerably dull, I'd say. Not a soul in the place worth note. Clarence only came to see Mrs. Jordan. Anyone would think he's seen enough of her for a lifetime.'

'Yes, but she's a marvellous actress all the same. One forgets she has borne all those little Fitzclarences.' Gussie sent Willy a frown, then her excitement returned. 'And I've heard all about the next act. There is a scene where she is supposed to take poison, and she falls down so bloodless there is no end of shrieks and fainting in the audience. There have even been wagers laid as to how many will swoon tonight. Isn't it exciting?'

'I prefer the farce,' said Willy. It was his tenth such dampening comment, and Catherine was wishing she had left him to the mercy of the footpads.

'But, Willy, don't you like drama at all?' asked Gussie, her fawn eyes like enormous pools in the dim light, and only Catherine noticed her blush at using his first name. 'Doesn't it thrill you to see the poor hero in such straits and his lady so unhappy she must bring herself to take poison?'

For the first time that evening Willy looked directly at her. 'Miss Lyndon, it seems somewhat bloodthirsty of you to be thrilled by suicide.'

The animation faded from Gussie's face as though she had been struck. Furious, Catherine was about to rebuke him when Lady Thorne turned her turbaned head their way.

'Willy, you are becoming as prudish as Giles. Next you will be telling us what a wicked place the theater is. let us have no moral homilies from you, if you please. I can't abide hypocrisy.'

Willy flushed, looking as though he longed to jump up and stride away. 'I beg pardon,' he said at last as Lady Thorne's gaze beat his down. 'I – I daresay my dismals tonight aren't pleasing anyone. I'm sorry.'

144

'Much better!' said his mama, and started to address a remark to the comtesse when Gussie, who had been sitting with her face averted, suddenly stiffened as something caught her eye.

'Catherine! Lady Thorne! Look there! I thought you said he wouldn't come.'

Catherine's eyes flew across the house, and at once she saw Sir Giles's rangy figure greeting friends in a box almost directly opposite theirs. His tawny hair stood out among less magnificent heads, and even at this distance she could catch the force of a carriage that was at once commanding and graceful. She gasped in a little amazement. Why had he come? *Peste*, it was perfectly timed in this moment when quiet preceded the raising of the curtain.

Lady Thorne raised her lorgnette. 'Giles? Good heavens, and with Bedford! Whatever is he up to? They never have anything to say to one another.'

At that moment everyone in the Bedford box took their seat, leaving Sir Giles standing quite at his ease in full view. A murmur passed through the house as his eye sought the Thorne box and found it. Suddenly Catherine felt her and Gussie's position at the front a too prominent spot. Sir Giles smiled and bowed to them, then sat down. The murmur swelled, drowning out the opening words on the stage.

'By Jove,' said Willy, impressed despite his ill-humor. 'He came just to single you out, Gussie! That's rather an honor, you know. You'll be the talk of the town.'

'Yes,' said Gussie in a small voice. 'I suppose I shall.'

Catherine sighed and glanced involuntarily past her aunt at Lady Thorne, and was surprised to find that woman's formidable gaze upon her, amused and highly speculative.

'We shan't know for sure, shall we, girl?' she whispered and turned her attention to the stage, leaving a highly discomfited Catherine to her own conclusions.

145

CHAPTER NINE

The day of the ball was spent at Thorne House. Lady Thorne did not intend to go home again until the next afternoon, so it was required of Catherine to pack two bandboxes, one for her ball gown and one for her necessities. She did this with mixed feelings, excited by the occasion but wary also of moving into Sir Giles's personal territory. He was too much a man, that one, the first she could not outthink or manipulate. She wondered what Milord would make of him, then grew impatient with herself. To moon over an Englishman was not her object. There was her uncle to be freed, and until she heard again from Armand she must continue with the plan.

But the resolve was difficult to maintain, thrown as she was into Sir Giles's company at frequent times of the day. He said very little to her, but one glance from his eyes was sufficient to convince her he had not saluted Gussie at the theater. Confused, and yet happy, Catherine hummed to herself as she retired that evening with Gussie to dress.

'Good, you are as excited as I,' whispered Gussie, pressing her hand for a moment. 'Oh, Catherine, can I bear it? A ball in our honor! I never dreamed I could be so happy. I –'

'Gussie.' Alerted by a hint of vapors in the girl's voice, Catherine clasped her firmly by the shoulders. 'What is wrong?'

'Why, nothing at all.' Gussie tried to laugh. 'Catherine, you have the oddest notions at times.' Abruptly she bit her lip and looked away.

Dressed in only her petticoats with her brown locks tumbled about her white shoulders, she appeared the veriest child. Catherine did not have to see her face to know the big eyes were filling with tears.

'You are miserable.' Catherine narrowed her hazel eyes. 'Because of Willy, *peut-être?* How silly! At the moment he can notice no one, but when he feels better he will not ignore you.'

'Ignore me?' Gussie tossed her head. 'He was *crushing –*'

'You must not regard that.' Catherine smiled. 'Seeing you together at the theater made me think you have chosen well. He is hey-go-mad now, but beneath that is substance.'

'Fudge!' Gussie dashed a tear from her cheek. 'How can you go on gammoning me? Oh, I know you wish to be kind, but don't be. Don't say things that are untrue. I don't want to be comforted in that way. It's false.'

'Catherine stiffened. 'I am not false with you.'

'Yes, you are.' Gussie drew herself up, shaking her head when the abigail came forward with her dress. 'I am not blind, Catherine. I make no doubt I am very foolish. Probably you have all been laughing at me. But I can see Willy hasn't the slightest use for me.'

Catherine shrugged. 'You have been with each other but once. Do you expect –'

'Yes! I did expect it. Think me a goose if you like.' She swallowed. 'I thought I cared for him. But if we were suited for each other he would at least have some recognition of the fact.'

Catherine sighed. She was not fitted to be an expert on matters of the heart. 'Gussie, you are being absurd. Do you know all there is about life? What tells you there must be love at first sight? Willy has been much enamored of another... female, and you would not wish him to be so fickle he at once forgets her at the sight of you.'

Gussie frowned. 'You are not kind.'

'*Mon amie,* if it is to be with you and Willy, the moment will come. But Willy is very young. Sir Giles had told me he will go into the army once he is done at Oxford. This takes time, *chérie.* You must stop wearing your heart upon your sleeve and be patient –'

'I can't be. Don't you understand? I don't have the leisure to wait for him.' Gussie put a hand to her trembling lips. 'My aunt has given me a severe talk. She reminded me this season is all I have, and it is half spent. She says if I do not soon accept one of my offers, I must go home.'

'*Dieu,*' said Catherine, deeming it time gentleness was abandoned. 'If you loved Willy you would gladly go home and wait for him. But I think this is mere cream-pot love, conjured up to escape your duty.'

Gussie paled. 'I had hoped – I wished for –' she gasped and could not go on.

'*Oui,* but when –'

'Stop! I don't want to hear more.' Gussie began to pace, back and forth, her hands twisting together. 'You don't understand, but then how could you? You aren't forced into a situation you loathe.'

Bitterness stung Catherine, but she made herself shrug. *Dieu merci,* she was past the age of wanting to best someone's tale of misfortune. But, oh, this ignorant child!

'If Sir Giles offers for me they shall never induce me to accept,' Gussie was saying. 'Never!'

'He shan't offer for you, *ma petite,*' snapped Catherine. 'No one could persuade him into a marriage he does not want. But you must stop thinking him a monster. He is a gentleman, of an excellence –'

'He is Willy's brother,' said Gussie, crimson flying to her cheeks. 'Could I bear being married to the brother of the man I love?'

'You mean, the man you think you love.'

'Oh!' cried Gussie, her bosom heaving. 'You are cruel

indeed, Catherine! I am forced to accept a duty that is odious, and you – one I thought my friend – can but stand there and offer no compassion at all.'

'If you are honest when you say you love Willy, then wait for him.'

'Wait?' Gussie laughed harshly. 'When my family faces ruin if I do not marry? When my sisters have no dowries if I do not provide for them? For Willy, I myself would not have cared that he has very little money, but wait for him? Wait? How could I face all that when I have no hope he would ever love me. And I have no hope, do I?'

Catherine hesistated, but it had to be said. 'That is not a thing to be promised, no.'

Gussie nodded. 'I shan't gamble on ending up a spinster, pitied, scorned, and a shame to my family. The other suitors it must be then. Wish me luck, Catherine. Shall I pick the first of them who walks through the door? Or the one who sends pink flowers?'

'Gussie, you are hysterical,' said Catherine with growing annoyance. 'How you vex me with these scenes. You can't go on being a child always.'

'That's what my aunt said. I suppose it's true.' Gussie turned away. 'Very well, I leave my fairy-tale hopes here behind me. When I go tonight into the ballroom, it shall be as one who is ready to take up a marriage of convenience.'

'Oh, Gussie, really –'

'I think you had better go now, or neither of us shall be ready on time. Besides, I am about to cry, and I would rather be alone while I do so.' She met Catherine's gaze. 'I'm sorry I snapped at you. Someday when I am married and Willy finds me desirable, you may tell him of how he could have had me had he not been such a fool. Excuse me now, Catherine, please.'

With a snort Catherine thankfully escaped. What a little tragedy queen Gussie was becoming. And how tiresome to

150

endure all that when one could so much better be occupied at one's toilette. She wondered who had really caught Gussie's fancy and whether it would endure past a day. But perhaps she should not be so scornful. Gussie did indeed have a duty to marry well. And Catherine knew what duty meant as opposed to one's wishes. It was best to criticize no more.

She found her aunt waiting for her in the guest chamber they were to share. Milady's dark hair was piled upon her head in a most arresting way; her dress was of the thinnest puce silk, gathered from the hem to betray glimpses of a gold petticoat.

Catherine gasped at the sight of her. *'Vous êtes très belle, madame. Vous êtes ravissante!'*

Milady sniffed. 'Flattery serves no purpose.' But then she smiled. 'Robert would be pleased, I think. *Mais vite,* child! The hour is almost upon us and you tarry.'

'I am sorry,' said Catherine, permitting the abigail to undress her. 'It was *nécessaire* to speak a word with Gussie.'

'It is more *nécessaire* to be beautiful,' said Milady, attacking Catherine's tousled curls herself. 'Tonight no one must outshine you.'

Catherine looked at her in surprise. 'It would be pleasant, but is it required?'

'Naturellement,' said Milady, plying the comb with enough vigor to make Catherine wince. 'Do you realize, child, that never has there been an assemblage in your honor?'

'The honor is shared with Mademoiselle Lyndon.'

'Such is not important. This is your night, child. This is something Robert and I could never give you, but which you should have. I thanked Milady Thorne for her kindness. In many ways I dislike her, but this I admire.'

Catherine smiled and kissed her aunt's cheek. 'I'm glad.'

'Listen to me.' Milady seized her chin and held it.

151

'Tonight, forget the intrigue. I permit it. I demand it. It is the only gift I can give you. Enjoy yourself. Think only of the dancing and the young men. Let them see not a part you are playing, but yourself, your *real* self.'

Catherine gasped, something within her leaping. Could she be hearing these words of release? Ah, *mâtin!,* it must be Armand's letter which had softened Milady. Warmth for her cousin rushed over Catherine. She seized her aunt's hands and kissed them. *'Merci,'* she whispered, so astonished and happy she could scarcely speak. *'Oh, ma tante, merci, merci!'*

And it was a gift, a gift such as she had never, for all her half-realized hopes, dreamed she would receive. Tonight she was free to be herself, to act as her birthright dictated, to reach out her hand for the honor due her without fear of the shadows which had lurked behind her since birth. The darkness of the Terror did not extend here. She was safe, and tonight she could relax and thrive on that safety. *Peste*, it was a heady promise!

An hour later she took her place in the receiving line assembled at the head of the stairs, Milady just a step behind her. That deference was another honor, a right she scarcely remembered as a rule, but which now lifted her on a surge of pride. For an instant she knew the squeeze of caution; were they mad to let her taste so deeply of these waters? But no. She swept the doubts aside and spoke prettily to Lady Thorne.

Gussie also was there before her, looking soft, appealing, and English in her pale blue gauze. Pink rosebuds were pinned at her waist and shoulder, and a string of pearls encircled her throat. She wore her brown hair pulled back with little tendrils escaping to frame her face. Her eyes were enormous and shone with the luster of brown velvet. She was certain to attract much attention. Catherine smiled at her, willing to forget the earlier scene, but Gussie turned away with a little toss of her head.

'My girl, that lace becomes you very well,' said Lady Thorne, her dark gray eyes sparkling. 'Stand here by me. Gussie can make room. I own, I had not thought you could wear that color, but you carry it off charmingly.'

'Madame is kind.' Relieved, Catherine inclined her head with a smile. She had feared these English would not like her costume, but with this show of admiration from one whose standards were high, she need not worry.

Her shoulders were bared to reveal her most beautiful feature, but from bosom to feet she was swathed in a cascade of old lace. She stood bare of ornament, save for a topaz pendant which rested in the hollow of her throat. A magnificent cluster of lilies nestled among her golden curls above one ear. Their heavy fragrance wafted over her like a siren's call of enchantment. She stood between Gussie and Lady Thorne, a full head taller, her porcelain complexion shining with a clear translucence. She knew her face, with its firm, strongly marked features, was not pretty, but, *peut-être*, · handsomeness had never shown to such advantage.

For a moment she knew a tremor of nervousness as she glanced at the guests now arriving, then her natural dignity and ease of manner took over. She saw Sir Giles, standing near the front portal and staring up at her. His expression was so arrested, on impulse she sent him a gay, artless little wave and laughed to see him blink. He had scarce time to bow in return before he began greeting the next wave of arrivals.

'I'm glad, Catherine,' whispered Gussie in her ear, startling her, but before Catherine could speak she was being presented to a turbaned matron with a swarm of daughters in tow, and the chance for denial never came.

With a stately cadence of its own the ball wound its way through the evening while the flowers drooped in the heat, the music flowed on, and guttering candles were replaced once, and then again. Sir Giles stood with his shoulders against the silk-hung wall, his blue eyes intent upon the scene. Catherine de Bleu had bewitched the entire company, and he had yet to have a dance with her. The right moment was not yet come, and some instinct compelled him to curb his impatience and wait. Good God, but she was a magnificent creature! Tonight she glowed with vitality and charm; there was something special in her eyes which had never shown itself before. It was as though she were relaxed and at her ease for the first time since he had seen her – almost bubbling, my Jove – and yet what dignity she possessed!

His powerful chest heaved a long breath, and his eyes gleamed. Once, like a fool, he had despised her and scorned her vain attempt to make a puppet of him. But gradually, as he endured more of her company, he had come to enjoy it, even, by God, to look forward to it. He could now see behind the mask of wit and dissembling she usually wore. He knew she was intelligent, cool-headed, and possessed of a spirit as finely tempered as God had ever made. She did not deserve to be under her worthless brother's thumb. She did not deserve to have the fine qualities of her mind and soul soiled by this plot of which she had run afoul. She did not deserve to be caught in Lord Reginald's trap and crushed there by his ruthless hand.

I serve my country and my prince, thought Sir Giles, noting she had agreed to dance with that buffoon, Lord Chesby. With a twist of his lips he also noticed little Gussie Lyndon flirting rather above her head with a rake of dubious reputation and strolled forward to escort her onto the floor. She was breathless, defiant, and highly overwrought, destined to end the evening in tears, or worse, to be kissed, but while he wondered what her duenna was thinking of to permit her this behavior, his eyes strayed back to Catherine. *But no matter the cost,* he thought, *I must save her.*

*

It was past midnight before the musicians took a rest. Conversation buzzed, and Catherine sank down upon a chair, not caring if it was half-hidden in a corner, and sent Lord Chesby and another gentleman away to decide between themselves who was to bring her lemonade. The room was far too warm. She wished now, as she vainly fluttered her fan, she had taken a seat near the windows, but it was impossible to cross the room alone.

'Would you care to take some air upon the balcony?'

Startled, she glanced up to see Sir Giles's rangy figure before her, striking in black brocade and snow-white linen. Her heart did a funny little leap, then she saw the glasses he held. Not lemonade, *Dieu merci!* She laughed and put out her hand. 'Monsieur, regard my enchantment. You are most kind to bring me claret.'

He gave her his slow smile, the gaze of his eyes blue and assured while she sipped her drink. 'Some women cannot thrive on orgeat. Shall we?' He proffered his arm.

She was delighted to go with him, and her delight increased as they made their way through the crowds. She observed how well suited their heights were for each other. And they were both fair, she thought, and not possessed of features commonplace. *Dieu*, but she liked to promenade with him in this manner.

All evening she had wondered, even when too sought after to be able to think of anything, why he had not chosen to dance with her, but now the consideration no longer mattered. It was *amusant* to see him beckon to a servant and order the tall windows opened, exactly as a man should hold himself and give commands. The fresh air rushed over her, bringing with it a heavenly coolness. She sighed and half closed her eyes, permitting him to guide her outside to a quiet spot a little apart from the other guests.

And now something ran through her. In astonishment

155

she opened her eyes to see him gazing down at her, serious as though he, too, felt the weight of the moment. The perfume of her lilies hung over them, enfolding them away from the others. She looked at his face as she never had before. It was dearly familiar and yet different as though at last she could really see him.

They made no movement, no sound. She realized he was staring at her with equal intensity, and was content. It was necessary they should learn each other's faces, so that no matter what time and distance brought, they would never forget.

Then he took her hand, and it was like a clap of thunder. Her contentment was ripped away, leaving her breathless and beyond herself. Surely he felt the same, for his clasp had tightened until her fingers were all but crushed. They did not kiss. They did not need to. A tempest roared through them and around them, cutting them off from the world and all normal things. Catherine saw one glimpse of sheer, maddening happiness, and swayed beneath the violence of it.

Then he was gripping both her hands and saying in a hushed, incredulous voice, 'Who are you? My God, I have searched all my life for someone... Who *are* you?'

He had guessed! Trembling, Catherine looked away in fright. But almost at once her own emotions reassured her, and she no longer feared to share her most guarded secret. She raised her eyes as she gave her trust to him.

'I am a princess, monsieur,' she whispered, clinging to his grasp for support. 'I am Catherine de Bourbon.'

'Good God!' He blinked and raised his brows as though this was not what he had expected to hear. 'You don't mean –'

'Yes.' The moment was gong. With all her will she strove to clutch it one second longer. Her hazel eyes looked straight into his. 'Swear you will not betray me. *Mon Dieu*,' she cried, as the realization gripped her. 'I have told no one before. Oh, *peste* –'

'Catherine.'

His calm voice soothed her, so that she believed him at once, before he spoke another word. Very gently he raised one of her hands to his lips, his eyes never leaving her face. Her whole body quivered at the daring of his caress.

'Catherine,' he said, so softly it was as though she heard him with her heart. 'On my honor and my life I vow I shall never bring you harm.'

CHAPTER TEN

'You are mad! I do not believe you have done this ... *non!*'
Milady turned away. 'It is impossible to contemplate –'

It was morning. Dressed to go out, Catherine sat on the
small sofa in her aunt's oval sitting room. She was stiff with
anger and hurt. After the sheer gloriousness of last evening,
to be jerked into a confrontation that shattered her bliss
infuriated her to the very core. Never in her life had she
known resentment such as was building in her now.

She looked up with a calmness that hid the fury. 'You
gave me the evening, Aunt Eustacie, the greatest gift of my
life. And now you seek to destroy it. Why?'

'Because I saw the glow on your face when you danced
with that Englishman,' said Milady with a flash of her dark
eyes. She jabbed a forefinger at Catherine as though to
accuse her. 'I heard you humming the music as you went to
bed. *Peste!* You are *éprise*, and for this you will throw away
all else. We are lost. I know not what to say.'

The words struck through Catherine. Her eyes dropped,
and she bit her lip. How had Aunt Eustacie guessed what
she herself scarcely knew yet? How dare her aunt know her
better than she did herself? Was this the way it was to be all
her life?

The anger in her flashed out. 'I have made my decision,
Milady. I am not going to approach the Regent.'

'Bah! Did we raise you and give you our lives to be repaid
thus? You are not worthy of the name you bear. Last night
you betrayed us, and today you consign Robert to his
death!'

159

'Enough, madame! You become hysterical.' With a sweeping gesture, Catherine stood up. 'I am tired of denying my birth and the name I have never been permitted to use. There is no price on my head in this country. And in France, Bonaparte sneers at us for seeking to keep a secret he already knows.' She paused, sensing her voice was becoming unsteady. Bravado or not, the danger was yet great; the fear of revealing her identity would never be completely vanquished. But she would die before she let Milady see her terror! She raised her chin to meet her aunt's eyes. 'As for Milord, we both have confidence, I think, in Armand. He will gain Milord's freedom. Nor is Milord himself helpless. I refuse to destroy England just to gain the mercy of that Corsican dog.' Her lips compressed, and her eyes did not waver from Milady's. 'And that, Aunt, is all I need say on the matter. I intrigue no more.'

She turned to go out, but as she did so Milady gripped her arm with fingers that dug hard. 'You throw away everything for an Englishman's caress. You are a fool, Catherine! A fool! His birth cannot match yours –'

'Birth?' Mockery stung through Catherine. She glanced at her aunt and did not trouble to hide the bitterness within her. 'The world has changed, Milady. There is no longer a place for me unless I make one.' Her voice hardened. 'And I shall. It is stupidity to cling to shadows of the past.' Wrenching free, she swept out, haughty in her anger but close to tears. One by one the ties to her family were being severed, and nothing was ever going to be the same again. Alone, she stepped toward the future. The thrones of France and the old ways were gone; there was no going back. Did she alone of them all realize it? Oh, *Dieu!* If only she could be certain of him. If only she could be sure that look in his eyes last night had not been just another of her dreams.

*

It had been generally held that no finery could outshine the lace Miss de Bleu had worn to the ball, but that afternoon she proved this viewpoint too shortsighted by arriving at a villa party dressed in zircon crepe draped across her bosom and falling in a narrow sheath to her sandals. Her white arms were bare and gleamed in the sunshine like alabaster, and she wore a broad chip-straw hat, under the brim of which her eyes shone a vivid green. Her cheeks were highly colored and flushed still more when Sir Giles came forward across the lawn to assist her, Gussie, and Lady Reginald Sperling from their landau.

It was an august gathering, as she quickly saw once her eyes could move themselves from Sir Giles. The Regent was standing beside a fantastically cut shrub, exchanging remarks with Lady Jersey. Lord Holland stood near them, blinking and looking half-aslep. Some distance away the Duchess of Bedford was laughing with Mr. Brummell, and lord Alvanley was putting Lady Sefton to the blush by ogling her pearls through his quizzing glass. These were among the most notable guests, but in the crowd she thought she also glimpsed York, and William Lamb, the dandy set, and Lord Palmerston, whom Lady Holland was scolding as though he were a child.

Peste, thought Catherine, it was a company in which she could do much mischief . . . only now when she need never again think of plots and intrigues, she found herself at a loss. What was she to do with all these people? As acquaintance they were of no use to speak to, and what should she speak to them about? Sketching in watercolors? Bah!

She glanced at Sir Giles, but immediately looked away. Last night she had been so sure, so happy. But in the light of day with the enchantment of an evening gone and Milady's words still blistering her heart, she could not be sure of anything. Everything which had passed between them in

161

that one crackling moment had been feelings, not words. She felt shy and wished it had not been necessary to turn her back on Milord and Milady.

'You are looking unwontedly serious today,' said Sir Giles in tones just short of boredom.

Catherine's head snapped up, but he was speaking to Gussie, who replied, 'Perhaps I have been too frivolous in the past, Sir Giles. Will your brother be here today?'

Sir Giles frowned as though something had displeased him. 'No. He –'

'Good,' said Gussie, her pique evident. 'I fear I am glad of it. He's such a child in many ways.'

'And so, my dear young woman, are you,' said Sir Giles coldly. He glanced at Catherine and softened at once. 'Excuse me, Miss de Bleu. I am being summoned by His Highness.' He strode away.

'Well!' said Gussie, her eyes bright with annoyance. 'Of all the unjust things to say! I have never seen anyone more odiously starched up.'

'Forgive me, but you deserved the snub,' said Catherine, weary of Gussie's petulance. 'It was impertinent to speak to him in that way about his brother. Last night you vowed you would never think of Willy again. Today you insult him behind his back. It is all very tiresome of you.' Ignoring Gussie's gasp, she moved away to speak to her hostess as she ought, and the woman was sufficiently charmed to present her to the Prince Regent.

Unable to think of anything save the plot against him, Catherine colored hotly as she swept a curtsy to the ground and was furious with herself for losing her composure.

'But what a pretty blush!' exclaimed His Higness, and leered down at her in a manner that made her rise swiftly with her chin high.

Bah! She was no goods for this fat fellow's ogling! With one of her coolest smiles she extended her hand, knowing

162

she dared much in this gesture, but nettled enough to be reckless. 'To meet England is much an honor, monseigneur,' she murmured.

The Regent laughed, visibly delighted. 'Well said, very well said. Thorne! Do you say this mamselle is a guest of your mother's? You must convey my compliments to her ladyship.'

He turned away to greet another lady, leaving Catherine to face the dry lift of Sir Giles's brows. She grimaced. 'He is adroit with his remarks, but *enfin* I do not much like the fat friend of Monsieur Brummell.'

Sir Giles was startled into a cough. 'So you've heard of that comment, have you? George had better be careful.'

Beginning to relax, she smiled saucily. 'Ah, monsieur, but which George do you mean?'

Sir Giles smiled back. 'Your Highness is quite a wit today.'

She clutched his arm. *'Dieu m'en préserve!* Do not call me that, not even in jest.'

He was watching her closely, as though he would observe even the pounding of her heart. She could not tell whether his eyes were blue or gray. Suddenly he seemed very distant from her, as though he had become a stranger. Her alarm increased.

'Catherine,' he said, taking her hand in a way she did not like. 'The Duc de Vendôme is here today. I wish you to meet him.'

The fear rose within her, battling her self-control. *Dieu,* but she had been a fool to speak! Sir Giles was English, this was England, she was safe here, but *non,* and *non,* she could not overcome the fear which had been drilled into her from her first years. No one must ever know who she was. Milord had taught them all that. He had frightened her out of all arrogance in her birth. The secret was chained too strongly within her for her to be able to bear this public disclosure. She had told Sir Giles because she loved him; *oui*, even her life she would give for him. But, *parbleu*, she must make him understand.

Her eyes rose to his in appeal. 'Sir Giles, please do not test my word. Forget what I said. Please do not test me. the truth is useless to anyone. I am nothing, or my uncle would have used me to advantage long ago. Please. I cannot bear this.' Trembling, she was so close to tears she had to pause to choke them back.

Sir Giles's hand tightened upon hers. 'You can bear anything. I've seen your courage. Come. The duc is waiting for us in the maze. He will be alone.'

She steadied. '*Vraiment?* Ah, but he will not know me. We have never met. We should not meet. Oh, monsieur, I can prove nothing! I do not wish to.'

'This is very important,' he insisted, his voice calm against her agitation. 'For your safety. Believe me.' he paused. 'Trust me?'

Helplessly she permitted him to lead her away to the tall hedge maze. He knew the key to its intricacies and guided her along past other couples who were quite happily lost. She did not think she was reassured. What did he mean when he said this was for her safety? How could she do this – when she had but hours before renounced the old France? How could she turn about and kneel to an exile who ought rightfully to sit in Bonaparte's place but who never would? This was madness; her mind told her so, but her instincts had left her. She had nothing to cling to but her trust in Sir Giles. Suddenly he had become the one secure point in a life gone beyond control. And yet, was he enough? She was so uncertain.

Then before she was prepared, they entered the spacious center of the maze. The hedge towered about them on all four sides as though they had entered a room. As Sir Giles had promised, a lone figure, richly dressed and pomaded,

164

stood waiting for them. Poised for flight, Catherine swept him with a glance. But, *oui*, the features of this man were clearly recognizable; the Bourbon nose was more strongly marked than her own.

The duc studied her with equal interest for a very long while. Beside her, Sir Giles was as taut as a drawn bow. Unable to bear the tension, Catherine sank into a deep curtsy and inclined her head. 'Monseigneur.'

'Ah.' Now at least he spoke, and his voice was sad as he said in soft French: 'In you, child, we see our sister once again. What is your name?'

For one startled instant she knew peace at these words, peace as though for the first time she glimpsed home and people who were really her own. It was not required to know any of them or even to be with them; this brief moment of recognition was enough. With renewed courage she raised her head. 'I am Catherine, your grace,' she answered.

'Catherine.' The duc smiled and raised her to her feet. 'So tall! And haughty *aussi*. Your eyes are your father's, I think, though I do not remember him well.' Then the warmth faded from his face, and he glanced abruptly at Sir Giles. 'We trust you, monsieur, Catherine and I. It is time to part.' Gently he kissed Catherine's brow and was gone.

There was a sigh, and with a start Catherine realized it was hers. She looked at Sir Giles, the warmth of relief spilling through her. How absurd her fears seemed now! He had not made a spectacle of her in any way. She knew by his actions today that her secret would remain under his protection. Slowly she held out her hand, liking his strong clasp he as took it. 'Thank you,' she whispered. '*Mon Dieu,* how I must thank you.'

His grasp tightened. 'You realize,' he said with a serious look in his eyes, 'that you are in the direct line.'

She smiled wanly and shook her golden head. 'I am a

female, monsieur. There are too many princes before me. It is why I live.' Then she grew pensive. 'No one has ever described my father before. He was Milord's friend, and that is why Milord adopted me as his niece. *Maman* was not guillotined, but –'

'Yes,' broke in Sir Giles gently. 'We'd better go back now before we are missed.'

But Catherine hesitated and with a frown glanced up at him. 'Why did you say this was for my safety? I do not understand the remark.'

He looked away, his lips compressed.

'Sir Giles?' Again she knew a twinge of alarm. Could he know? But it was impossible!

'I'm sorry,' he said at last. 'I cannot answer.'

She cocked her head to one side. 'Is it a hunch, *peut-être?* I have much faith in them.'

'A hunch?' He looked quizzical, then nodded. 'Yes, I suppose you might call it that. Come.'

CHAPTER ELEVEN

Creed, the valet, opened the door of the dressing room in response to an unexpected knock. Glancing round with a rebuke upon his lips, Sir Giles blinked to see Lord Reginald standing upon the threshold instead of Willy. Swiftly he fashioned his features into a more welcoming expression.

'Why, good evening, my lord,' he said, tossing down his brush to go forward. 'I confess I did not expect –'

'There shan't be any chance to talk at your mother's dinner, Giles,' said Lord Reginald, unusually brusque. He stepped inside and shook Sir Giles's hand briefly. 'You haven't been calling of late. I'm disappointed.'

Sir Giles held back a frown. While from boyhood he had been accustomed to looking upon Lord Reginald with the respect and affection one naturally accorded an old friend of the family, he found less he liked in the man. Socially there was no one more charming than his Lordship; concerning the threatened safety of the realm, no one more grim. Least of all did Sir Giles appreciate this visit. It smacked very much of a confrontation, and Sir Giles was not in the mood for one.

But he permitted none of his annoyance to show as he handed the water ewer to Creed and began to lave his hands. 'I have a good reason, sir. As you no doubt have observed, there is a young lady I am seeing much of.' He dried his hands and dismissed Creed. 'My bedroom is a better place to talk.' Once they were seated by the fire, however, Sir Giles did frown and permitted his voice to become sharper. 'Good God, my lord, aren't you being a trifle imprudent in bringing this discussion here? I am all but living in Miss de Bleu's pocket now. If I call on her with more frequency it will have to be as a suitor, and under these circumstances you will find I balk at such a step.'

'I know this whole matter is distasteful to you, my boy, but do think of me!' Lord Reginald leaned forward. 'I must report to the others, and there has been nothing since you told me the girl is being forced to do this by her brother. Where the devil *is* Jacques-Pierre de Bleu? That's what I want to know. He slips by our surveillance at the ports, makes one flamboyant appearance during which he shoots a footpad, and then disappears completely. My God, it's maddening. Napoleon can't hold a fleet and army immobile forever. No, Giles, he's got to move soon, and it will be either us or Russia. We've lost our informant at the Tuileries, and by the time a new one is in place, anything could happen.'

'You know Prinny has not been approached,' said Sir Giles coldly. This weaseling about behind a network of lies and deception was enough to turn his stomach. But he saw his duty and would not shrink from it. 'I am certain Catherine can be brought round to our side,' he went on, trying to choose his words with care. Somehow he must make sure she did not come to harm in this.

'Yes, of course,' said Lord Reginald, tapping his fingers upon the chair arm and not really listening. 'But when, Giles, when? She must know where her brother is hiding. She must know when he plans to strike. As for approaches to the Regent ... she has met him, that I know.'

Sir Giles rose to his feet. 'Good God, am I spied upon as well? I warned you once, sir, that I had little taste for this. If you can't trust me –'

'Giles!' Lord Reginald stared at him. 'My dear boy, there's no need to lose your temper. I wouldn't be here if I

168

didn't trust you. In fact, your house is safer than mine. Sit down, my boy, do sit down. The Regent is watched, not you. And it was remarked that her manner was daring with His Highness, but preoccupied.'

'Because she was about to meet the Duc de Vendôme,' said Sir Giles through his teeth. He continued to tower over his guest, with silk-encased arms folded over the breast of his scarlet dressing-gown. The faint alarm which had been nagging him of late now twisted sharply. Try as he might, he could not be at peace regarding Catherine's fate. She was too vulnerable. And Lord Reginald, damn the man, seemed unimpressed by his mention of the duc. He must try again. 'She is connected to his grace, you know,' he said, striving to keep his tone impersonal. 'I am not sure, the more I learn of her, that she is a part of this.'

'Of course she is a part of this. Good heavens, man, don't get besotted with the little jade! She's using your mother, isn't she? And she's hiding Jacques-Pierre. She's clever and glib, and simply too useful. You must pry from her the whereabouts of her brother.'

'She may not know,' said Sir Giles, trying not to bristle. Heaven knew, he was not accustomed to the rôle of a pacifist, but someone must defend the girl. 'I –'

'Then put Willy on the scent. He has a reason to find De Bleu, hasn't he?' Lord Reginald rose and held out his hand.

Sir Giles hesitated before he took it. 'I think, sir, that we'll leave my brother out of this.'

'Shall we?' Lord Reginald opened the door for himself. 'Perhaps. I'm looking forward to this dinner of Lady Thorne's. It shan't hurt to take a closer scrutiny of the De Bleu girl myself, as well as her dragon of an aunt. Goodbye.'

The door shut softly behind him.

'Damn!' said Sir Giles and swung around – only to pause, his anger dashed as he saw Willy standing in the entry to his dressing room. Willy's hand gripped the porcelain knob with knuckles as white as its surface. His face was set, his green eyes smoldering.

'How could you, Giles? How could you?' he demanded in a low, awful voice. 'As though it was not enough that you set Harriette against me – yes, and flung me the insult of *buying* her off, so that now I am the laugh of the town. I never meant to marry her; I just said so to wring your withers a bit. But, no, you must deal with a heavy hand. And now – *now* you seek to denounce Jack as some sort of filthy assassin. Oh, yes, I heard it all,' he said with a sneer as Sir Giles started to speak. 'I came to borrow a neckcloth and instead find you planning to do in the man who saved my life.'

'That's enough, William,' said Sir Giles, stung on the raw. 'There is a plot against –'

'I don't care!' Willy clenched his fists. 'Damn you, Giles, the man may be the most wretched creature alive, but he saved my life. I should think that would mean something to you, but apparently it doesn't. You think of me as a bother and an embarrassment, I know. I daresay you'd prefer me to be as cold and stonehearted as yourself. Well, I'm not, and shan't ever be! I know what friendship and honor mean, and I don't intend to let you destroy Jack in this calculating, odious way!'

He started to fling himself out, but Sir Giles seized the boy's arm. 'Have done with this fustian, William. You aren't going anywhere until you under –'

Willy's fist glanced off his jaw with enough force to stagger him. Wrenching free, Willy glared at him. 'All my life I've looked up to you. I thought you were everything a gentleman ought to be. Now I know otherwise. I daresay it's a good thing you never married. Any woman would die of shame to see what you really are behind that mask of ice. To think someone as good and fine as Miss de Bleu taken

170

in, I –' Abruptly tears welled up in his furious eyes and he ran out, slamming the door with force enough to rattle the panels.

Still holding his aching jaw, Sir Giles wrenched it open with a violence that all but sprang it off the hinges. 'Willy!' he shouted, frantic to stop the boy. A startled footman appeared on the landing, and Sir Giles swore at him. 'Stop him, you fool! Oh, damnation!' He clenched his fists as the fellow gaped, and was about to hurl himself down the stairs when he realized he was still in dressing-gown and slippers. By now Willy was probably out of the house.

'May I be of assistance, Sir Giles?' It was Creed, trying to hold to his training despite the fact that his eyes were fairly popping out of his head.

With a snarl Sir Giles strode back into his chambers, flinging off his dressing-gown as he went. 'I am leaving this house in five minutes. I want the bays outside the door, waiting. Get my cravat; one neckcloth will do.' He glared at Creed, who was staring at him in horror. 'Move!'

Never before had he cursed the vagaries of gentleman's fashion as he did now. Satisfaction in meeting the challenge of arranging a cravat to perfection was gone. Sir Giles flung the cloth around his throat and knotted it with a savagery that pained Creed. Sir Giles's lips compressed to a thinner line, and he shrugged on his coat himself, not permitting anxious hands to straighten the shoulders.

Creed bowed anxiously. 'Shall you require the square of fawn-edged handkerchief, Sir Giles?'

'Damn your eyes.' Snatching up gloves and hat, Sir Giles brushed past the valet and thundered downstairs, striding past his footmen and butler without a glance, springing to the box of his curricle and whipping up his horses before the groom could scarcely scramble out of the way.

The streets were dark, preventing him from making the speed he so desperately needed. Looping the rein, he swept round a corner and struck his team to a canter, not caring that his wheels shaved a sedan-chair by inches or that the less-spirited horses of another conveyance were set rearing in fright. He had to reach Catherine before Willy betrayed him. He had to stop the boy from telling her what wasn't so. One moment of carelessness, and all the hours of nurturing that young lady's trust and faith in him . . . gone, as though they had never been. He could not permit it to happen.

Worse, that anguished look in Willy's eyes was like a dagger plunging in. Who had thought the boy would come along in time to hear? Devil take Lord Reginald for his impatience! The man had undone everything. Like all eavesdroppers, Willy had heard imperfectly, did not fully understand, and yet his accusations had cut painfully near the bone. Of course he did not know Jacques-Pierre was here to murder the Prince Regent and open England to invasion, but he was right – curse him! – about the despicable treatment which had been dealt Catherine de Bleu.

Sir Giles shifted on the seat, knowing his falling in love with her, when he thought no female would ever touch his heart, did not excuse his seeking her company and encouraging her to trust him while half the time he was watching for any slip she might make. A sliding of one wheel on the cobblestones forced him to slow the horses as they clattered through a narrow alley and turned into Half-Moon Street. The knife plunged in again as he saw the lights in his mother's windows. Dear God, he must be given the chance to explain how he had made such a mull of things. He did not want to trap Catherine; he wanted to free her, to cherish her always. She must not be allowed to listen to Willy, who was wild enough with anger to blurt out anything. She must be made to understand.

But as he strode inside he was met in the hall by Willy coming down the stairs, panting and savagely triumphant.

172

'Too late, Giles!' he said, and despair crashed down upon Sir Giles, bringing him to a breathless, hopeless halt. 'I've spoken to her, and told her what you and Lord Reginald mean to do to Jack.'

Sir Giles could only stand there and stare at him as the dreams of his future crumbled. 'You poor little fool,' he said.

Willy's dark face flushed. 'Am I, Giles? I know what a devilish time we've been having with this war. My friends are being killed in it, too.' His chin came up. 'But I also know what my honor demands. The French may be sneaking connivers, and Jack may be the worst of them. But he save my life, and now I've returned the favor. I shan't ever want to see him again, nor you, because you're just as base as he is! I'm going back to Thorne House to get my things. The stage will take me to Oxford, where I can find something to do until the next term begins. Goodbye!' Then he paused and looked back as Sir Giles set a hand upon the newel. 'She won't see you. You may as well not try it. Besides' – and his voice was a jeer – 'what would you say?'

Upstairs, the silence was ominous. Catherine sat in her aunt's oval sitting room with her hands gripped together as tightly as the band of self-control around her throat. The blow had been final, and to escape its devastation she had leapt for refuge into this motionless silence.

'And now, Catherine? And now?' Abruptly Milady began to pace the floor. 'We are trapped. Oh, it has been very clever, *non?*' She wiped the tears her anger could not dissolve. 'We suspected nothing. Robert would despise us.' She sniffed, her dark eyes blazing. 'As for this Jacques-Pierre you insisted on creating – how long until they discover there is no such being and come for *us?* We must flee. We have failed.'

'Non!' With a gesture Catherine rose to her feet. Her crushed pride sparked a savagery of purpose within her. The glow of the past weeks was gone; she could think with swift clarity. Now she knew what Milord meant when he warned her against entanglements of affection. 'We have not failed,' she said with a flash of her eyes. 'And we are not yet trapped. As for Jacques-Pierre, without him to fool these *Anglais*, we would be in prison by now. He has been useful, madame. He will continue to serve us.'

Milady drew in a sharp breath. 'You will not appear in that guise again –'

'Did I say this was necessary?' asked Catherine coolly. 'But now that they know we know of them, it is time to strike, I think.'

'At the Regent?'

'No, at Milord Reginald Sperling and Sir Giles Thorne. It would be easy to trap them. A word of Jacques-Pierre in their ear, and they would come running.' Catherine's eyes narrowed; to hate was her only defense against the terrible pain. 'Dogs! We will –'

A knock on the door silenced her. It was a lackey, come to say Sir Giles was downstairs and desirous of her presence.

Catherine stiffened. 'Inform monsieur I am indisposed to his company. And please say to Milady Thorne I have the headache and will not make my presence at dinner.'

The door closed behind the fellow, and Milady frowned. 'Is it wise to hide?'

'I will not see him!' Sweeping up her skirts, Catherine left her aunt for the sanctuary of her own chamber. There, having secured the door, she threw herself across the bed and began to weep, her fury and bravado gone, her dreams shattered all about her.

Later, when her tears were spent and she was left with ragged little sobs of exhaustion, she heard a pecking at her window. She jerked upright and gasped at the face pressed against the pane.

Then her heart began to beat again, and she eased out a long sigh. 'Joseph!' She flew to open the window for him. 'I am so happy to see you! Is all well? Have you brought Armand and Milord? If you only knew how eager I am to be rid of this vile country.' She knew she was babbling as one never did to a servant, even one of as long standing as good, sturdy Joseph, but she could not help herself. The strain of these weeks had been too great, her own horror at this moment too painful, for her to retain any composure now that her uncle was safe at last and back to command her every action.

But Joseph's weathered face was frowning. 'You have been weeping, mademoiselle. Such a thing is not like you.'

'Oh, Joseph.' Catherine wiped away the tears still on her cheeks. 'It is merely a foolishness we need not regard.' But how did one stop regarding a broken heart, she wondered, and winced at the worn phrase. The description was too simple, too trite to convey how much this void ached within her. She felt as though half of her had been ripped away and was still bleeding and would go on suffering unspeakable agonies for the rest of time. *Trust me,* he had said, and oh, *Dieu*, she had! She had! He had but to have lifted his finger, and she would have thrown away all she possessed for him. Never in her life had she given away her heart or her trust, and now it was as though he had defiled her by stealing what could never be replaced. Despite her pride she must tell Milord some of it. He would call Sir Giles out and shoot him down, and while that would solve nothing, at least she could claim the paltry satisfaction of revenge.

'Where is Milord?' she asked again, with increasing eagerness to see his austere face and to listen to the drawl which masked a lightning wit. 'Does he wait outside in the street? I must see him at once, and you will help me, Joseph, to bring Milady away from dinner. It –'

'Mademoiselle.' Joseph took her hands between his calloused ones. 'I am sorry. I bring bad news.'

Something clutched through the pain within her. 'What?' She pulled free, her eyes widening. 'Not –'

'Yes, mademoiselle. The letter from Monsieur Armand was a forgery. Monsieur sits beside Milord – at the Palais du Lexumbourg. We were arrested two days after reaching Paris.'

'Both in prison? But –' Catherine's eyes narrowed. 'Why the letter, assuring us all was well? *Sacredieu,* do they play with us?'

'Yes, mademoiselle.' Joseph's brown eyes were troubled. 'And now I am sent to give you a new message. 'The Emperor grows impatient.' That is all. I think it clear enough.' He sighed.

'The dogs,' she muttered through her teeth. 'We are rushed from all sides. *Morbleu.*' All this time she had been delaying, moving slowly, trying to give Armand a chance when there had never been a chance for him at all. How Bonaparte must be laughing. A thousand curses upon his head! And upon Sir Giles's, too. Had he not tried to trap her, she would have gone to him for his help. Somehow they could have gotten round this stalemate. But now she had no one to turn to but herself. Well, the devil with her heart and her sentiment! As a female she was a fool, but that would be said about her no longer. *S'il plaît à Dieu,* she would show them all her steel and her mettle. The time for mercy was past.

'I must return to the Emperor with your reply.' Joseph's eyes were upon her again. 'We have no choice, mademoiselle. Milord himself has said it.'

She gasped, refusing now, even at this late stage, to fully believe it. '*Non!* There must be a plan of Milord's. Joseph,

176

there must be! I know him too well to believe he is caught forever. Did you bring me nothing of a plan?'

Slowly Joseph shook his head. 'If there is a way for him to escape, it has not been confided in me.'

'I will send gold to him!' Catherine turned to hurry across the room to her dressing-table. 'He can bribe his way out –'

'Mademoiselle, it would be taken from me before I could see him.'

She shut the drawer, nodding reluctantly. Every avenue seemed closed. And Napoleon Bonaparte could not be trusted. Nothing could make her believe he would release Milord and Armand if she did what he asked. But perhaps... Ah, *peste*. Thinking was beyond her. They had no choice.

Her head came up. It was time to turn away from the world she had reached for, and go back to her place of shadows and intrigues. 'Tell the Emperor we will strike,' she said.

But Joseph was not content. As Milady had asked, so did he: 'The Regent?'

This time it was a very long while before Catherine answered. Once again she felt tempted to run to Sir Giles and beg his help. But it was absurd. He was an English gentleman with a heart like ice. He knew her to be an adventuress and had treated her as such. And even if all that was not between them, even if she was not standing here now torn with love and hate for him, she knew there was not one thing he could do to save her uncle.

With a sigh she looked up, and when she spoke at last her voice did not waver. 'It is the Regent. Within a fortnight.' Her glance met Joseph's briefly, then she opened the window for his departure.

He paused while climbng out to look at her. 'God keep you, mademoiselle.'

She looked down, feeling cold, and lifeless, and hard. 'God has abandoned me. *Allez,* Joseph. Do what you can for them.'

CHAPTER TWELVE

The following morning she awoke as the maid drew back the curtains. Declining a tray of steaming chocolate and croissants, she dressed and went to her aunt, where in a terse, cold voice she gave Milady the bad news. Milady turned white, and the cup slipped from her hand to shatter, unheeded, upon the floor.

'Robert,' she whispered, and crumpled.

Catherine caught her just before she could fall among the china fragments and with difficulty maneuvered her to the day-bed. Then she rang the bell and stood in the center of the room until Aglaé appeared.

'Milady has swooned,' she said as Aglaé rushed forward and began chaffing the limp hands. 'There is news *très mauvaises* about Milord. He has no hope of escape.' She hesitated. 'You will comfort her, Aglaé.'

Walking out, she was about to go downstairs when she received a summons to Lady Thorne's boudoir. This was a chamber she had not entered before. With one swift glance she knew she did not like it. There were too many flowers, too many frills, too much pink upon the walls. The lapdog bounded forth to sniff at the hem of her riding habit. She pushed him away and looked up to see Lady Thorne's gray eyes upon her.

She inclined her head, impatient already with this visit she must endure. 'Madame?'

'Sit down.' Lady Thorne's voice was equally cold as she pointed her lorgnette toward the chair. 'I see you are recovered from your indisposition.'

'Yes. Thank you.' Catherine sat on the indicated chair, and put down a hand to prevent the dog from bouncing into her lap. He licked her fingers. Revolted, she drew her hand quickly away.

'You needn't thank me.' Lady Thorne leaned forward, her eyes piercing. 'Tell me why you have seen fit to hurt Giles.'

Catherine blinked, her cold preoccupation struck from her. 'I have done nothing to him.'

'That's a lie. I may be an old woman, but I am not a fool. I know Willy came posthaste to see you last night, after which you refused to come downstairs and sent Giles a most rude *congé*. And now this morning Willy has been thrown out of Giles's house.' Lady Thorne's brows drew together. 'Never, on any score, have they disagreed so violently. If that young idiot has offered for you, and you have accepted him, you shall find yourself in the street before the hour is out!'

'Willy?' Catherine could but stare. Milord had been right; entanglements were the devil with which to deal. Annoyance sent her to her feet. '*C'est incroyable!* There is nothing between us, *non*, and could never be. But to offer me such insults –'

'Be quiet. And sit down. I shan't have you towering over me,' said Lady Thorne, with such ferocity Catherine complied. 'What are you doing, then? If Willy did not offer for you, I'll wager he tried. You needn't cozen me into believing no hard feelings have sprung up between the brothers. And I know you are at the root of it.'

Catherine laughed without amusement. 'Indeed, madame? Willy has a right to be vexed with Sir Giles. But the only demoiselle in love with him is Mademoiselle Lyndon. You see, she does not like Sir Giles at all. And Willy does not care for her –'

'I shan't be led off the subject,' said Lady Thorne, brandishing her lorgnette. The dog fawned his way onto her lap but she ignored him. 'Surely you are not so hen-witted as to believe I ever really intended that vapid chit for Giles! As soon as I saw you, I knew you were perfect for him, though of course to say so would have set him against you at once. Everything was going splendidly. You had him, you know. And now you have done or said something dreadful to him, and as long as I live I shall never forgive you for causing the misery I saw in his eyes last night.'

The words did not seem real. Catherine sat gripped by disbelief and despair, part of her wanting to believe and part of her scornful. Perhaps... but was she a fool, to accept an old woman's fantasies? Sir Giles did not care for her. Ne never had. He was a liar and a cheat. He had played the game better than she, and had almost won it. But he would not win. She swore he would not.

'Lady Thorne,' she said, her voice low. 'Your son has never cared for me. He sought my company because he thinks I am a spy for the French. Willy told me this last night, and if you think I am eager for the chance to hurt Sir Giles, you are right. I should like to trounce him into the dirt! *Mon Dieu*, madame, that was not misery you saw in his face, but chagrin. Because now I know what a dog he is, and he knows if he dares to approach me again, I shall – I shall – oh! Good day!'

Furiously she walked out, glad she had left Lady Thorne stricken and white. But beneath the anger and the hard resolution burned her memory of the ball, when their souls had met and she had lost her heart to him. Snatching up a vase from its pedestal near the stairs, she hurled it the length of the corridor. Oh, *Dieu*, why could she not forget?

The interview with Lady Thorne did not alter her plan for the day; in fact, it set her more quickly to work. Returning to her room, she spent an hour at her toilette, going over every detail until she was satisfied all was perfect. She regretted very much that the bodice of her habit was cut high to the throat, but in compensation she rouged her lips and practiced melting looks in the mirror. In this latter activity she was not successful, for how could she look warm and appealing when inwardly she raged? Very well, she must instead scorch Monsieur le Prince with a little fire.

The hour was upon her. Throwing down her comb, she took a deep breath and arranged the short veil on her hat. Then out she swept, crop in hand, to the front steps, where the bay horse Romulus awaited her. The groom who was to accompany her was already mounted. The footman helped her up; she took her time about arranging her skirts to sweep just so over Romulus's side, though inwardly she quivered. *Peste*, no nerves now! She spurred Romulus to a trot.

It was a busy, colorful time of day. The morning was sufficiently gone for the *beau monde* to be stirring about the streets. She was hailed often by acquaintances and answered prettily, reining up here and there to chat a moment with young ladies she knew well enough now to speak to. And always she kept Romulus at a showy, leisurely pace, careful to give the impression that she was out to show off her habit and the fine turn of her wrists. But her strong hands held the reins firmly and short, and her every fiber was on the alert. While she smiled and simpered and pretended to admire the setting, her hazel eyes were sweeping the grounds of the park for any signs of a phaeton-and-six.

Dieu! Suddenly, there it was, halted mere yards away while the Regent spoke to the occupants of a curricle. Her breath caught, and she leaned forward with a quickening of her senses. Ah, *très bien*, it was the quarry at last. Timing her moves carefully, she held Romulus to a dawdle until from the corner of her eye she saw one of his horses sling its head and the others come alert. The prince was gathering his reins, ending the conversation with the other man she could not see because of the angle of the carriages. Now was the time for her move.

Laughing, she threw a glance over her shoulder at the groom. 'James, is that not a clever rise before us? I wish a canter!' As she spoke she sent Romulus forward with a bound, gratified that he responded so nobly to her commands, but too intent upon what she was doing to praise him now. The phaeton's wheels were rolling; still laughing and pretending to notice nothing but what a splendid outing she was having, Catherine kept Romulus on his collision course. He snorted, but she was firm, counting the danger, but confident of her horse and herself.

There was a shout; she glanced up to see they were upon each other. Romulus was already checking as she screamed. She spurred him and yanked hard on the reins to make him rear just a few feet short of the startled team also plunging to a halt. Romulus was made to rear again, and this time Catherine let herself slide off in a fall that was expert, designed to hurt little, and looked much worse than it was. She lay still while the tumult of oaths and exclamations raged over her.

Since her sudden canter had left the groom behind, and the Regent's own tiger ran at once to the horses, there was no one closer to her than the Regent himself, who was obliged to throw his reins away and clamber down to her assistance. His hands lifted her with more strength than she had expected.

'My dear young lady, are you all right? Good God, what a stupid thing to –'

She opened her eyes before he could finish and gasped. 'Did I fall? What happened. Oh, *mon Dieu*, I was so afraid!'

'There, there, you mustn't cry,' he was forced to say as

183

tears spilled onto her dusty cheeks. 'You're quite safe now. Er, yes, quite safe indeed. And I'm sure no one meant to harm you. Just a silly accident. You've no cause to be afraid now.'

'*Vraiment?*' Somehow she had become cradled in his arms. He smelled nicely, and his linen was exquisite, but, *peste*, such corpulence! She raised her brimming eyes to his, knowing their color was at its loveliest behind tears, and tried to smile. 'Yes, I feel much better now.' Then as he began to look intrigued, she blinked and blushed furiously. 'Why, you're – oh, *Dieu! C'est le beau prince d'Angleterre!* Forgive me, monseigneur, I have given you offense.' She struggled in very weak confusion to pull free of his embrace.

He shook his head, even smiling a bit. 'My dear, not at all –'

By now the horrified groom had come rushing up, and others as well. She could hear the babble of voices around them.

Just as the Regent looked discomfited by the crowd and started to release her, she gasped and put a hand to her head. 'Oh, *peste*, I feel so dizzy.'

The Regent stood up, surrendering her to someone else's arms. 'Put her in my carriage. She must be taken home at once.' He patted Catherine's hand. 'You mustn't worry, my child. You shall be all right and tight again in no time.'

She shook her head, bringing forth another blush. 'Monseigneur, I *have* caused you the embarrassment. I –'

'Nonsense. It was all my fault,' he said, looking charmed with her. 'Why, I believe we may have met somewhere. Have we?'

Again she colored. 'Oh, yes. The villa party.'

'Yes, good God, yes! Mademoiselle de Bleu, isn't it?' He smiled. 'There, you see? I remember you quite well. You needn't be frightened now. Promise me you won't be.'

'Because you wish it, I – promise,' she faltered, raising her eyes to his in a way that made his pale blue gaze grow warm.

'Good.' He patted her hand again, gave her one last interested glance, and beckoned to someone. 'See here, Thorne, drive her home, won't you?'

'Yes, of course, sir. My curricle is at your service as long as you require it,' Sir Giles was saying with proper deference, but Catherine scarcely heard him for the flame of fury engulfing her. *Sacredieu!* Not that man again!

He came forward and stared at her with the glint of mockery so prevalent in his steel-blue eyes she would have raised up to strike him had she dared. He knew, devil take him! He knew, and his contempt was plain enough to flick her on the raw. Ah, the fiend! When Lady Thorne said there was misery in him, it was not true! There was nothing left to do in this situation but pretend to faint. And she did so, lying still and limp while the phaeton drew her away from the little scene, the groom leading Romulus along behind.

The dreams were gone now, gone as though they had never existed. She had been such a fool! But she did not repeat mistakes, and since Sir Giles must be her enemy, she would show him what an enemy was. The intrigue was hot; the battle lines were drawn. And if all went well, that poor fat prince now driving himself home in a borrowed conveyance would never know who was the victor or why. Soon he would know nothing at all.

Naturally news of the contretemps spread across London. Naturally there were any number of people who had seen the royal phaeton in Half-Moon Street. Naturally it was discussed at great length over tea and cake. Naturally everyone waited to see what advantage Miss de Bleu would take of it.

185

She began by not appearing for two days, sitting in the privacy of her chamber, bored to tears but pleased with the flowers and note of apology sent by His Highness. And when she did go about again, she made light of the matter, insisting it had been very much her fault, since she failed to watch where she was going. Then when she did encounter the Regent at the opera, she did not seek to gain his attention or his notice, thus leaving him free to approach her if he wished, which he did with every evidence of pleasure. In avid public view they exchanged a few moments' conversation, during which Lady Thorne was at her most gracious and Lady de Chalier at her most haughty. After this Catherine found herself popular.

But while satisfied with the manner in which her ploys were working, she could not make herself be pleased by them. She could not be happy at all. The pleasant, sane world of these English was denied to her forever. And her artificial existence of elegant duplicity seemed like a prison. She hated it and what she was doing. She hated the fact that if she and her people won through this, there was no future for her save to start another adventure in Milan or perhaps Vienna. She was denied her birthright. She was denied the chance to be the wife of an Englishman. Having glimpsed – no matter how falsely – a view of life more shining and ecstatic than she had ever imagined, she could not be happy or content with anything less. And she could never have anything but less.

There were many rounds of activities to attend, and mercifully these kept her busy. But matters were still strained between her and Lady Thorne, and Sir Giles never approached her at all. She was at once puzzled and hurt. He never again showed his scorn as he had on that day with the Regent, but she was not reassured. Worse, now that her first blaze of fury was spent, she was dismayed to find she could not stop thinking of him. The ecstasy had been so

186

short, so brief! One evening and one day, and then it had all blackened to ashes when Willy had burst in with that awful tale. Oh, *Dieu*, she was so wretched! She loved Sir Giles. She wanted to be his wife, his lover, the one he thought of with delight. She wanted her hands held in his strong ones. She wanted his lips upon hers. She wanted to see his low, distant smile, the way his eyes changed color when he was pleased or angry. She wanted to banter with him and hear his wit. She wanted to be with him, to share the days with him ... *peste*, yes, even to bear children for him. It was mad, it was folly, but beneath her hate, and anger, and hurt, she loved him still, with an ache that grew stronger and more insistent as the days crawled by.

What good was her cleverness and her talent, when she was denied all that was meant by being a woman? Milord's life, and now Armand's, in exchange for England, in exchange for a countryside lush and charming, as full of gaiety as France was grim. Must the blood staining Europe run here, too? She had grown to like this island, especially the early hour of morning when the birds were still and the mists had not yet rolled back and the sun barely spilled over it all. It was a place of enchantment, a place where the monarchy still stood, a place where the man she loved made his home. What would happen to him when the invasion came?

He would fight, of course, for she had learned Englishmen were swift to drop all to meet a challenge. Only who could defeat Bonaparte? No one had. The man was blessed by Satan, and if ever he was brought down, she prayed it would be by the English. They deserved that honor, for they alone stood against him.

But what chance would they have if she opened the door to invasion? The answer was inescapable. Once touched by the boots of the French, England would go down. Sir Giles would be killed on the bayonet of a Norman farmer. Lady

Thorne would lose her home to poverty. Lord Chesby would be put to work in the kitchens. The people on the land would starve. The royal family would either flee to share the exile of their French cousins or be destroyed; *oui*, even the mad old king would receive no mercy. Bonaparte would not win easily, but he would win. And she would make this carnage possible, because life did not always permit choices, and the question of saving her uncle and cousin was precisely such a matter which allowed no choice. In all decency and love she had to save them, no matter what the cost. But could she? How long would her strength last?

And then, just when she began to think her conflicting desires were going to rip her asunder, a gilt-edged invitation was brought round my messenger. She read it once, slowly and with a numbness which drove away the flurry of her distraught emotions. It was too late to question now. The time had come. She went to her aunt and showed her the card with its flowing inscription.

Milady accepted it, her dark, hollow eyes remaining on Catherine. 'What is it, child?' she asked, but her question seemed to be something other than what she spoke.

Catherine understood, and her eyes answered as she replied, 'It requests the presence of myself and that of my duenna at a select dinner party.' She paused, because it was impossible to say it all smoothly. 'At Carlton House.'

Milady's eyes filled with tears as she gripped Catherine's hand and kissed it. *'Merci,'* she whispered.

And after that there could be no more consideration of wavering from the purpose.

CHAPTER THIRTEEN

But first it was necessary to attend Almack's, the Duchess of Devonshire's rout, two card parties, and an assembly to announce Gussie Lyndon's betrothal. The latter was squeezed into the social calendar by a relieved Lady Reginald, regardless of the confusion it wrought with other hostess's plans. Since she had been brought out with Gussie, Catherine was obliged to go. She did so with mixed feelings. Despite their recent differences she still liked Gussie and wished to see her happy, but she knew this would be the last occasion she would see people she had grown to care for. She felt very much a Judas that evening as she sat upon a chair of Sheraton design and drank a toast to the future of Miss Lyndon and Mr. Barclay.

She had seen the gentleman before yet knew nothing of him. He was slim but well made, and sported the coachman style of cravat. In a good-natured way he seemed to be enjoying the naïveté of his prospective bride. Catherine herself was startled, for he was Sir Giles's age, and Sir Giles's friend, and she could not at first imagine what had induced Gussie to accept his suit.

But after hearing how wealthy he was, Catherine lifted her brows and decided as a first husband he might do well. He would teach Gussie poise and sophistication and probably be considerate enough to grow old and die before she was much past forty. This thought amused Catherine enough to enable her to felicitate Gussie.

An anxious look cleared from Gussie's large eyes.

189

'Thank you, Catherine, ever so much. I was afraid you would not like him, and I do so want to be your friend again.'

Pain twisted in Catherine. After tomorrow she would be no one's friend. But she smiled. 'We have never stopped being friends, *chérie*. But do *you* like him?'

Gussie blushed and laughed a bit. 'I confess I didn't at first, not at all. He is so much older, but not stern like –' Her blush deepened, and she clasped her hands to her breast, crushing the rosebuds pinned there. 'Oh, Catherine, please don't despise me! I . . . Willy does not intend to return to London, does he?'

'No.'

She gave herself a little shake. 'Mr. Barclay always makes me enjoy being with him. He has wonderful address and manners which must always please. As his wife, next year I am to bring out both my sisters. And he is going to settle Papa's debts and add a little to Cordelia's dowry to make it respectable, and besides, he has kissed me once and it was rather wonder –'

'Please excuse me,' broke in Lord Chesby, who was suddenly before them and bowing. 'I hate to interrupt this little coze, but, Miss de Bleu, if I could –' He stopped to clear his throat as they both turned to gaze at him. 'Well, er, would you mind too much if I –'

'Oh, Uncle Chesby, not a poem, please!'

He turned red above his rumpled neckcloth. 'Not at all," he said to Gussie. 'I'm sorry to disappoint you, but I don't write verse now. I've given it up. Useless.' He nodded and brought out a vast handkerchief to mop his brow. 'Taken up painting instead. Oils.'

'You will find it most rewarding, I am sure,' said Catherine, wondering why he lingered.

'Yes.' He bowed and smiled at her in a nervous way. 'Miss de Bleu, I wonder if I could prevail upon you to come with me for a moment?'

'*Oui*, but of course,' she said, puzzled as to what he could want to discuss. It was certain to be tedious.

But he gave her no inkling as he clasped her hand in his moist grip and drew her away to the palm room. She recoiled at once from the abundant foliage and humid air, but before she could speak or move away, he had seized her other hand and knelt before her.

'My dearest, dearest Miss de Bleu, there is no other creature in this world I honor more than –'

'Milord!' She looked at him in alarm, reading suddenly the earnestness upon his chubby countenance, and knowing, with revulsion for the wrongness of his instincts, she must prevent him from speaking further. 'What are you saying? A declaration? I must not let you. It will not do, *non*, not at all!'

She did not wish to be cruel, but her words were forceful enough to bring him faltering to his feet.

'But I've scarcely begun,' he said, his eyes wide.

She sighed, spurred by compassion. '*Oui*, I know. And it is very hard when I do not permit you to finish the speech you have memorized with such care. I am sorry, milord. You honor me much, but –'

'I want to marry you! You're the only woman who understands me!'

'That is not true,' she said, making herself stand firm, though it was like striking a bewildered dog. 'I have patience with you, but that is not enough. I am sorry.'

'Nonsense.' Again he clutched at her hands, but this time she pulled away. 'Catherine, dearest, we would get on famously. I have the most charming little establishment on Mount Street. You would like it. I know you would. And I keep my paintings hidden upstairs where the light is better, so that needn't be a bother to you. And you could give little soirées . . .' He paused, frowning as she continued to stand unmoved by this description of domestic bliss. 'May I call you Kitty?'

191

'Never!' she said with a gesture and flash of her eyes that visibly startled him.

'Oh, very well. I – I had rather hoped I could,' he said slowly. 'It's such a pretty little name.'

'Je le déteste!' How dare he force her to linger here? He perceived her so wrongly she could have stamped her foot at him. Bah, she should have been cruel and sneered at him in the past, for now his foolish brain had romanticized her into some sort of pedestal beauty to be cherished and pampered and spoiled rather than swept away from herself by a man who was, *parbleu*, a man!

She caught her breath, abruptly brought to tears. 'Give me leave to go. I will talk of this no longer.'

'Yes, well, all right. I've come at you too quickly, I suppose.' To her vexation he blundered along to escort her out. 'Please forgive me for presuming and all that. You shan't ever guess what it's taken to speak my heart to you, not that I've said much.' He reddened and cleared his throat. 'Oh, my dearest Miss de Bleu, I wish you would be kind and think it over.'

He said more in this vein, but she did not listen. Her eyes swept the assemblage and rested stormily upon Sir Giles's tall figure. Gad! How could her pride bear it, this love for such a scoundrel of a man? He had used her, insulted her, done everything in his power to betray her, and still he could go on being calm and distant. It was insufferable! Did he know she supped tomorrow with the Prince Regent? Why did he not speak to her about it? Why did he not come and attempt to explain away what Willy had told her? Ah, the arrogant devil! It was plain he did not care what she knew. Her fists clenched. She would never forgive him for this contempt.

But, while her eyes flashed and her pride burned she knew deep inside with a withering little thrust of shame that, were he to step forward now and ask her to trust him she would throw away everything.

'And will you think it over more carefully before you give me your final answer?' pleaded Lord Chesby.

She scarcely heard him. Her eyes were still upon Sir Giles. 'Excuse me,' she said, and walked away. She could not go to him, though her heart cried for her to do so. Her pride would not permit it.

But before the evening was over he had sought her out, appearing at her elbow just as she rose to make her departure with Lady Thorne.

She lifted her brows at him in a cool manner. 'Why, Sir Giles –' she began, but he merely looked at her and she could not finish the intended piece of banter.

In faith, her breath was fairly caught from her, and for a moment it was as though she were being squeezed by an invisible hand. Her cheeks felt cold; she wondered if she had gone white. Yes, surely she had. Oh, *peste* . . .

'I shall call upon you tomorrow,' he said in a clipped voice that forestalled any rebellion. Never had he looked more masterful than at that moment.

A spark of hope came to life within her heart, and no amount of common sense could quench it.

'So, Giles, you take notice of us at last,' said Lady Thorne, turning back to them. Her eyes swept his set mouth and Catherine's frozen hauteur, and she sniffed. 'Squabbling again, I see. I wish you both in Jericho! Come, Catherine, don't dawdle.'

But Sir Giles laid his hand on her arm, detaining her when she would have obeyed. His gray eyes, as hard as steel, raked hers. 'Tomorrow I will come.'

Was it a challenge? Through the flame engulfing her at his touch, her spirit could yet leap in answer. Her gaze did not falter. 'I will see you,' she said, and releasing her, he walked away without another word.

She waited all morning, but he did not come. And the afternoon brought delivery of a small package from Messrs. Smyth and Ginnis, gunsmiths. In the bolted privacy of her chamber she unwrapped the burlwood case, which contained a small silver-mounted pistol, finely wrought to fit a boy's or lady's hand. On a wicked impulse she had instructed the initials *J-P. de B.* to be engraved upon the butt. But now it seemed a small joke.

With steady hands she loaded the pistol and primed it, then slipped it into the bottom of the beaded reticule she was to carry that evening. Her gown was detailed to perfection and hung upon a stand in the corner so its folds should not become crumpled. Her invitation lay upon the dressing-table. She stood a moment and stared round at it all: the preparations, the elegance of the chamber itself. The pistol had brought menace here. Deadly purpose seemed to hang in the air, though it had not before. She still kept Milord's firelock, but it was far different from the little silver-mounted pistol, which had been ordered and crafted for a single purpose. Once the purpose was accomplished, it would never be used again. Monsieur Bonaparte could have it as a keepsake. *Dieu*, but she hated him!

Fists clenched, she slammed herself out of the room and headed downstairs in order to work out her building tension upon the pianoforte. But she encountered – this time without design – Sir Giles in the hall and was obliged to halt. Warily she greeted him.

He bowed.

'I was going to the *salle de musique*,' she said, while the hope which had first stirred last night now beat with vigor. *Par les saints,* he was a man, *non?* If he was, he would stop her. He would strike her, he would abduct her, he would woo her to distraction, but, *voyons*, he must stop her. There was no one else who could, not even herself. 'Please come with me. We can be private there.'

Without a word he followed her to the golden room she had once found advantageous for a confrontation. But as soon as she stepped across the threshold and saw again the harp and the crystal bowls, now serving as prisms for the sunlight spilling through the windows, she realized she had erred in coming here. For it reminded her of the joy and relief she had felt upon receiving Armand's letter, and those emotions had proven to be spent on falsehood and lies. Armand had not been able to spare her from the diabolical task. It was she who must somehow now find the strength to save him.

She looked straitly at Sir Giles, pausing a moment to steady herself – for inside she was trembling – and lifted her brows at him. 'Yes, monsieur?'

He frowned with his tawny head slightly bent and walked forward to lay one arm upon the mantel. Then he looked at her, his face grim and set. 'Let us cut line, shall we?' he began in a low voice. 'I – am very well aware that there is a plot, authored by Bonaparte of France, to assassinate our Regent.'

Catherine gripped her hands together, chilled at how dreadful his flat utterance made the words sound. Oh, *Dieu*, how he must despise her for what she was doing! But she could not explain; she could not beg for help.

'I know this assassination was entrusted to your family. You yourself have told me of your uncle's imprisonment. There is no other reason necessary to explain why you are engaged in helping your brother carry out so dastardly an act.'

This recital was cutting too near the bone. If only he would speak to her as he once had, with gentleness and understanding. She did not wish to hear more relentless accusations. Up came her head. 'Monsieur, please. Willy explained your knowledge to me.' And could she ever forget that moment when he had burst in, white-faced and beside himself, to blurt out: 'You must warn your brother at once! Giles knows all about him. That's why he's made up to you, Miss de Bleu, to trap Jack. Jupiter, but it makes

195

me sick, all of it!' And before she could speak or fully grasp what he was saying, he had departed, leaving her to suffer the brutal implications without hope of learning more.

'Willy explained nothing,' snapped Sir Giles, losing that dispassionate calm, which was, after all, more fragile than it had first appeared. 'Miss de Bleu, I know he has made you hate and – distrust me. He was wrong to do so, because when I swore to you I should never bring you harm, I was not lying.'

'You assumed a great deal that night!' she flashed. 'I know only that I told too much to a viper waiting to betray me at the first chance.' She bit her lip to keep it from quivering, but her head was very high. 'When does the watch come to make its arrest, monsieur? I have done nothing against you, yet you took my trust and twisted it into dishonor. I cannot forget such a thing.'

He winced but came forward, seeking to take her hands. She turned and walked several feet away, then faced him once again.

'I think not, monsieur.' Only God could know how violently her heart was pounding or how weak were her limbs. She could barely stand there before him; if he touched her, she was lost. But still she held her ground with all the remaining strength she possessed.

'Very well.' He came no closer. 'You do not believe me, but I speak the truth when I say I am trying to help you. I know you are in this against your will. Do you think I don't realize how terrified you are of Jacques-Pierre? Is it betrayal to ask you to tell me where he is? You could be free of this whole matter. But you must help us put a stop to it. Won't you?' He swallowed hard and looked as if he would say more, but did not.

She stood there, stiff and with her face averted, believing him in spite of everything and despising herself for doing so. Dear God, how could she think when every fiber of her being ached to run to his arms? But he had not said he cared for her, and she must hear him say it. Again she longed for him to stop her, not plead with her as he was doing now, but to stop her. Nothing less could serve. He must know that. He was not a fool. And yet he continued to curb his impatience and desperation like a gentleman, trying to give her a fair chance, when she did not want such a chance. She wanted him to throw aside his sangfroid and his civility and *act. Dieu,* by now he should know that someone like her, who rode and shot like a man, played cards to win or lose at will with a skill that went beyond mere trickery, and manuevered almost anyone to her own choosing, could not be treated in the way one would a timid little damsel of sheltered sensibilities! Could he not, for all his cleverness, see that? Was this distaste for involvement and action the man's flaw? How she longed to tell him what to do! But she had said once she never cheated on the important things, and she could not do so now. She could not help him when he would not make her.

The ache which had gnawed at her since Willy's shattering outburst now became a knife of pain. But still she faced Sir Giles, squarely through her agony of knowing he had failed her in this when she most needed him not to fail, and said in a low voice which gave none of her turmoil away – save by its quiet tone: 'And what of my uncle?'

Sir Giles gestured helplessly. 'Oh, my dear Catherine, we both know that is something I cannot –'

'Yes, I know it,' she said, still quietly. 'Monsieur, I think we have nothing more to say.'

He went white to the lips and started a protest which was stilled by her steady gaze. Then, after a long moment, he bowed and left, shutting the door after him with a care that turned the last of her shattered hopes and desires into contempt. She raised a hand to her cheek, her insides as dry as though they had been scorched by the bitter fires of disappointment, and knew that for her nothing would ever be the same again. The ideal man had faced one final step to claim her, and either because he did not love her or because he was a fool, he had not taken it. She could never forget. She could never forgive.

The dining room at Carlton House was ample, impressive, and overheated. Catherine did not care for the taste which had decorated it. She considered the meal ostentatious to a fault and a burden to eat. The claret was too sweet; the ratafia too mellow. She was obliged to sit beside Sir Giles, and if it had not been for the fact that he was visibly puzzled at her *failure* to procure a place for Jacques-Pierre, she doubted she could have borne his proximity at all. As it was, she gave the performance of her life, chatting to him on every trivial subject she could think of until he looked vexed to distraction, then dazzling the Regent with her smiles. The fact that at some time during the course of the evening she must endure his sensual lips for a kiss was sufficient to rob her of what scant appetite she possessed.

But she ate, and she conversed, and she charmed, while inside she was ice cold. Something else seemed to be guiding her words and actions, but the horror within her continued to grow.

'I must warn you, Miss de Bleu,' Sir Giles was saying over an untouched dish of creamed spinach, 'that His Highness is prepared to accept no invitations to meet the rest of your family.'

She had just swallowed a sip of wine, and her fingers tightened on the glass with a sudden urge to hurl it at his head. Instead she gave him a sinister smile. 'Why, Sir Giles, you need not give yourself the concerns. Jacques-Pierre is not in London at this time, and my aunt has already this evening charmed the Regent much. Did you not see when he spoke to her?'

'No,' he said through his teeth. 'Her ladyship is honored.'

'Merely to be here is an honor,' she replied, and then mercifully at last the meal ended, the port was brought out, and it was time for the ladies to withdraw.

Free of the royal eye, they fanned themselves and exclaimed over the heat of the apartments while consuming the tea brought to them. Catherine took little part in the conversation – which mostly was taken up with coy speculations over the absence of Lady Jersey – leaving Milady to do so for her. She was too preoccupied, and besides she was so cold she feared she would begin to shiver soon and spoil everything. How long, she wondered with growing desperation. How long?

It seemed forever, but barely half an hour passed before the gentlemen finished their port and were with them again. A harp was wheeled in, and Lady Cowper consented to play.

Lady Sefton leaned toward Catherine. 'How very melancholy it makes me to recall a similar gathering last year in this very room. Dear George Brummell was putting me to the blush with his wit. He removed my earrings once in full view of everyone, did you know, and paid me such a darling compliment that no one could be offended.' She sighed. 'How I wish he and Prinny were on good terms again, but I suppose now that His Highness has kept Mr. Brummell's snuffbox, there is no hope of reconciliation. It's such a pity.' She turned away, freeing Catherine of the necessity of replying to such dismal commentary, and punched Sir John Lade awake just as he threatened to snore.

Presently, however, the musical interlude ceased, and conversation resumed. Looking up, Catherine perceived Sir Giles coming toward her with a markedly determined expression upon his face, but Lady Cowper waylaid him with a request that he help her put away the music.

Catherine was watching this when a bluff, hearty voice inquired at her elbow, 'Why, my pretty mademoiselle! You've not permitted me to show you a very fine painting I've just acquired. Come, it's just outside.'

She rose, allowing the Regent to take her hand, and accompanied him from the drawing room. Now that the moment was upon her, she had ceased her inward quaking. Her nerves were contolled and her voice steady when she duly admired the painting which was, indeed, only a few feet from the door.

'Monseigneur is possessed of handsome apartments,' she murmured, and tightened her grip on her heavy reticule even as she summoned all her willpower to give him one melting look of appeal from beneath her dark lashes. 'But may we not go further? One painting is not enough to slip away for.'

He laughed his assent and drew her hand closer through his arm. 'I have a little antechamber full of miniatures. You will like seeing them, I think.'

It was necessary to round a corner before the reached the chamber, which suited her purpose. She noticed how firmly he closed the door, though she pretended to give the paintings her full attention. The Regent began pointing them out to her, but quite abruptly his arm had encircled her waist even as he went on talking.

Braced though she was, the action startled her. *Peste*, the man wasted no time! Neither then should she, for they would not be left alone longer than a minute or two. With a deep breath, she put her hand inside her reticule, gripping the pistol, and broke from the Regent's grasp. He exclaimed, and she drew the pistol to aim it at his heart, her eyes as narrowed and as hard as his were bulging.

'Good God!' he gasped, becoming rather blue in the face. 'Good God!'

All that was required was a tightening of her finger upon

the hair trigger. She was surprised and a bit proud to find how steady was her hand and how suddenly calm and purposeful she had become. The Regent still stood gasping before her, his raddled, corpulent figure heaving in distress. The faint lingering signs of his past good looks were now erased by fear. But he was still a prince, and, *parbleu*, she was still of the blood royal. Her decision was made at last, with finalty. The horror of what she was doing was upon her. She faced it, and knew now there could be no turning back.

'Miss de Bleu! Good God, I –'

'Cease calling upon our Lord, and listen,' she snapped, and with a half-sob of his breath he fell silent.

'This pistol upon you was ordered by Napoleon Bonaparte,' she said in a clipped voice, giving him no chance to interrupt. 'If I pull the trigger, England will be invaded. Even now the spies listen for the sound of the shot. They are saddled, ready to give the word across the Channel. The fleet of the French waits for that word, monseigneur. But it will never come, because I choose not to pull this trigger. Not because I have fear, but because I choose not to. I am kinswoman to Vendôme. If you wish, you may ask him about me. But never again, my prince, abuse the French, not even in your thoughts. For I am of France and much has been brought to bear upon me, but the Corsican will not get the chance to lead his army against you.' She lowered the pistol with a fierce flash of her eyes. 'Remember this day, and what might have happened. Adieu!'

Swiftly she crossed the room and laid the pistol down upon a chair, then flung open one of the windows and looked out, her heart pounding as though she could already feel the breath of the hunter upon her. Ah, it was not far to the ground, and there were shrubberies to cushion her landing. Sweeping her skirts over one arm, she swung herself over the sill and dropped, landing with a crash in the shrubbery and scratching her face and arms, but getting less of a jar than she might have. In a moment she was on her feet and hidden from the Regent, who was now leaning out of the window. Anger flashed through her. Did the fool not know he made a perfect target?

He moved back inside, and her own grief overtook her. But urgency gave her the steadiness she needed, and like a slim shadow she flitted past the sentry through the rear gates and across Pall Mall before anyone could sufficiently realize what was happening or try to stop her. There came a shot, but she scorned the easiness of it as she hurried along with her skirts held up off the pavingstones and hoped these complacent Englishmen would learn not to be so trusting. But now she must find a job carriage and swiftly, for in this female guise the danger of the streets was too great for her. At last she did find a hackney, although the jehu on the box did not much want to stop for her, standing there as she was, without wrap or escort. She promised him a shilling if he'd spring his horses to Half-Moon Street. The result of this generosity got her to Lady Thorne's house much too quickly to permit her the chance to think over what she had done.

It was harder to get to her room unseen, but she managed it. Now she must move more quickly than ever, for Milady was certain to be here at any minute. Catherine could not depend upon her being detained. Milady would know something was wrong when no shot came. She would know Catherine did not have the courage to go through with it, and she would come with a vengeance. Catherine refused to let herself think about Milord. It was done now.

She yanked off her gown and the ribbon confining her curls. The breeches, shirt, boots, coat, and cloak were ready in their hiding place. Money and Milord's old pistol rested secure in the pockets. Throwing open the window, she dropped out a bandbox containing feminine attire and threw her cloak after it. Then, clapping on her hat, she pulled herself through the window and climbed down the creeper, growing reckless as she heard furious sounds of an approaching carriage. *Vite!* This was no place to be caught.

She jumped the remaining feet to the ground, wincing at the jar, and bent to snatch up her cloak and box. Without warning, a shape loomed toward her from the shadows. She whirled with her heart in her throat and tried to dodge, cursing herself for having the pistol in her cloak pocket where she could not reach it. Powerful arms seized her in a hug none of her struggles could dislodge. Another man approached with a length of frieze cloth, which he flung over her head. A rope lashed her arms to her sides and she was trapped in the makeshift sack, half-suffocated by the stench of sweat and filth, and panicked when one of the men swore coarsely in French.

'Muret! Hurry, will you? Someone comes!'

Who were these devils? Ah, *bon sang de bon sang,* could Bonaparte reach her so quickly?

Still struggling with all her might, Catherine was picked up bodily and heaved onto the floor of a carriage. Through the sack she heard a shout, and her heart leaped within her. Oh, *Dieu*, could it be him?

The Frenchman cursed, a whip cracked, and her carriage was rolling. She heard more shouts, and the scrambling clatters of hoofbeats, and cried with all her strength, 'Giles! *A moi! A moi!'*

'Be quiet!' snarled a voice, and she was shoved down with a rough hand.

She panted, striving to hear in the blindness of her prison. A horse screamed; they had still failed to gain speed. The carriage lurched, and she heard Sir Giles roar, 'Damn you, man! Block their way! They've got her –'

A shot rang out, shattering her breath, cutting off Sir

Giles's command. She knew then what had happened, and bolted up in terror.

'*Non!* Giles –'

'*Merde*, this creature!' snarled the man beside her. 'Drive on, Philippe!' And something hard struck Catherine's head, breaking her darkness with a shower of light. Agony flooded over her, and then she knew no more.

CHAPTER FOURTEEN

Pain eddied over him, waves of it. Not in one spot, but everywhere, around him and inside him, so that there could be no escape from it. He hoped if he did not move perhaps it would go away, but in the end there was nothing to do but fight it.

Gritting his teeth, he abruptly opened his eyes – not to find himself lying in the dark street as he had expected, but in a bed, a vast one with a white counterpane that reflected the candlelight into his face. He winced and shut his eyes, too weak to brave more discomfort. But something moved beside him. A hand took his, and he opened his eyes once again to find the candle moved away and Willy's face hanging over his.

'Giles,' he whispered. 'Oh, Giles.'

Sir Giles realized then with an odd sort of puzzlement that he must be injured grievously to bring his brother to him. He had never expected Willy to look at him again with anything but contempt and disappointment. He waited, studying the lines of Willy's features as he did so, but still the pain did not ease. He thought, however, he could now locate the source of it in his shoulder and tried to put his hand to it, only Willy was still gripping his fingers.

Much moved by the boy's grief, he managed to speak and was surprised at how weak one word could leave him.

'By Jove, you are better, aren't you?' Willy blinked and glanced round. 'I'd better fetch the doctor up again. There –'

'No,' said Sir Giles, his voice rasping a bit. The first moments of disorientation were behind him, and now he had to know. He must ask. 'Willy, where –'

'Deuce take it, Giles, I *am* sorry!' Willy bent over him again, and there was the sheen of tears in his green eyes and a quiver in his dark face. 'I swear I am. I should never have said such things to you. They don't matter one jot, and I should have seen that at once if I hadn't been such a fool. And now that you've been out for five days, raving and then so quiet sometimes I thought you must surely be going, and Mama beside herself with anxiety, I –' His voice broke, and kneeling beside the bed, he began to sob.

Sir Giles let his hand rest on the bent head, waiting for the boy's tears to subside. Five days, had Willy said? Good God, anything might have happened in that time. But the dread gnawing at him was smothered by his weakness and the awful, clawing pain.

'Willy,' he said at last, his voice so faint he doubted the boy could hear him. 'You needn't apologize. You were right. You were right and I so wrong...' For a moment bitter regret washed over him. Damn him for being such a fool.

But the pain sucked his strength like an ebbing tide, and he noticed the candle growing dimmer. Then it was gone, and there was just one last sob from Willy echoing faintly in his ears before the darkness came and swept him away.

He dreamed fitfully, remembering the night when Willy had told Catherine the truth. He had betrayed that girl. He, Sir Giles Thorne, knight, baronet and gentleman. He sought her out and taught her to trust him, but for reasons which were base, especially once he realized she was the woman he must have for his wife. Had it been fair to either of them to continue taking her trust and never speaking the truth to her? Good God, he had been a fool! Only a fool could go on biding the time and hoping she would eventually confide in him. He wanted her to come to him so he could save her. But she was not a person to ever be weak like that. No, she would have kept the terrible secret of her mission to the grave if need be. He should have seen that at once. He should have faced her squarely after the ball and told her the truth. She might have left him, but she would not have despised him as she did now. Oh, God, how hard it had been to stand his ground that night when she would not come down to face him and they had both known why. And besides, what sort of explanation would he have given had she seen him? How could any man explain such stupid, futile behavior as his had been?

He had handled her wrongly, he knew that now. Catherine was not sprung from the common breed. She was fierce, and courageous, and intelligent, someone who moved by her wits as well as by her reason. He had recognized those qualities and come to adore her for them, but all the same he had failed her, the only woman who could ever be for him.

Worse, he had actually believed she would go through with this plot to destroy the Regent. That hideous moment when he escaped Emily Cowper and realized the two had slipped out he actually stood in horror and believed she was going to do it. Damn them all for worrying over Jacques-Pierre! He was nothing but a blind, and like fools they believed it. And like a fool he had forgotten Catherine's mettle and believed she would bend to the pressure upon her. What could anyone else have done but pull the trigger of that exquisite little pistol? But she had not, and she had told the Regent why, as cleanly and as proudly as she had done everything since Sir Giles had come to know her. He felt deep shame then, upon bursting in on the stunned prince, a shame that drove him past his self-pity and damaged pride and sent him tearing after her in the hope of

207

raking away all the stupid misunderstandings.

Only she was gone. He called for her, remembering his panic when he came up in his curricle and saw those ruffians throwing her into a job chaise. Napoleon's hand reached everywhere, and it had seized her at the very moment of rebellion. Damn the French! How could they use a child of their own country like that? And now she was gone . . . dead, or else in God knew what danger, her trust in him destroyed by his own stupidity, and with no one else to turn to. She *needed* him, and where was he?

Shot, damn it, and helpless, probably dying, and without the means of doing anything about it. The pain gave him no ease, and fierce panic suddenly gripped him. He would let no doctor cup him again. Devil take the leech! No!

His eyes flew open, and he found himself sitting bolt upright in his bed, the darkness of before exchanged for sunshine skittering across the floor. He was panting, and a swirl of dizziness made him clutch hard at the covers, but he withstood it and looked around, blinking from the nightmare and the fact that in reality he was quite alone.

How much time had he lost? The answer mattered only if he did not waste any more. He had to find her. He could not bear to fail her again. He could not endure the agony of wondering if she were already lost to him.

But, no. Good God, why didn't he think? If they had meant to kill her, a single shot would have done the job. No, they had gone to the enormous trouble of kidnapping her. The aim, then, must be to get her back to France. And that was where he must go.

Gritting his teeth, he pushed himself out of bed, all but swooned, and finally got himself standing upright. Briefly he caught a glimpse of his pallid face with its unshaven cheeks and gaunt eyes in the looking-glass before he turned away to ring the bell.

The door to his dressing room opened almost at once,

and a worn-looking Creed stood gaping in the doorway. 'Good heavens, sir, you must get back into bed at once! I'll help you.'

For a moment Sir Giles feared the world was going to spin on him again, but miraculously it steadied, and he was able to lift his head and say, 'You will send for hot water and my razor. I am going to shave.'

The valet relaxed visibly, even brightened. 'Why, of course, sir! You must be feeling a great deal better. But first if you will be good enough to get back into bed, I am sure –'

She had called to him, hadn't she? Yes, now he remembered her cry for help just before that ball had ripped him apart. Hope flashed through him, giving him the strength to go on glaring at his valet. If she had called out for him to save her, then he knew in time she could be brought to forgive him, even, if God were merciful, to love him.

He did not move from his stance. 'When I am shaved, Creed, I shall dress. I also desire food. A small beefsteak will do. If my brother is in the house I wish to see him, and you will send a message round to Lord Reginald Sperling.'

Creed blinked unhappily. 'But surely, sir –'

Sir Giles lifted his brows. This resistance was fatiguing, and he could not afford to go back to bed and become an invalid again. He must act! 'Did I ask for your opinion, Creed?'

And he spoke so coldly the valet obeyed in spite of himself.

Willy arrived almost as soon as the shaving water. 'Giles! For heaven's sake, can't you forgo your dandy instincts this once and get back to bed? Creed can shave you there.'

Sir Giles paused in the act of easing his left arm into a makeshift sling. 'My dear Willy, if you think I am going to take these boots off again, you may revise your thinking.' His shoulder had begun to throb, making him wince as he settled back in his chair for Creed to apply the shaving soap.

'It's all very well for you to adopt that lofty tone,' said Willy, looking vexed. 'But you're as white as that napkin around your throat. And when you collapse on the floor and reopen your wound –'

'Good God,' said Sir Giles, faintly so as not to startle Creed, who was now passing the razor over his throat, 'I believe you are nagging me. Don't.'

And the sudden hardness in his tone kept Willy silent until the shave was over. Then he turned from the window where he'd been fidgeting. 'See here, Giles, I'd better send for the sawbones. You've been in a bad way, and you needn't try to gammon me into believing you're suddenly as right as rain because I can see you're not.'

'Very well.' It seemed pointless to argue any more. Sir Giles stood slowly as Creed came forward with his waistcoat. The gingerly easing of that garment over his wound caused him to sway, and he sat down before he really meant to.

'Giles!' Willy rushed forward.

'I was afraid of this –' Creed began, but Sir Giles dismissed him, then sighed and said to Willy, 'I am afraid I must depend on you rather more than I intended to. Willy, if you can bring yourself to forgive me, will you help me find Catherine de Bleu?'

'Forgive you?' Willy choked. 'I – I should rather think so! Oh, Giles, I wish you'd forget all those things I said. I was such a scabster about the whole –'

'Will you help me find her?'

Willy swallowed hard and tried to shrug. 'Oh, very well. pass it off if you like, but it's I who am in the wrong. I should have trusted you.' He paused. 'And I am in a fair way to forgetting Harriette already. Now that all that's said ... yes, Giles, I'll do anything you like. You know I will.' With studied lightness he set his hand upon Sir Giles's sound shoulder. 'Now, why don't you let Creed put you back to bed? It will take a day or two to get the necessary papers to jaunt all over France. That's why you want Lord Reginald, isn't it? And I'll have to see about making arrangements to have our yacht brought round from Portsmouth.'

Sir Giles looked up. 'Not that. We can take a Dover packet.'

'Hardly,' said Willy, shoving his hands into his pockets. 'There are few packet captains who want the headache of transporting a chaise and a team of horses.'

'Good God, Willy! I never said anything about taking a chaise to France.'

'You shan't be fit to ride a horse,' said Willy with a practicality that was becoming quite exasperating. 'Mama's chaise is beautifully sprung; you had it built to those specifications, remember? And French roads are impossibly rough –'

Sir Giles frowned. 'Don't be such a featherhead! I cannot make any sort of rescue idling along on pillows like some tulip! Next you shall suggest we play cards along the way!'

Willy grinned. 'That mightn't be such a bad notion. Oh, come, Giles! Do think for a moment. Even if you were fit enough to ride hell-for-leather, how far do you think you would be able to do so? We'll be in *France*, for God's sake. You can't go haring over someone else's turf, especially when we aren't on the best of terms with the frogs. Besides, if she's anywhere at all, she'll be in Paris. And if you want to get *there*, I should strongly advise you not to proclaim what you're about.'

'You're saying I should dawdle about like some hen-witted looby, out to see the sights,' said Sir Giles through his teeth.

Willy shrugged and fetched a candlestand to hold the

211

tray brought in by a servant. He raised a lid to smell an aromatic dish of broth. 'This looks devilishly tempting. I'm saying, Giles, that you really don't have much choice in the matter. Do You?'

His eyes met Sir Giles's, firm and unyielding, and in the end it was Sir Giles who had to look away. Damn the boy for having grown years older in less than a week! He sat frowning, trying to curb the impatience within him. 'No,' he said at last, grimacing at the broth which he did not intend to swallow, however much Willy might coo over it. 'I suppose I don't. But we must find her, Will.' And the desperation in his voice broke through.

Willy nodded, giving him a wan little smile. 'We shall.'

Sir Giles fumed through the days before their departure, pushing himself past his strength to show them how fit he was, then trying desperately to hide his subsequent exhaustion. He came to the conclusion the night before they were to leave for Dover that he had not fooled anyone – except perhaps poor Comtesse de Chalier, who sat about in fierce grief and did not notice anything. This final day had been endless. He'd seen Lord Reginald twice within the space of two hours and managed at last to convince the man that Catherine ought to be saved. Sperling's obstinacy still infuriated him. Good God, the man was callous.

And then there had been the Regent's visit, the prince having somehow caught a whiff of Sir Giles's intentions and desiring very much that Miss de Bleu be told of his respect for her. Of course His Highness had been sincere; certainly it could not be doubted the experience had affected him. But all the same Sir Giles felt a stab of cynicism. Respect her indeed. They ought to do more than that. She had sacrificed her uncle's life and saved England from invasion out of her conviction of what was right. There ought to be more than Lord Reginald's reluctant pursing of his lips as he signed the paper giving Sir Giles the cachet of his government. There ought to be more than the Regent's rather pathetic 'I should like to thank her myself, you know.'

Devil take it! He had hours to wait until they began their snail's-pace journey to Dover. And once across the Channel it was a good one hundred and fifty miles to Paris, perhaps more. Time continued to slip by while he stood trapped by distance and ill-health. What if he could not reach her in time? The question gnawed at him and undid the good wrought by rest and care.

But the next morning he awoke with a new vigor in him and looked out the breakfast room window with a challenge in his eyes. At last he could do something!

'Willy,' he said, still looking out, with his good hand fidgeting at the lace draperies, 'I begin to think I am a poor sort of fellow. None of this seems very real. It should have ended that night of the Regent's dinner. I should have saved her then. By now we could have matters worked out between us, and . . .' He rubbed his jaw, hearing the scrape of Willy's fork upon his plate. 'Surely you realize what I mean. There was so much tension when everyone fretted over Prinny's safety, and now suddenly it's all over. Only it isn't over, not for Catherine, and not for me. But while I know that, I cannot shake off this feeling of anticlimax.'

'Stuff!' said Willy in the bracing tone he'd adopted lately. 'My word, Giles, I shouldn't expect anything else of you. The wind's been pretty well taken from your sails. Now do stop talking this fustian and eat something, won't you? I thought you looked pretty chipper when you walked in, but if you're going to sink back into the dismals, Mama shan't let us go.'

With a wry smile Sir Giles lowered himself into a chair and studied the plate of food set at once before him. Steaming hot and dripping with fresh butter, the rolls

213

tempted him. He began to eat, and as he did so he knew once again a quickening of energy and spirit.

'Thank God,' he said, 'that her ladyship is safely in her own establishment again. It's unnerving to find her so much in the cosseting mood.'

Surprised by this sally, Willy grinned. 'By Jove, it is, rather! But she snapped off my nose yesterday, so I think she is returning to her usual humor.'

'Let us hope so.'

But the butler was in the doorway. 'I beg pardon, Sir Giles. Their ladyships, Lady Thorne and the Comtesse de Chalier, await your convenience in the lower drawing room.'

Sir Giles frowned and started to rise, but Willy reached across the table to stop him, with a scowl for the butler. 'Priggins, what a dolt you are! Did you not say we are at table –'

'Hush, Willy,' said Sir Giles in a quiet voice. 'You're forgetting your manners. Finish this slab of ham while I go and talk to them.' Rising, he silenced Willy's protest with a glance. 'No doubt it's only advice and nostrums they mean to hand out. But hurry. I wish to leave a half hour earlier than planned.' Giving Willy no chance to speak, he went out on the heels of the butler, expectant of gaining his mother's blessing despite the fact that this journey could only be described as arduous and was very much against his doctor's wishes. He had no doubt she was as eager as he to get Catherine to safety.

'Well, Mama?' he said, smiling a bit as he entered the drawing room past Priggins, who shut the door after him. He glanced round at the long narrow room with its cream-and-pale-blue furnishings and lifted his brows. 'Where's the comtesse?'

'Never mind about her,' said Lady Thorne with a wave.

'She has become such a watering pot of late I can not depend upon her to keep any sort of composure. I sent her away to the library, and if you like, you may speak to her later. Now come and sit down.' She pointed to a petit-point chair. When Sir Giles had obeyed, she went on, her lips a little compressed: 'It is time I told you what I think of this bacon-brained scheme of yours. What possible assistance can you give the girl now? She is either in prison or ruined, and I cannot see what you can do for her.'

Startled, he regarded her for a moment, then drew his breath with a narrowing of the eyes. 'I mean to bring her back, ma'am.'

'Oh, good heavens, don't sit there and make such pronouncements to me!' She began to tap her lorgnette upon the arm of her chair. 'I have humored you and encouraged William to humor you because that cloth-head of a doctor said we must, but really, Giles, this is beyond the pale of what can be allowed. You must reconsider. You cannot go careening across an enemy nation in search of a bloodthirsty little adventuress. It smacks of something out of an Arabian fable. It isn't like you.'

'I shall marry her if I can,' said Sir Giles, quite set now with annoyance. Had her fondness for Catherine been nothing more than a pretense?

Lady Thorne threw down her lorgnette. 'No! I shan't have it! Giles, you have gone mad.'

The dull discomfort in his shoulder made itself felt, but he ignored it as he rose and faced her with a grim expression. 'Never in my life have I seen you enact a Cheltenham tragedy –'

'Never have I been obliged to see my son dragged in bloody and lifeless,' she snapped, clenching her small fists. Horror came through her voice, and appeal. 'Giles –'

'Of all people, you ought to be in favor of this,' he said,

ignoring her. 'I thought you fond of her. And now, when I have made up my mind to marry her, you jib! Pray tell, why?'

'Because she will never have you, not after the way you've treated her,' said Lady Thorne with a fierceness equal to his own. 'Catherine has great pride and a natural hauteur which can be hurt only so much. She will never trust you again. Why should she? And you may be sure she won't be thankful for this glorious rescue you've planned. Save her, indeed. If you are sincere about marrying her, why didn't you sweep her off to the altar when you had the chance? Why? Because you thought she was an adventuress? Don't tell me you were such a gudgeon as to think once you'd stopped her, and betrayed her, and used her as you pleased, she'd come flying into your arms.' Lady Thorne sniffed. 'Yes, you did think it, didn't you? But she's got too much spirit and pride in her to ever do that, even if she hadn't been carried off by those ruffians. I know that girl, Giles, and I know she never wants to see your face again.'

Sir Giles stood appalled. Never had he been spoken to in this way. Was she blaming him? 'I thought you cared about her, ma'am. I – I had supposed you to be concerned about her welfare.'

'Of course I care!' she cried sharply enough to convince him. 'But Catherine is like a cat. She will land on her feet. And besides, though you can't know how it cuts me to say this, if she does need rescuing, you aren't the man for the task, Giles. No, and I very much fear you never will be.'

For a moment he could but stare at her, furious and chagrined that after all these years she still misunderstood him. Stiffly he said, 'I suppose you are referring yet again to Alice.'

'No, I am not,' she snapped. 'But since you bring it up, Alice Mayfield would have made you a splendid wife. It was hardly her fault her father embroiled himself in such scandal the whole family was sunk beneath reproach. You were within your rights to break off the betrothal when she offered you that choice, but I have never respected you for doing so. At least I did not until I saw Catherine and realized that while Alice was excellent, Catherine was ideal.'

'Then why –'

'Giles, will you be blind all your life? Can you not understand that you are self-centred to a fault? There has always been an aloofness, a reserve about you, which has caused you time and again to stand aside from a problem and let it go on to its own solution. All these weeks, if you knew you were in love with Catherine, why didn't you resolve the matter? But you did not, and to my mind you relinquished any claim to her then. I cannot see what you mean to do once you're in France. If the poor girl has any self-respect, she will cut you dead for your stupidity and presumption.' Lady Thorne's eyes pierced straight into his. 'In her place I should.'

'I see.' There was nothing else to say. Tight-lipped, Sir Giles turned on his heel and strode out, ordering the carriage brought round at once as he passed through the hall. He would have gone on, but a whisper reached through the fury engulfing him. He stopped and glanced over his shoulder to see the comtesse approaching with a faint rustle of her stiff skirts.

She came up to lay a detaining hand upon his good arm, and gasped as her haggard eyes looked into his face. 'Monsieur! You are white. Are you unwell?'

Yes, he was. The bitterness in his heart over his failures was nigh to killing him, but with a rough swallow he shook his head and forced himself to be civil. 'Not at all, my lady. How may I be of service to you?'

She paused, twisting her thin hands together and gazing

at the floor before she replied in a low, sorrowful voice. 'Because of Catherine I – I have lost my husband and my son. It is not easy to forgive, but can monsieur understand that I cannot bear to lose Catherine *aussi?'* Milady glanced up, her regal features stricken. 'No matter how she has failed us, I . . . oh, *mon Dieu*, I love her as my own child! Bring her back, monsieur. I beg you to do all you can. There is no one to save her from those monsters but you.'

Something caught at him. He drew a quick breath. 'Then help me! I don't know where to look or how.'

A gleam flashed in her eyes; it was almost as if she had come to life again. She seized his hand between hers. 'Ah, *bon!* I will tell you. Go to the Palace of the Tuileries. Go to Savary, to Dessaix, to Napoleon. They have her imprisoned. They are the dogs behind this plot, and unless something is done, they will keep her forever just for the joy of having a Bourbon in their power. Be bold, monsieur, and hard. Forget the English civility. Catherine needs now your steel and your honor, not your good manners.'

Despite the weight within him, his heart quickened at her words. Good God, in her day the comtesse must have been a formidable woman! But though hope had returned to him, he could not keep from saying, 'She no longer trusts me.'

'Bah! And of what importance is that?' Milady snapped her thin fingers. 'Are you not a man? Do what you must, and she will go with you. She is not a fool, monsieur. Do not think her one.' Milady's dark eyes looked straight into his, challenging him, forcing him to draw on his very spirit to face her. 'Now go,' she said, and it was like the command of a general. 'God keep you. I do not live until you return.' Then the fierceness faded from her eyes, and she was only a woman stricken with grief and tremulous hope. 'Both of you,' she whispered, and turned from him.

CHAPTER FIFTEEN

The road from Calais to Paris was rutted and potted and swamped with endless sheets of rain that drenched them throughout the journey. The wind bellowed and howled, gusting the rain about with such force the coachman could scarcely see the straining horses before him, and damp was constantly blown into the chaise, tightly made though it was. Sir Giles half-reclined upon one seat, wincing in silence each time the jolts wrenched his shoulder. Willy and Creed, who'd taken a sniffly little cold, huddled on the other.

'Lord, it's small wonder the frogs are trying to take over the rest of the world,' said Willy from within the folds of his caped greatcoat. 'Who'd want to live here?'

It took four days of steady traveling to reach Paris, four days of jolting progress, incessant rain which thwarted all attempts to glimpse the passing countryside, and beds in miserable inns. They reached the capital, but it was doubtful they could have done so without the strong axles of their chaise and the stout hearts of the English horses they'd brought to pull them along. Three teams of Sir Giles's own blood-cattle had been left at various stages along the road, and the coachman volubly misdoubted they'd ever see the animals again.

'For it's sly, heathenish people what lives here,' he confided to the miserable Creed at one halt. 'Eatin' snails and horsemeat like they do, what's to promise us Sir Giles's beauties will be kept properly rubbed down and warm?

Like as not there'll be naught but a winded jade to pull Sir Giles home again. A shame, I calls it.'

But Sir Giles himself voiced no complaints. Despite the harrowing conditions of travel and his own impatience, his shattered self-confidence had mended. Each mile brought him more inner strength and certainty, and when at last he reached their lodgings in the fashionable quarter of Paris and stood in his chamber, free of Creed and Willy, he snuffed out his candle and went to gaze out the window. The dismal weather had broken during their supper, and now the moon shone low and full above the unfamiliar spires of the city. The hour was late; the streets and houses were dark. Left to its own radiance, the moon dappled the buildings and splashed silver over the black velvet waters of the Seine.

Slowly Sir Giles pushed open the window and leaned out. A breeze, still damp with the recent kiss of rain, stirred his hair and brushed lightly over his face. Paris smelled differently than London. He had been here before as a lad on his Grand Tour, and of course he had noticed no such thing then. But there was a crisp smell to Paris, a smell of vitality and life... and yet, something more than mere gaiety and military power, something gentler and more entrancing. The memory of the scent of Catherine's lilies stole into his mind.

He sighed, longing for her, and looked once again at the great white moon. No more would he think of Paris as an evil place where blood ran black in the streets. The evil was in the hearts of its present masters, but Paris herself was sweet and vital, like Catherine. She was here, somewhere. He no longer despaired of finding her. She was here, and if he had enough courage he could yet gain her for his own.

Peace came to him, not the peace of satisfaction, but rather a sort of calm sprung from the knowledge that he had been right, after all, to jilt Alice Mayfield so many years ago. At the time he could give no reason, but now he realized it had not been cowardice but rather an instinctive desire to wait for the one meant exactly for him. Catherine was that one. Never again need he hide behind a wall of hauteur and icy high standards. There was no more reason to despise himself.

But now he must coolly know what he was about and why. He smiled to himself, feeling more of a man than he had in days. He was under no obligation to Lord Reginald, as he had been before. Nothing would stop him from speaking to her as she should be spoken to, nor from kissing her as she should be kissed. But first he must find her and gain her release, and, if God were merciful, he would.

In the morning there was nothing about him to betray that he had not slept. He rang for the landlord and bespoke a hearty breakfast. He rang for Creed and dressed himself in morning attire so exquisitely cut and fitted to his figure that Willy gave an involuntary whistle as he entered.

'Jupiter, Giles! There's everything prime about you today. Are you thinking of cutting a dash upon the Grands Boulevards? I must say, it's worked out devilish fine, being situated so close upon the river. Just an hour ago I met the prettiest little chit, a boatman's daughter. She never understood a word I said to her, so you wasted your blunt upon that old French tutor I had, but what prodigiously pretty dimples! I –'

'Willy, I should prefer you not to wander too far, in case I must send for you.' Finishing his breakfast, Sir Giles rose and accepted his hat, gloves, and stick from Creed. 'I go to call upon the Emperor of France.'

'Wait, Giles! You didn't think I'd forgotten why we were here, did you? Of course I haven't. Just allow me a moment to grab a roll –'

'There is no need for you to accompany me,' said Sir

Giles, lifting his brows as Willy flushed.

'Thunder take it! Am I not a part of this?' he demanded, stuffing a croissant into his pocket. 'You shan't leave me behind. I'm not such a loose fish as to let you!'

Sir Giles bowed, then unbent enough to smile. 'Very well, you insistent wart. But I warn you –'

'Oh, I shan't find it dull,' said Willy blithely as he took up his hat. 'Facing down an emperor couldn't be.'

But the Emperor was not granting audiences, not to Englishmen, which one had but to regard as obvious, nor to anyone else. The Emperor had gone away to the country, to Malmaison. The Emperor was not well.

'How could he be after we put such a spoke in his wheel?' murmured Willy sotto voce, and Sir Giles trod upon his toe.

'Then I ask to see whoever is acting for him,' said Sir Giles and nodded at the papers from Lord Reginald, which the secretary now clutched.

But the secretary was nervous. One gathered the Emperor had departed in a rage days ago to sit in an empty house in the country, the former empress's house. The new empress was distraught.

'Achilles, sulking in his tent,' murmured Willy, not to be suppressed.

At any other time, Sir Giles would have envied his ability to take these things in stride. But just now such jauntiness grated him on the raw. He cut short the secretary's lamentations to turn upon Willy. 'My dear boy, I fear I've left my handkerchief in the carriage.' He let his drawl harden a fraction. 'Fetch it, won't you?'

Willy went out with a scowl at the dismissal.

'Now,' said Sir Giles, returning his attention to the secretary, who had paused to dab at his lips and brow. 'I must and shall speak to someone. The matter is not trivial, I assure you.'

Eventually he was taken to another salon, stuffier and more gilded than the first, with sea-green cushions of watered silk. He was introduced, in an incomprehensible torrent of French, to a thin, balding man whose name he could not discern but whom he gathered was a minister of some sort. Sitting down in a *fauteuil* with the graceful but chilly hauteur he had cultivated through his years in society, Sir Giles made his request, only to be answered by an expression of blank confusion.

'A Mademoiselle de Bleu? *Qui est-ce qu'elle est?*' The man shrugged and shook his head. '*Pardon.* I know nothing about such a young woman.'

A stab of impatience sharpened Sir Giles's tone. 'Good God, man! Next I suppose you'll tell me you don't know anything concerning the recent plan to invade England.'

'England?' The man's pale eyes protruded; he turned a shade red. '*C'est impossible!*'

'Quite.' Sir Giles looked him straight in the eye.

After a moment the man blinked and began dabbing the moisture from his face. An aide looked in, then retreated hastily. The place, Sir Giles thought without amusement, was certainly at sixes and sevens.

'*Oui,*' said the minister, adjusting the order across his chest with absent fingers. '*Oui, oui! Mais sacrebleu!*' He glanced at Sir Giles, gave him a distinctly nervous smile, and began to pace. His narrow feet were clumsy. '*Pardon*, monsieur. You think us *imbéciles* perhaps. Now the anger of the Emperor is explained. This plan, since it has failed, may I know of it?'

'No,' said Sir Giles. 'There are people in question whom I wish released.'

'English?'

'I have told you the young woman's name. Also one Comte de Chalier and his son, Armand.'

'De Chalier!' Again the man's eyes popped. '*Non!*

223

Impossible!' He crossed his arms and shook his head.

'Has the comte been executed?' asked Sir Giles grimly.

'I think not, but...' The minister's brows crawled up. 'You know of this intention? You know why?' He dabbed at his lip. *'Dieu!'*

Sir Giles did not know nearly enough, but he was no stranger to the art of bluffing. 'Must we discuss it?' he said, his eyes glinting gray. 'With royalist connections the comte is –'

'No more!' The minister glanced about as though he expected ears in the walls. Again he paced. 'Savary should be here. This is his province, not mine.'

Sir Giles started to rise. 'Then I shall speak to him.'

'Non! It is not possible!' The minister sighed. 'You come at a poor time, monsieur.'

Sir Giles settled back into his chair, and now he did not trouble to keep his demeanor civil. 'I want the lady's release. What are your terms?'

'But I have informed monsieur I know nothing of this demoiselle.' The minister threw up his hands. 'Nothing. It is hardly a matter of concern here. *D'accord?'*

'On the contrary,' said Sir Giles and threw down the first of his trump cards. 'Her family name is Bourbon. Does that jog your memory?'

The minister sank into a chair, staring. 'I go mad! What do you tell me?'

Sir Giles frowned, beginning to believe the man really did know nothing. 'I need not repeat myself.'

'This must be verified.' The minister tried to pull himself together. 'Where is she now?'

'My good man, if I knew I should not be here,' snapped Sir Giles, his patience going to shreds.

'Pardon. Of course. This must be discussed. You will wait, please?'

'I will wait,' said Sir Giles.

And he did so for more than an hour, a grim, determined figure in the dainty salon. More than once the door was thrown open and hastily closed again while French shrilled outside it. Irritated, Sir Giles held his ground. He might be obliged to kick his heels all morning, but he'd be damned if he'd simply go away!

At last, however, his minister scuttled inside and paused to shrug. '*Mon Dieu*, when this day ends I shall thankful, be. Monsieur, I regret to say we cannot release these persons.'

'What?' Sir Giles was on his feet, towering over the minister, who blenched and shrank back.

'The comte is marked for trial. The son Armand is in the Palais de Luxembourg, a prisoner of the state. These are royalists, seditionists, makers of trouble. It would take a lengthy trial to free them, and, *je vous assure*, there will be no freedom granted.' He shook his head. 'There is Monsieur Savary, you know. His star wanes, but still he is a powerful man.'

Sir Giles's jaw grew taut. 'I am not concerned with your internal politics. What of Miss de Bleu?' His eyes bored into the pale ones of the minister. 'Do you dare put her on mock trial as well?'

'But, *non!*' The minister bit his lip, and Sir Giles felt a strong urge to throttle him. 'Only, monsieur must understand a matter of this weight can be put only before the Emperor.'

'Then I shall see him.'

'*Mon Dieu!*' The man was close to wailing. 'The Emperor cannot be approached. If you but understood –'

'I understand the tantrums of despots well enough, thank you,' said Sir Giles, and his gaze did not waver, so that it was the minister, despite his visible outrage, who looked away. 'Pray tell me what plans have been made for Miss de Bleu. Is she to be kept a prisoner the rest of her life?

What purpose will that serve the Empire? I should think the royalists would appreciate a symbol to rally around.'

'*Le Bon Dieu* knows why she is here,' burst out the minister, sorely tried, then gasped at his own reckless tongue.

Sir Giles accorded him a slight bow. 'I do not think you dare kill her. In fact, how you mean to rationalize the trials of any of them when Bonaparte has seen fit to pardon the rest of the nobility is –'

'Please, monsieur,' said the minister, pained. 'There are those who can never be pardoned. The fools who refuse to give up their royal masters –' He shrugged. 'The lessons of the Revolution die hard. Besides, what are these people to monsieur?'

Hesitating, Sir Giles pulled out his snuffbox to gain time. He was not sure he should give away all his reasons, especially to this fubsy-faced excuse of a fellow, whose origins had plainly not prepared him for the position he now held. Still, he was in no mood to pass by this chance to strike a home blow.

'There is,' he said, raising a pinch of snuff to each nostril, 'a dispatch written and sealed, waiting to be delivered to St. Petersburg.' Coolly he aimed his gaze at the minister, who had come alert. 'France's alliance with Russia is floundering. We needn't pretend otherwise. I think the Czar would be interested to hear of the assassination attempt on our Prince Regent.' The edge in Sir Giles's voice became more cutting. 'War is war, sir, but such a ploy reeks of dishonor and base cowardice.'

Gasping, the minister started to bluster a protest, then suddenly he shrugged. 'Of course we know England is upset, but as you have said, monsieur, war is war. The code common does not apply.' He raised his brows, but Sir Giles had no intention of being led into a moral argument.

226

'Then I see we must part, sir. It is time to deal with St. Petersburg.'

'*Attendez!*' Ashen, the minister did not wait for him to take even a single step toward the door. 'We would prefer, of course, that Russia remain in ignorance of affairs which concern only France and your country.'

'Then give me Catherine de Bleu,' said Sir Giles through his teeth. He was not a man who deuled, nor would his breeding permit him to call this fellow out, but the temptation to bloody something was growing within him. He clenched the fist at his side, damning the sling which held him inactive.

The Frenchman's eyes flickered. 'Monsieur, the decision is not mine. Your terms will be discussed. Wednesday we shall give you ours.' He shrugged, wary but holding his ground. 'I can say no more, monsieur.'

Frowning, Sir Giles left. On Wednesday, however, after a wait of two hours which left him in a cold fury, he was brought to Monsieur Savary and not the man he had dealt with before. Weariness struck at him. He foresaw an endless round of delays while he was shuttled from one authority to another and obliged to explain again and again. Well, it would not happen. This chief of police would be the end. He was treading hopeless ground, but he was not some diplomat they could deal with at their leisure. By God, they would at least learn that.

'Do you take snuff, Sir Giles?' asked Savary, opening an enameled box and extending it. 'It is fine Martinique, the purest blend.'

Sir Giles's nostrils twitched in distaste. The snuff had been drenched with scent. He refused curtly. Somehow he must discover her whereabouts and get her out by force. It was the only avenue left, apparently. 'I have come for your terms, Monsieur Savary,' he said, his words clipped.

227

Savary frowned. 'You are impatient, Sir Giles.'

'I believe I have some right to be.'

'And your poor arm. Have you been unwell?'

Sir Giles smiled thinly in what was more a baring of teeth than an expression of civil amusement. 'A ball in the shoulder. A French ball.' He was annoyed enough to make a reckless guess. 'Muret – one of your men, I daresay – decided to attack me outside my mother's house.' He paused to savor the expression on Savary's face that told him he had guessed rightly. 'Needless to say, I am not enamored of the French. Nor is my prince.'

Savary's lips twitched, but his dark eyes were still cool and watchful above that nervous gesture. 'Yet you are here concerning the release of French criminals –'

'I hardly think that term applies to Princess Catherine or her uncle, the Comte de Chalier,' snapped Sir Giles, and this time Savary flushed.

'Do you represent the government of your country, Sir Giles?'

Sir Giles met his eyes with steely composure. 'Do you, Monsieur Savary? Let's cease this sparring, shall we?' Calmly he sat down, unasked, and smiled at Savary's frown. 'You know my position. What is yours?'

'It is true we have no present use for the girl,' said Savary, beginning to drop his suave manner. 'But she is valuable.'

'She is not a bolt of cloth.'

'She is a cause of trouble! She does not do as she is told!'

'Then see that she leaves your country,' said Sir Giles, not raising his voice to match Savary's.

The chief of police sneered. 'And what does England intend to do with her? You call her a princess. Bah! She is an adventuress. All her life she has lived without the law, fleecing men at cards, knowing a beggar's existence. She is a disgrace to France! She can be of no interest to anyone else. What would she do in England? Drink tea?'

'I doubt it,' said Sir Giles and betrayed nothing of how close he'd come to landing Savary a facer. To think of Catherine held captive by the order of this knave! It was more than damnable. 'It is none of your business, but I intend to marry her. She shan't return.'

'Marry!' Savary swore under his breath, plainly astonished. *'Pourquoi?'*

'That is definitely none of your concern.'

Crooked teeth appeared in a grin. Savary raised his brows. 'A royal French jade with no dowry wedded to an Englishman?'

'There will be no jests in St. Petersburg,' said Sir Giles in a low voice that took the grin from Savary's face. 'And, sir, if you insult Miss de Bleu once more, I shall take every satisfaction in thrashing you within an inch of your life, with one hand if need be.' Slowly he lifted his gaze to Savary's set face and held it there.

Savary scowled. 'You are in no position to threaten me! My signature keeps her here. Only my signature can let her and her uncle go.'

Nothing was being gained. Sir Giles concealed his pang of disappointment and rose, so that his rangy height towered over the Frenchman. 'You may be damned,' he said and turned to walk out.

'Wait.' Now Savary got to his feet. 'You have not waited for the terms, Sir Giles.'

Grimly Sir Giles halted. So the threat of going to Russia was going to work after all. Savary had been toying with him as a poor sort of vindication. What a miserable cur! He bowed, loathing the man, yet keeping a rein on his temper.

Savary began to play with a letter opener. 'You may have Catherine de Bleu, Sir Giles. But if she sets foot again on French soil she will be shown no mercy. I concede the plan was wild, but it would have worked had she not served it as a traitor. Were it merely up to me she would not –' He paused to clear his throat. 'If she returns, she will be arrested.'

Sir Giles was almost too relieved to answer. But he kept his calm. 'I have already given my word on that. She shan't return. And her uncle and cousin?'

Savary bared his teeth. 'They will die, Sir Giles. Before she leaves Paris she will sign a denunciation, condemning De Chalier and his son. Well, Sir Giles? What is your decision?'

Sir Giles faced defeat and could not escape it. He had lost her, as surely as though he had never come to this godforsaken place. Without any chance to regain the love she had once begun to show for him, he had no hope she would ever make the choice he longed for. Indeed, his honor demanded that he not seek to make her sign the death warrant of her own family. The horror of such a thing was almost beyond belief. She must stay then, for these curs would never alter their terms, and he could not ask her to meet them. She had forsaken her uncle once. It was too much to demand more of her.

But at the same time his own emotions rose up in protest. How could he give up and walk out of here? How could he leave France without her? As a gentleman he must, but as a man he could not.

The words of his mother came to him. He looked into the future and saw himself embittered and alone, growing old with the knowledge that once again he had failed. Damn it! What was fair and right? He loved her more than anything else he had ever known. He could no more walk away without her than he could cut off his hand and leave it at Savary's feet. If she cared for him, or if she hated him, it did not matter. He would not give way this time.

With his jaw taut and his eyes like granite, he faced Savary. 'The decision must be hers, not mine.'

Savary blinked. '*Peste!* You will not spare her? She must be asked?'

Sir Giles did not hestitate. 'Yes. She must be asked.'

CHAPTER SIXTEEN

Catherine could not call her prison a harsh one. Her quarters consisted of a small suite of chambers in the palace, well-aired by windows which opened over a walled garden. At four each afternoon she was permitted to stroll about its confines, always, however, within the sight of a guard. Her tiny sitting room possessed a harp, which sometimes she plucked on, as well as a needlework stand, which she scorned. Books were brought to her, but she found them a dead bore. Twice a stupid, nervous woman had come to converse with her upon the latest French fashions and gossip about the opera. But mostly she was left alone and although she knew she was guarded closely enough to prevent escape, the watch upon her was otherwise negligible. That suited her, for her spirit was chafed enough.

It had not taken long to recover from the blow to her head and the laudanum forced down her throat to keep her quiet until she was in Paris. Since then, though she gave every appearance of meek resignation to her situation, she had not been idle. Her days were spent in a leisurely fashion, but her eyes and wits were ever alert for the chance to escape. She did not intend to sink into a decline over an Englishman, even if he had died from that shot she'd heard . . .

She could not say she did not care, for the anxiety within her bit hard. But she gave no rein to it, telling herself repeatedly that whether he breathed or rotted was of no

233

concern to her now or ever. He was a closed chapter in her life, a memory to be locked away. And, besides, the shot had probably gone wide and hit no one. She could ill afford to worry over something so uncertain.

But all the same, she could not put Sir Giles from her mind. Had she not once searched his face so as to never forget it? What a fool he'd made of her! And now it galled her to think of him sitting in his club – the picture of complacence since she'd spared his fat prince – and never thinking of her again while she languished in this genteel prison. God strike the piece of arrogance! Of a surety he had forgotten her, while she sat here, undeceived by her surroundings, knowing that at any moment the axe could fall ...

A light tap on the door broke her thoughts. Solange, the pretty little *bonne* assigned to serve her, and who had been so easy to bribe into devotion, stood curtsying.

'*Pardon,*' she said, her blue eyes round with self-importance. 'Mademoiselle is to meet with Monsieur Savary this night at the Place Vendôme.'

The place of blood! With a gasp Catherine was on her feet, pretending fury to mask the panic that clutched her. 'I refuse! The man is a goat.' But even as the spirited words rang out, her fear had checked and she could think again. No, no, they would not announce her execution in this way. She must seek to turn this to her advantage. If escape was granted, she would ... ah, no, gad, but she was tired of the game, tired of it all. The fire of her hurt and longing and injured pride was not enough to sustain her. She had lost part of herself, the vital part, and although she sprang to the ready on instinct, her heart was not in it. *Sang de Dieu*, then, she thought wearily. What was left to her but to enter a convent? One might as well die.

'Mademoiselle does not listen,' reproved Solange. 'Mademoiselle has no choice but to go. Three men – Muret and two others – will take you there. All this I have heard and came at once to prepare you.'

With an effort Catherine forced herself to acknowledge this service. 'Go on.'

Solange dimpled, pocketing the tiny gold coin. 'These two are not of the usual guard. They are from Savary. But still, though it will be hard, you may be able to flee them. It will be dark, and if you take courage –'

'Do not advise me,' snapped Catherine. She turned away as Solange curtsied, and began to tap her chin in thought. Ah, *peste*, she must know more. 'What does the goat want of me? And why the Place Vendôme? The irony of that does not escape me. But Savary is not a man for these gestures. If he wished an interview with me, he would come here, as he has before. Bah!' She glanced at Solange's intent face. 'What else do you know?'

Solange shrugged. 'Nothing more. But there are rumors. The Emperor still sits in Malmaison. The Empress has bewilderment. Who would not? She is a fool, but she knows she has not yet won him away from Josephine. And your Joseph says he held the horse of an Englishman today when he was watching at the palace gates. One he did not know.'

Catherine sneered. 'A reproof, *sans doute*, for the attempt on their Regent's life. Bah, these English and their manners civil!' She glanced across the room at her escritoire and frowned. But there was no need for more weighing of judgment. The chance had been handed to her; perhaps it was a trap, but at least she would make the try.

Opening her writing tale, she scribbled two short notes and affixed a plain white seal to each. These she gave to Solange. '*Entendez*. Deliver these now with haste. And tell Joseph what you have told me.' She gave the abigail a faint smile. 'Go! I must think and think on the plots of Monsieur Savary.'

'*Bon.*' Solange whisked herself out, deftly tucking away the *louis* from Catherine's slim fingers.

As soon as she was gone, Catherine pulled shut the draperies and knelt upon the floor. '*Cher Dieu,*' she whispered, clasping her hands. 'Grant me the cleverness to outwit them. If the English monsieur still lives, bless his life. Stand with me this night, I beg. In the name of Jesus Christ, amen.' And then there was naught left to do but wait.

The knock on her door rapped a few minutes short of midnight, startling her despite her readiness. A bit unsteadily she rose and drew near the cloak Solange threw about her shoulders. They were early. She tried to swallow, but her throat was too dry. God alone knew what evil or good fortune the night was to bring.

Her guards awaited her in the shadows of the unlit corridor. Candles were conserved in this wing of the Tuileries. Only the moonlight streaming in through the narrow windows of the gallery gave any illumination, and it was too stark to show her much of those who stood before her. One was tall and broad-shouldered; the other of neater proportions. Neither were of the palace guard. Both were spurred and muffled in caped greatcoats that added to the grim air about them.

For an instant her courage failed her and she felt panic. What devilry did she face? The Place Vendôme was still tainted with the memory of the blood which had run from its guillotines. A shiver ran through her. How long until the nightmare that had been the Revolution ended?

With impatience the smaller man strode toward her, his spurs ringing. He put out a hand to seize her elbow. 'Come,' he snapped. 'We are late.'

She stiffened, and would have spoken, but Muret's bulky form suddenly appeared. In his hand glinted the worn outline of a pistol. Catherine gasped in fresh alarm.

'Venez,' he said. And when the tall guard questioned the need for his drawn sidearm, he snarled out an oath. 'You are either new to serve Savary or else a fool. Woman or not, she's as fierce as any man. I don't trust her and you'd be wise to do the same. Come.'

Out they went, the cool air of the night blowing across Catherine's cheeks. A carriage awaited them at the side door they used. The men were all close to her and bundled her in before she could scarcely glance up the street. *Diantre,* she thought, her mettle rising.

'Hie!' shouted the coachman, and with a clatter of hooves they surged forward, the silence within the coach as ominous as the shadows were dark. Minutes later they halted at the Place Vendôme. Slowly Catherine climbed down, her wary eyes taking in all details of the scene. Near her the fountain with its elaborate statues burbled and splashed. The fat, yellow moon hung distantly in the sky, throwing eerie light over the tall column and the men standing between two equipages already there. The horses blew and jingled their harness.

'Come,' said Muret, pulling her forward while his companions followed a few paces behind.

But by now Catherine's gaze was upon those before her. She picked out Savary at once, but who were the two men beside him, and the one leaning from the chaise window?

'I might as well have stayed in Jericho for all the help I've been to you,' that latter one was saying in English.

He said more, but Catherine did not hear. She jerked to a halt. The voice belonged to Willy Thorne! And if he was here, then so was his brother. Ah, *oui,* now she saw him, standing a head above Savary. Her heart lurched within her, taking her breath, destroying her thoughts. But, oh, the joy that followed! He was here! He had come for her! Oh, *Dieu,* it was not to be believed. He did care for her; he

237

must, for he had come. A wave of relief rushed over her, and had he been near enough she could almost have swooned into his arms.

Shaking off Muret's hand, she went forward swiftly now, her eyes shining in the moonlight which spilled across her face. She saw the useless arm in the sling and understood at once. She forgave him for all of it. Wounded, but still he had come! Oh, *Dieu, grâce à Dieu!* It had not all been a lie ...

'Well, Mademoiselle de Bleu, at last,' said Savary, stepping forward so that she was forced to halt before she reached Sir Giles. Her eyes swept past Savary to him, longing to feel his hand upon hers, to hear his voice again. Savary cleared his throat. 'I have received a most persuasive argument on your behalf.'

Still incredulous, she drew in her breath, and again her eyes flew to Sir Giles, who stood in silence. She frowned a little now, but, in faith, she herself was as taut as a bowstring. Was it all to be so easy? Whatever Sir Giles had done to obtain her release, she did not care. She ...

'Mademoiselle,' said Savary with peculiar intensity. 'You may have your exile from France. On one minor condition.'

Now Sir Giles did move, as though in pain. But he did not speak. Perhaps it was his continued silence as well as Savary's own words that struck such a chill into Catherine. She drew back as though a viper had bared its fangs.

'Condition?' she said sharply. 'What is it?'

Savary pulled a paper from his pocket and proffered it. 'You will sign this.'

For a moment she was immobile, unable to comprehend. Around her the tension stretched until her nerves screamed from the pressure of it. In the moonlight Savary's face was quizzical, and behind her that vile Muret began a soft chuckle deep in his throat.

'Mademoiselle?'

She snapped to life. 'I will read it first!'

He bowed. 'But of course.' He raised a finger and one of the coachmen brought forth a lantern. In a trice she had read the paper, and the audacity of it rocked her. Almost she flung it into his face.

'I, condemn my uncle and cousin? I, sign their warrant of death?' She tossed her head and shoved past Savary to face Sir Giles. Her hope and joy were cinders in the fire of her outrage. All other considerations dropped her mind as she confronted him. 'So this is what you bring me. You knave!' She would have ripped the paper in half, but Sir Giles's hand caught her wrist and crushed it until she gasped.

'Catherine, I –' He caught himself. 'The terms are Savary's, not mine.'

'Yet you accept them!' she raged. 'You bring them to me. How could you? I thought, when I saw you, that you cared. I thought you were here because you –'

'Damn it, girl! I love you more than my life!' Still grasping her wrist, he pulled her close to him. 'I want to marry you.'

'Marry!' she gasped, reeling from the shock of it. Deep within a clarion call sounded through her, but there was her pride and her scorn blazing too mightily over it. No! He was too late. She could only abhor him now.

'You may do your wooing when the paper is signed,' said Savary. His hard eyes swept Catherine, and his lips curled slightly at her fury. She burned to slap him.

'Never!' she cried.

'Catherine,' said Sir Giles, and it was a cry from his soul.

She nearly broke then, but she couldn't. She couldn't. The eyes of the men behind her seemed to burn through her back to her very core. Indecision and longing swayed her. He loved her; he wanted to marry her. In exchange for that she could throw away the world just to put her hand in his.

239

But what he asked was too much. It would be so simple to sign. But her principles held her hard.

'I cannot!'

'Bah, such a stubborn little fool,' said one of the guards from behind her, and she almost whirled on him.

'Quiet!' thundered Savary, and the murmuring ceased.

It should have been enough, but Catherine began to tremble, her eyes upon Sir Giles as they filled with tears. Did he realize what he asked, nay, what he demanded? How could he stand there, offering all she most desired and ached for, when her every conviction stood against that paper? Even were Milord a thousand miles beyond the clutches of this goat and his friends, she could not sign.

Shaking, weeping, she shook her head.

'Oh, Jupiter,' said Willy in almost a moan. 'Giles, help her! You know she can't do it.'

'She must,' said Sir Giles, and there was a note in his voice that tore at her so her chin came high in a final gesture of defiance. *Dieu*, how he undid her! Before, she had despised him for stepping back, for being too much the gentleman at the crucial time. Yet now he stood as stone when decency demanded him to yield. She must persuade him to yield. He demanded all of her, and she could not give so much!

'Giles, please,' she whispered, putting out a hand to him.

He did not take it. *Sang de Dieu!* Instead he took the pen Savary had just dipped in an inkpot and extended it to her.

'You savage! she cried.

'Sign,' he said. 'I don't care how much blood is on your hands. I shan't leave France without you.'

Willy was coming out of the chaise. 'Giles, for God's sake –'

Sir Giles ignored him. 'Sign.'

Savary was like a snake, breathing over her shoulder. But she took the pen, not heeding when he snatched it from

240

her and dipped it once again in ink before forcing it back into her stiff fingers. What was she doing? It was wrong! It was wrong! She could not love Sir Giles this way. He was destroying her piece by piece. Did he not see?

But it was too late. Weeping, she scrawled her name with one shaky flourish, and Sir Giles pushed her into the chaise even as Savary snatched up the paper from where she dropped it in the street.

'You've got what you want,' said Sir Giles to him as Catherine huddled in a corner, spurning the hand Willy placed upon hers. 'Give me our pass out of Paris.'

Savary thrust something at him. 'It will take you through to the harbor at Calais.' And the triumph in his voice scraped Catherine on the raw. She buried her face in her hands, paying no heed to her guards, who had come quietly up. 'Yes, the two of you get in,' said Savary and cut short Sir Giles's protest. 'The girl is no common one, Sir Giles. She will escape you at the first opportunity and make the futile attempt to free her uncle and cousin. These men will make sure she steps off France's shore.'

'Poor Catherine,' murmured Willy.

'*Tais-toi!*' she snapped, turning her back to him.

At the carriage door the smaller guard bowed his obedience while already the tall one was leaping in to jostle Willy, who cursed him. Muret hesitated, his pistol reluctantly going into his pocket.

'Well, well, Muret!' said Savary, giving him a slap on the shoulder. 'Aren't you glad you gave up the army for a career in my employ? *Oui*, my man, put away the gun. The mademoiselle is no longer our concern. And as for Sir Giles, it is not required that you shoot him again. Come! I have a reward for your good work. Adieu, Sir Giles. You will forgive me if I do not welcome you to come again.'

Without a word Sir Giles climbed into the crowded chaise and said wearily, 'Oh, let be, Will,' when his brother

241

asked why couldn't the cursed frogs ride on the roof where they belonged.

Catherine sighed and shut her eyes, neither moving nor listening as the chaise bowled through the cobbled streets. What good had any of this served her? She would go to England and become his wife, but he had killed her heart. How could she bear to look at him again? How could she endure the daily horror of facing the ruins of what could have been a glorious existence? Oh, why had the fates given her the worst of choices? She would live, she would be free, she would have Sir Giles and the home she'd always dreamed of, but happiness was denied her. She could only look at him with – no, not aversion. But what was it she felt? Oh, *Dieu*, she did not know. Every sensibility was bruised. To be conquered in this way, to be made to grovel, was horrid. It was degradation.

They passed the final sentry and the gates of Paris. The horses's hooves ceased ringing on the paving stones and thundered over the earthen highway. The north road to Amiens and thence to Calais stretched out before them with the great yellow moon shining overhead. And still no one spoke until several miles later.

Suddenly the fierce air of hostility was dispelled. The tallest of the guards sighed and pulled off his hat. 'It seems, *mon père*, that pursuit is not Savary's plan.'

His companion, likewise doffing his hat and divesting himself of his disreputable muffler, at which he grimaced and flung out the window past an astonished Willy, agreed. 'You are a man of parts,' he said to a staring Sir Giles and held out his hand. 'How do you do? I am Lord de Chalier, and this graceless object is my son. We are deeply in your debt.'

'Good God,' said Sir Giles, nonplussed.

'But you were escaping when we –' blurted out Willy. 'How –'

'I fear we were making the attempt,' said Milord with gracious deprecation. 'As to how –' He waved one hand. 'A tedious affair. Once Catherine returned to France and sent her *petite bonne* to us with gold, it was a matter of the simplest to bribe an escape. We have merely been awaiting the moment when Catherine would be brought away from the palace. Thanks to you, messieurs, we may leave France in comfort instead of disarray, laughing all the while at the little coup de grâce Monsieur Savary has performed upon himself.'

'But surely you haven't been her watchdogs all along?' asked Willy. 'I say!'

'Non,' said Armand in his lazily deep voice. 'An exchange made only for this evening. But, Catherine, you do not speak! I am all admiration for the way you performed.'

With an effort she raised her head, and the tears of her devastation were all too clearly in her voice as she replied, 'Armand, you and Uncle Robert must forgive me. *Voyons,* this should be a moment of joy, but to think I failed you by signing such a vile –'

'Tais-toi,' said Milord. 'We regard such a trifle not at all.'

She frowned. 'Of course now that you are free – I mean, I knew you stood behind me and thought me a fool, but –'

'Child' – and there was gentle reproach in Milord's voice – 'what is this stance on principle? Do you threaten to become respectable?'

But she could not laugh, nor answer. It was impossible to voice the grief within her. To have Sir Giles, and yet not to understand him...

'Coachman! Stop the carriage,' said Sir Giles suddenly through the window, and as the chaise drew to a halt Milord leaned forward.

'But, monsieur –'

'There is a matter I must deal with first,' said Sir Giles,

243

inflexible purpose in his voice. 'Get out, Catherine.'

She could not disobey; he all but dragged her out over Armand.

Milord leaned out the door. 'A warning to be quick, monsieur. Savary will enjoy complacent sleep tonight, but by the morrow he will know of our trick. We must keep the advantage of our start.'

'I understand,' said Sir Giles, seizing Catherine by the elbow and pulling her along to the rear of the carriage. He glanced up at a face looking down at them. 'Creed, strike up a conversation with the coachman.' And the face promptly disappeared.

Catherine pulled free. 'What shall we discuss, monsieur? You perhaps expect me to kiss your feet with gratitude? I despise you!'

'Why?' he demanded. 'Because I forced you to be a woman for the first time in your life?'

She would have struck him, but he caught her hand and forced it down.

'Don't be a fool,' he said, giving her a shake with his one good hand. 'I've read your eyes, Catherine. I know you thought I couldn't match you. But I can, and we both know it. Don't we?' And without waiting for her fierce retort, he jerked her close and set his lips upon hers.

Lightning streaks ran through her, and it was as she had once feared. His touch was enough to rip the strength from her very core. Ah, *Dieu*, it was madness... it was heaven!

Too soon, he released her, and breathlessly – for she could no nothing else – she sank to her knees and remained there, head bowed, the tears streaming down her face. What was she to do? He changed every feeling within her. She knew not who or what she was; she knew nothing – save that she loved him. And how could she find the meaning of that?

'Catherine.' Tenderly his hand gripped her chin, forcing

244

it up. The moonlight glistened on her tears and set, frightened face. 'There is such a thing as trial by fire. I love you. I love you more than anything I have ever felt before. But I had to put you through this; I had to make you see that you love me as you long to. Put away dreams, Catherine! You're not a puppet anymore! Put away the acting and the self-deceptions and the pride! It's been devilishly hard for us, but it shan't be from now on. The dross has been seared from what we feel for each other. I will never fail you again, nor permit any harm to come to you. I know your keen spirit is like no other woman's in this world, and I thank God for you.'

The horror in her was stilled and swept away. A great peace took its place. The fact that she knelt in the dust at his feet, the fact that on the morrow they would be fugitives from the wrath of France, did not matter. He had not destroyed her nor conquered her. No, it was as he had said. They had been passed through more than many people would ever experience. Together and apart they had survived and drawn closer because of it. She saw now his reasons and understood her own, and was awed.

Slowly her fingers touched his face as he bent over her. 'Giles. *Mon Dieu,* it is incredible. Despite everything, we have the honor of loving each other.' She got to her feet, her eyes upon his to draw strength from him. 'You said you would marry me. You did not ask. I ought to have insult, but, *peste*, with you I am pleased to be commanded.'

'My darling,' he said, his voice low and shaken. 'I will do so only with your consent.'

She laughed then, pure and freely. 'Oh, you mad, adorable Englishman, *oui!*'

Swiftly he kissed her again, pouring fire into her soul to replace all he had stolen. Then he held her near with her head cradled upon his sound shoulder. 'Oh, my Catherine,' he whispered. 'I love you. I love you so.'

'And I love you *aussi*,' she whispered back, then caught her breath in fresh joy. 'Gad, but think of it, Giles! We have won!' She caught his hand. 'Come. The intrigue is finished. Pouf!' And she snapped her fingers.

Sir Giles followed her back inside the chaise, smiling at Willy and giving a little nod as Catherine hugged her startled cousin in a fierce embrace.

'Armand! Uncle!' she cried, throwing herself radiantly into Milord's arms. 'Is it not wonderful? He loves me! I rest content.'

Milord cleared his throat, and Armand began to laugh. 'So, little cousin, you *have* become respectable!'

Willy's white teeth flashed in a grin. 'I say, Giles!'

Calmly, Sir Giles let down the window. 'Coachman?' he said. 'Spring 'em!'

FLOODTIDE

Suzanne Goodwin

Stella grew to womanhood in a land torn apart by the
Boer War, but the thunder and flash of guns on the
distant horizon did not trouble her until her sixteenth
year. To the battle-hardened British troops the fire at the
farm was just another brutal act of war: to Stella it was a
blazing beacon burning her past to ashes and lighting the
way to a strange new life in distant lands.

Who would not pity a wounded soldier dying in the
parched veldt far from his English home? How could
Stella fail to nurse the pale, aristocratic Rupert Coryot
back to health – to give him her frank young love? And
how could she suspect that his summer passion for her, a
Boer farmer's adopted daughter, would change in the
colder climate of his ancestral home?

Viscountess, lover, actress and mother, Stella flees from
the scorn and hatred of Edwardian high society to seek
fame in the theatre. But as the Great War shatters the
world she knows, she learns that her love will never die.

HISTORICAL ROMANCE   0 7221 3974 8   £1.95